T0162658

DANCE OF THE
BLUE
CHAMELEON

HERBERT TORRENS

Order this book online at www.trafford.com
or email orders@trafford.com

Most Trafford titles are also available at major online book retailers.

This is a work of fiction. All of the characters, names, incidents, organizations, and dialogue
in this novel are either the products of the author's imagination or are used fictitiously.

Printed in the United States of America.

ISBN: 978-1-4669-6703-8 (sc)
ISBN: 978-1-4669-6702-1 (e)

Trafford rev. 10/31/2012

 www.trafford.com

North America & international
toll-free: 1 888 232 4444 (USA & Canada)
phone: 250 383 6864 ♦ fax: 812 355 4082

For Tuffy

ACKNOWLEDGEMENTS

I knew I was going to write a book about the lives and times of people around the "Downs," from the minute I stepped into the scene in 1983. Bonsall, and especially the Downs, was such a special place in the mid 1980s, full of charm, mystery and tales. Good times.

I wrote "Chameleon" in the late 1990s. It was my first book and just finishing it was an accomplishment, and experience like no other. I had high hopes. I spent more than a year, editing it, getting input from friends and editors, and making revisions (yes I know a few more revisions could be made). I spent about another year trying to find a home for it. No luck. It got to the point where if I even got a response from an agent or publisher I was happy.

After too many rejections, I walked away. Dance of the Blue Chameleon became a file that was on one of my machines and somewhere in the back of my mind. I continued to write for a living as a media and content specialist, and I published an autobiographical sketch of surfing in the 1960s called "Paraffin Chronicles."

In 2012, I felt like getting back to writing fiction. I started a couple of ideas, but kept coming back to Chameleon. I always loved the story and the times I spent living and working in that area. One day while driving through Bonsall I saw all the construction and found out they were going to put a six-lane road through Kelly's Corner and the little bar I loved so well. The chameleon inside awakened.

Dance of the Blue Chameleon is a labor of love for me. I no longer have dreams of being a famous fiction writer. I don't see this work as a life changing accomplishment. No movie. No riches. No redemption. I simply want to share a story about some places, and some characters that are simply gone. Maybe something will live on.

Herbert Torrens

INTRODUCTION

Dance of the Blue Chameleon is set in the northern regions of San Diego County and southern regions of Riverside County, California in the mid 1980s. It's a time before cell phones and the internet when communications were manual, if not practical. It transpires in a region that would change dramatically in the years to come.

This is a fictional story; however, many of the streets, highways, towns and areas mentioned are or were real, or as real as I can remember them from the time. Some are close to being accurate; some are purely the result of my imagination. The characters in this book, with the exception of one, are all fictitious. Some may be based on composites of various people I may have run across, but none are real. My intention with this book was to capture a special place in time with a story and characters that were representative of that time.

Herbert Torrens

CHAPTER ONE

Lady Luck

It wasn't a big crash. But it was big enough to win the pool, and that was what really mattered.

A bright-red BMW t-boned an old blue-and-white Buick Riviera. It happened at the intersection of Olive Hill Road and State Highway 76, at about 2:30 in the afternoon. It was a Thursday in early November. The pool would pay $140 and change, before expenses.

A half-second screech of tires on asphalt, and clank. Metal meets metal. The all too familiar sound bounced off the stuccoed—green walls of the corner bar. Inside, a creak of naugahyde was almost instantaneous with the yelp of the tires. Four customers spun on their seats as if one. In a second they were on their feet jostling for position at smoke-covered, louvered windows facing the street. Through partially opened slits, they quickly sized up the situation.

"It's minor," noted a stocky, cherub-faced young man wearing a beat up black Stetson, and a Chicago Blackhawks T-shirt.

A pony-tailed woman sipping her beer through thick lips agreed: "No doubt, Bob."

A lanky cowboy-type with a Texas drawl and sideburns pointed his long-neck at the scene unfolding on the street: "Classic T-bone. No injuries."

The bartender: "Beemer needs a tow. No way it's drivable."

"Shit, five bucks says the Buick drives away," said Little Jerry, a scratchy-cheeked diminutive jockey-type wearing a cap too big for his head.

Bartender: "Buicks can always drive away."

Chicago Bob was smiling now. "Nice-lookin' blonde in the Beemer."

The driver of the Buick was first out. He bailed through the driver's side window like some kind of paratrooper, rolling as he hit the ground and gone before the next car rounded Kelly's Corner. The remaining occupants, six in all, were slower to react. In fact, they actually took time to open one of the doors. Soon they were following their driver, running full-tilt up Olive Hill Road toward the safety of the canyons and groves.

"Ten bucks says the coyote gets away and the pollios all get caught," said the cowboy.

The little jockey smirked. "Shit, that's a lock."

The bartender grabbed the phone on the wall and dialed 9-1-1. "We've got a two-car vehicle TC at Olive Hill and 76. Nobody down. Looks like minor injuries, but you better send a tow truck and get CHP out here quick or there's going to be another wreck."

"Shit, you got that wired, Logan. They should pay you. You're like a regular dispatcher or something, 'cept you left out the part about them illegals."

Little Jerry began almost every sentence with the word shit, his pronunciation setting the tone for whatever he was about to say. A long "Shhhhhhiiiit," usually indicated some major revelation, while a short "sht" sufficed for conversational reactions to whatever point someone had made. The same two terms preceded by the word "no" rounded out the bulk of his otherwise limited vocabulary.

Logan smiled. "Sorry, I forgot to check for green cards. Let the Border Patrol worry about it."

"That's no shit, Logan."

Logan Mullhaney had taken the bartending job at The Paddock two years before. Now he was manager. A little over six foot, with slightly thinning curly light brown hair, gray blue eyes and a thick mustache, Logan was captain of the dayshift at The Paddock.

He'd been married once. In fact, still was legally, although he hadn't lived with his wife in fifteen years. A little over forty and still carrying an athletic build from years of paddling a surfboard, he now focused his sports activities on golf, gambling, and cavorting with his friends. There was the occasional fling. Usually with an out-of-town woman sporting money and style. He enjoyed his music, having a few drinks, sleeping late, and eating sunflower seeds. He loved The Paddock, and he loved the country hamlet of Bonsall. He didn't love wrecks at the intersection of Kelly's Corner. They happened too frequently out in front of the bar and restaurant. Too much destruction and carnage on Kelly's Corner to remember. He'd almost been a part of it himself on more than one occasion. He had stopped counting the number of wrecks he'd seen before Mori had made him manager.

Chicago Bob was transfixed to the window. "Nice-looking lady," he said wistfully.

"Shit, Bob. You're a dog in a man's body, you know that?" said Little Jerry. "There's cars stuck in the middle of the highway, wetbacks running for their lives, probably another wreck about to happen any second, somebody just won a two-month wreck pool, and all you can say is 'nice looking lady'."

"Besides that, you don't have a chance with a chick like that," said the pony-tailed woman. She was wearing blue jeans and a tight-fitting dull white T-shirt that showed off her biceps, and other points of interest. Marsha was one of the boys. Almost.

"Like you do?" shot back Chicago Bob. She just smiled at him, and went back to sipping her beer.

"You know, right now, there's some pencil-necked geek in a Caltrans office who's been waiting for this wreck to happen," said lanky cowboy, otherwise known as Gary Scott, unofficial leader of the small group of horse people. The native Texan seemed never short of words and he was somewhat of an authority on wrecks at Kelly's Corner.

"He knows that this particular crash qualifies this particular intersection for a traffic study. And that means he can spend six more months fucking around with his numbers and bull-shit routine, before recommending they put in a damn signal.

"In less than a year, there's been fourteen vehicle-versus-vehicle traffic collisions; eight vehicle-versus-bicycle TCs; five vehicle-versus-pedestrian events; at least a dozen vehicle-versus-dog fatalities; and one vehicle-versus-horse traffic mishap. All tolled that's three fatalities—not including dogs—ten serious injuries, and a shitload of minor scrapes and bruises. All at the intersection of Olive Hill Road and State Highway 76. In eleven months. Now," he let the word drift out the louvered windows. "Now, fucking Caltrans is going to do a study?"

"Shiiiit," said Little Jerry in amazement of his friend's knowledge of the statistics.

"Now is that real, or you just guessing on those stats?" asked Logan.

"Real," said Scott. "I like keeping track of things."

"Yeah, I remember the chick on the horse out there. Quite a scene. Glad the horse was okay," said Marsha.

Little Jerry, who at four-foot ten befit his nickname, jumped down off the barstool he'd been straddling and strode out the door toward the intersection. In a minute, he would be out on the highway directing traffic like a maestro conducting an orchestra. At least until the CHP showed up. Gary Scott, Marsha Bowman, and Chicago Bob followed the little man out to supervise.

Logan filled a Tom Collins glass with soda and topped if off with a long pour of the house vodka. "Never a dull moment," he exclaimed to no one in particular. Reaching behind the cash register he retrieved a manila envelope and extracted a hand-drawn calendar with a series of names and initials scribbled in the squares. His finger ran across the sheet to November Fourth.

"Hey, I won. I'll be damned. Maybe my luck is changing. Hey! I won the pool; November fourth was my day. I won it!"

Logan was alone in the bar, but he didn't mind, he could talk to inanimate objects, and space. He poured out the contents of the envelope. The counter was clear except for four half-empty longnecks and two empty shot glasses. Logan started counting.

"Alright, a hundred and forty bucks!" he announced, again to the empty bar. Tony the cook came from the kitchen with a load of clean glasses. "Wreck in the intersection, and I won the pool," Logan said to Tony.

"Bueno, now you pay for drinks," replied Tony with a smile that showed a large front tooth made of silver. Then squinting out the windows, he surveyed the scene with interested eyes. "My friends, I think," he said, looking at the blue-and-white Riviera. "Maybe they make it anyway."

The Border Patrol was first to arrive. Followed shortly by sheriff deputies, CHP, a tow truck, a fire truck, and an ambulance. Little Jerry along with Ed, who ran the liquor store next to The Paddock, had managed the traffic like pros until help arrived. Soon the intersection was teaming with authorities, lights flashing and radios squawking.

Something out in the intersection caught Logan's eye. He angled the louvers on the bar windows for a better look. Instantly, his attention was drawn to the driver of the BMW. She was pure California. Shoulder-length blonde hair flowing over a navy blue Hawaiian print dress. She had a deep tan and elfish features. Magazine looks, and all good. The safety belt had protected her from injury. A good thing, thought Logan. The same could not be said about her car.

By 4:30 p.m. the road was clear again. The abandoned Riviera had been pushed to the shoulder and the BMW was being towed to Fallbrook for repair. The bar was nearly full when she came in through the main entrance and took the last available bar stool. Logan casually placed a cocktail napkin down on the counter in front of her.

"Quite an ordeal out there. Can we buy you a drink?" He couldn't help but notice her enticing blonde hair, perfect tanned features, accentuated by gold, hoop-style earrings. Attractive? It was a given. That assessment came in all of a half-second.

"Stoly on the rocks with a splash of soda, and a twist," she said, while fumbling through her purse for some misplaced belonging. Logan made the drink and brought it over.

"This one's on the house. The Paddock's victim-relief program, for survivors of Kelly's Corner," he said with a smile. "Those who survive deserve a drink. Those who don't, well we drink to them."

She acknowledged the gesture with a slight smile and a nod, then took a long sip from her drink. "Well, I'm not exactly glad that I'm stuck here." Logan saw the look on her face. Nerves? Fear? Maybe a little of both. And the way she was looking through her purse. An almost neurotic prodding.

"The lady's room?" she asked. Logan pointed through the dining room. More than one pair of eyes traced her journey from the bar through the restaurant.

The Paddock bar was buzzing. It was the busiest time of day, like a factory when shifts overlap. The afternoon shift consisted of mostly horse people: trainers, exercisers, outriders, and occasionally, the owners of thoroughbred hopefuls. The hardcore started early, when the restaurant opened at 11:30. Some such as Little Jerry, Chicago Bob, and Marsha would stay through Logan's shift, which was over at five. At about three, the construction workers would start to roll in. They were the rowdiest lot, often surly after a long day doing what they didn't want to do. By five, the regular eight-to-fivers would start to arrive. Real estate agents, sales reps, and suits in for a quick one on their way home.

"How's it going, Logan?" Lenny was Logan's nighttime counterpart. He had a deep baritone voice that could be heard over most any crowd. He was a large man with curly red hair. Heavy set and well over six feet, he had his bag of change in his hand and was ready to take over the helm.

Logan responded with a smile. "I've got them all warmed up for you."

"I'll say you do," said Lenny, whose eyes were trained on the shapely blonde walking through the dining room. "A little action on the corner, I heard."

"That's right, and guess who won the pool." The smile was a dead giveaway.

"You son-of-a-bitch.," said Lenny in jest. "Now you going to buy back your board?"

Logan smiled again, "Yeah, that might just be the ticket."

The blonde sipped her Stoley and seemed not to notice the din of the bar at happy hour. No one really noticed when she left. One minute she was there, the next minute the seat was empty and so was the glass. Two one-dollar bills were left on the counter.

"That was kind of strange, don't you think?" Logan was a little perplexed. He'd planned on talking to her a little more.

Lenny laughed. "Hell, no stranger than anything else that happens around here. You going up to The Club?"

It was a regular deal. Like a job. After his shift at The Paddock, Logan went up to The Club for a drink and conversation. The Club was really Bonsall Downs, a public golf course, restaurant, and bar. To the locals it was simply "The Club." And it was a country club of sorts. But it was also a club, where people of diverse backgrounds came together and mingled in its spacious lounge looking out over the golf course and valley. From the long bar one could see golfers on the first tee, on the practice putting green and on the driving range. It made for some interesting action.

Logan liked The Club. There was always some kind of game going on. Cribbage and gin were commonplace. Friendly, and not so friendly, golf matches. Talk at the bar was about sports of any kind, races of any kind, and events of any kind. There was betting. Lots of betting. Formal and informal. Formal meaning serious betting, through a book. Informal meaning between friends, acquaintances, or anyone who wasn't a cop. Or who was a cop but was off duty. Of course, a valley full of thoroughbred ranches and a full-blown training facility meant there was also a little action to be had at the track. Del Mar, just an hour or so away, offered thoroughbred action at its finest. And from its mutual betting facility, you could bet on almost any race card in the country. Of course, there were the seasons at Santa Anita, and Hollywood Park. And, if you liked quarter horses, some did and some didn't, there was old Los Alamitos.

This night, Logan arrived to a rousing response from the crowded bar. The winner of The Paddock Wreck Pool had obligations. Big Mike was there, along with Spike, whose real name was also Mike. Logan saw Tuffy, the local historian, Bob, the salesman, and the usual crowd of golfers, horse people, and after-work drinkers.

"Did you see it happen?"

"How much was in the pool?"

"Heard it was a van full of aliens."

"The chick's fault, right?"

"It's always the chick's fault. God should have never given them licenses."

"God?"

"Hey Logan, coyote got away, wets all got caught, right?"

Logan just smiled. "Set 'em up, Al. I'll buy the corner, and that's it." Logan grinned as he produced a roll of worried bills from his front left pocket. Al, the big bartender with a handlebar mustache, started setting up the drinks. Mostly beers and a few shots. Big Mike and Spike always drank mixed drinks. On this evening it was Canadian Club over ice. Tuffy had an imported beer.

Logan sat at the corner of the bar nursing a Coors and taking in the idle conversation. His mind wasn't on drinking, his golf game, or even playing cards. He was thinking about other things, not the least of which was a quiet blonde who sipped Stoly on the rocks. There was something about her that he just couldn't quite put his finger on. Something that wasn't right. She was good looking, no doubt. Maybe it was the stress, the look of nervousness about her, like she was afraid of more than of what just happened today. Lines under her eyes, a slight case of the sniffles. Drugs? Maybe, maybe just a cold. Whatever, she had made an impression on him.

"Fifteen aces!" Big Mike was looking at Logan, he had a dollar bill folded in quarters in his right hand, a tumbler of CC over rocks in his left. "I say fifteen aces, Logan! Fifteen fucking aces."

Logan looked at him blankly. "Mike, I'm not playing liar's poker. Does it look like I'm playing? Do I have a bill in my hand?"

Mike mumbled an apology and turned to Bob the salesman, who was holding a bill. "Fifteen aces."

"Beautiful, just beautiful. The guy doesn't even know who's playing and he calls fifteen aces for an opener," Bob said as he scrutinized his own bill. The corner laughed.

The door from the parking lot scraped open with a distinctive clanking sound that always triggered a Pavlovian response from those at the corner of the bar. There was an equally familiar yet different sound from the same door when opened from the inside that usually signaled a departure. Arrivals and departures from The Club lounge rarely went unobserved.

Two plainclothes detectives made their way in from the evening glow. It wasn't the funky jackets or the polyester slacks that gave them away. It was everything. The look, the demeanor, the walk, the eye contact that froze everyone in the room at first glance. Detectives on duty. Officers in uniform were rare at The Club. Plainclothes officers were even rarer. Folded dollar bills at the corner vanished quickly. Replaced by quiet, very cordial conversation.

Logan watched them walk in. One was noticeably taller than the other and had reddish blond hair and pale blue eyes that were a bit too close together. The other was a bit thicker, Hispanic, with straight black hair, dark brown eyes, and an olive complexion.

"Mullhaney here?" asked the shorter of the two. The bartender pointed at Logan. The corner murmured. Never one to skirt an issue, Logan walked over and greeted the officers. He knew the shorter one: Manny Cassio. A former Fallbrook cop, Cassio made both official and unofficial visits to The Paddock.

"How ya doing, Manny?" said Logan, in friendly tone.

"Did you call in the TC this afternoon?" Cassio asked. If there was ever a face that had no expression, this was it, thought Logan. His eyes were piercing yet blank and devoid of expression. Cassio was all business today and right now that business, whatever it was, was serious.

"Sure did. Had 'em rolling within a minute. Of course it took Chippies a half hour to get there." A feeble attempt at humor by Logan. One that most sheriff's detectives would appreciate, but there was no laughter from these two, not even a smile.

"Did you talk with the girl who was driving the BMW?" asked the other officer, whose name was Brado. He took out a small spiral-bound tablet and made an effort at taking notes while he asked the questions.

"Yeah, she came in for a drink."

"You ever see her before?"

"Nope. But, I wouldn't mind seeing her again." The anticipated chuckle never materialized.

Cassio reached inside his jacket and produced a small folder. He laid a three-by-five snap shot on the table in front of Logan.

"Is this the woman that was in the wreck?"

Logan looked at the photograph. It was her. She was getting in a car outside of what looked like a hotel. A man with longish black hair and a goatee was holding the door of a Mercedes sedan.

"I don't know. It could be," said Logan, starting to feel a little defensive.

Cassio, leaned over the table to get closer to Logan. "Could be? How about you being a little more specific."

Logan backpedaled a bit. "It's hard to tell by this photo. It's a little grainy, and far away."

Cassio took another photo out. This one was in color and done professionally. It was her again.

"How about this one?"

"It sure looks like her. Except, the girl that came in for the drink was older."

Cassio seemed to take that as a yes. Brado, the cop with the beady eyes, jumped back in to the conversation.

"Did you notice any other people talking to her while she was there?

"Not really, but it was happy hour. The bar was full."

Brado pointed to the man in the picture with the blonde. "How about him? Did you notice him at the bar? Take a good look."

Now Logan was definitely feeling edgy. But why? He had nothing to hide, he'd always had a pretty good rapport with the cops.

"He could have been there, but I doubt it. It was just the regular crowd, and she didn't talk to anybody that I saw."

Cassio took over. "Who did she leave with?

"That was the funny thing. I never saw her leave. One minute she was there, and the next time I looked, she was gone."

"Logan, did she look like she was on something when she came in?" Cassio said, emphasizing the use of the first name. Now Cassio was the "good cop." Logan thought about it and hesitated before answering.

"She looked nervous, but hell she had just been in a wreck. It wasn't her fault. The coyote just pulled out in front of her. She never had a chance."

"A lot of people are doing drugs down at your bar," said Brado in a flat tone. Definitely the bad cop.

Logan shot him a look. "Excuse me? I really don't think so. We've got a regular crowd of hard working people and you know damn well, we don't have a lot of disturbances. If people are doing drugs there, I don't see it."

"Sure, you don't see it," said Brado. "Just like you didn't see anything this afternoon." He had a sarcastic smile. It was obvious that there was more to this case than just an accident at Kelly's Corner. Brado took out another photograph from the envelope.

"Now, I know you know this guy." Logan glanced at the print. Headband Dave and another guy who looked like a biker. Headband thought of himself as a biker, but hadn't owned a motorcycle since he crashed his Honda Scrambler about a year ago. The two in the picture appeared to be exchanging something. Could have been anything, but there was an obvious insinuation in Brado's voice. More alarming was that the photo showed The Paddock sign in the background.

"No drugs at the Paddock?" said Brado. "Think again."

"Look, I just serve drinks and mind my own business. When there's a wreck at Kelly's Corner, I call it in. As far as I know, this guy is just a want-to-be biker. That's it." Logan felt the anger building in his stomach.

The good cop felt it too. "Take it easy Logan, we know you're not involved with this shit. We just have to check out all the leads. You know?"

"Yeah, I know just doing your job. But what does this wreck today have to do with anything? You guys can't be investigating a DUI. What's this really about?"

Cassio sort of rolled his eyes in a jester that suggested that it was no big thing.

"Just checking a few things out up here," he said, still using friendly tones. "We've been getting reports of increased drug use in the area, and we want to cap it before it gets any worse."

"And you think this chick is involved?"

"Why don't you just call us if she comes back in," said Brado, laying one of his San Diego County Sheriff cards on the table. "And, tell your friend Headband Dave, we're watching him."

Brado put the notepad in his back pocket, and they stood up to leave. "Thanks for the help," said Cassio.

Logan felt relieved it was over. Still, he wondered what the hell was going on. Had there been more drugs around lately? Violence? Maybe some of the construction workers had been a little more rowdy. Headband Dave was mellow, but it wouldn't be too much of a stretch to put him with the meth crowd. Still, no big deal. There was a roar of laughter from the bar, as the game of liar's poker started up again. Big Mike had probably made another ridiculous bid. Maybe he was on drugs.

A tall man at a corner table behind the crowd of poker players got up and left through the door leading to the putting green. Logan watched as the door closed behind him. Something in the way he went out struck a chord. Like a guy running out on his check.

CHAPTER TWO

Lights Out

It was nearing six by the time Pete finished unloading the red BMW from the platform tow truck. The sun had set almost an hour before, but there was still a mild glow above the hills to the west. Pete's Towing was located on the west side of Fallbrook, in an industrial area bordered by Camp Pendleton Marine Base to the rear, a sewage treatment plant to the south, and a trailer park that had seen better days to the north. Surrounded by a six-foot chain-link fence with coiled razor wire at the top, Pete's was a secure, if not attractive, place of business.

Pete snubbed out the butt of a frazzled White Owl with the sole of his greasy black boot and walked to the driver's side of the BMW to retrieve the keys and secure the car for the night. This is weird, he thought, it should have been a simple matter of towing the car up to Gary's Auto Body and Paint. Let Gary hassle with the rich bitch and he'd collect the towing fee, and a small commission from Gary. But the call from the sheriff dispatcher had changed those plans. This car was to be impounded, by order of San Diego Sheriff's Office. Drugs? Pete wondered. Probably, just about everything had to do with drugs these days. They would send a truck up in the morning to retrieve the car. Pete would receive a voucher from the county, payment to be received after due process.

A cold evening breeze whispered through the assortment of wrecks as a pack of coyotes yipped up a fuss from the nearby base. Pete rubbed his hands on his pants. It was getting downright chilly. And smelly. The wind that blew up the valley carried the essence of the treatment plant right through Pete's yard. Pete usually didn't notice it, sensory fatigue had set in long ago and the unmistakable aroma of compost was just another "feature" of Pete's world.

Something tonight was different though. He smelled the sewer and felt the chill of the wind around his ears and down his back. There was no comfort in the serenade of coyotes in the distance. Yet there was something else. He didn't feel alone. What about Red? Pete's trusted Doberman mix hadn't barked since he pulled up in the truck.

The yard was illuminated by two mercury vapor streetlights casting a yellowish glow over most of the area. The large garage and adjacent structure Pete called home were both well lit. Still, there were shadows on the perimeter of the yard.

The phone rang so loudly it made Pete jump, which didn't happen often. Tonight, for some reason, he was a bit edgy. It rang that way by design, of course. One of those outdoor jobs that could wake up a drunk from a sound sleep. It rang so that Pete could hear it from anywhere in the two-acre yard. Neighbors had complained about the ring, but for the most part it was an accepted fact of life on the West Side. This was not Rolling Hills, or Glenn Ivy. Pete went into the barnlike garage and answered the phone. It was Gary.

"What the hell, Pete. I thought you were bringing me in some work. I've been here for a fricken hour and a half waiting." Gary was miffed.

"Sorry, I was gonna call. I just got done putting the thing to bed myself." Pete was in no mood to explain, but he was bound by professional courtesy. That and the fact that Gary contributed substantially to Pete's well-being during the course of a year. "Listen, I was on my way up the hill when S.O. called and told me the car was to be impounded. They're going to send a truck from downtown to get it tomorrow. Shit, I'll be lucky if I get paid within six months."

"Police matter! I've never heard of them sending a truck up from San Diego before. What the hell is going on?"

"Hey, all I know is it's a late model BMW that's been kissed in the front end. For all I know, the thing may be full of drugs, or money, or guns, or who the hell knows what?"

Pete was thinking out loud and suddenly realized there might be something of value in the car. But then, that would be tampering and he wanted to stay on the good side of the county. After all, they provided him with a lot of work. That, and there was the cowboy sheriff who was known to come down pretty hard on "offenders."

Gary still wanted the job when the cops got done, and Pete left it at that. No way they would bring the car back to Fallbrook, but what the hell, Gary could dream. Pete finished up some paperwork and decided to go out and check the car again, for curiosity's sake. He strode out the door and waited a second for his eyes to adjust. Where is Red, he wondered as he walked over to where the car was parked. He never heard the footsteps, but he surely felt the blow over the head before the lights went out.

Red lay motionless under the bed of a '69 Ford Ranchero. He'd eaten the drugged meat in a heartbeat. Steak was hard to resist for a working junkyard dog who was usually paid in generic-brand dog chow. The sound of Pete's rig leaving with the BMW back aboard went undetected by watchdog and master. In minutes, the rig was rolling down Alturas followed by a nondescript late-model Ford pickup. The two vehicles were out of sight and well on their way to the main highway before two headlights from a black sedan illuminated the dark, narrow driveway across the street from the towing yard. The car crept slowly from cover and followed the procession briefly before turning off.

It happened off of Market Street in the Gaslamp Quarter of San Diego. The woman came running out of an alleyway screaming. Her short red skirt was torn and she was holding what was left of her blouse in her hand. A black-and-white San Diego Police unit rolled to a stop and two cops jumped out. One stopped with the woman, the other ran up the alley.

Within minutes, a crowd had gathered. The woman now had a blanket wrapped around her. She was olive skinned, with short curly hair. Too pretty to be working the streets down here, thought the cop who had stayed with her. Still, she was a prostitute. That much was obvious.

High-end, from the looks of her. Another unit rolled up and two more cops got out and started moving the crowd along. Soon an ambulance arrived and was directed down the alley.

"Why don't we sit in the car and you tell me what happened?" asked the cop.

The woman was breathing hard but had stopped crying. She was nearly hysterical when he'd first stopped her. He and his partner had been on routine patrol when they got a call about screams and shouts coming from an alleyway. They were close by and came around the corner to find the half-naked woman running from the alley.

"You're not going to arrest me, are you?"

"That depends on what you tell me, and what went on up that alleyway."

She told him she had been on a date. He was a well dressed man she had just met. They had gone to dinner and were driving to another club when the man, his name was Dawson, turned his car down the alley. He had stopped and pulled out a small packet of dope. She suspected it was coke but wasn't sure. He used a business card to sniff a couple of little piles. He offered her some, but she declined.

He was okay for a couple of minutes. Then he started breathing funny and his eyes got big. The next thing she knew he was pawing at her. He frightened her with his aggression and animalistic mannerisms. She said he looked as if he were foaming at the mouth. His eyes were bulging. He grabbed at her and she jumped out of the car. He chased her and caught her. He wrapped his arms around her in a bear hug and started pressing into her. She kicked him in the groin with her knee and he let go. Running around the car, she got away. He stayed on the ground for an instant, then started rolling over and kicking. She thought she hurt him with the kick, but he wasn't holding his groin. He was rolling and kicking in wild convulsions. Then he started bashing his head on the pavement. She ran away and that was when the cops arrived. The cop listened and took notes. Sounded pretty weird. His partner came out of the alley and over to the patrol unit.

"Who else was in the alley with you, ma'am?"

"No one, it was just him and me."

"So you bashed his head on the cement and killed him?"

She looked up horrified.

"No, I told him what happened." She looked at the cop who had been taking her story. "He snorted some dope and just went crazy. Like an animal. He did it himself."

After escorting her to the back of their patrol car, the two cops walked a few steps away and talked. The officer who had discovered the body was a seventeen-year veteran of the streets. He had seen a lot of weird stuff down here but had never heard of a guy beating his own head in.

"We've got an I.D. and we have the dope. Let's go down to the station and see if we can sort this thing out. The guy is from Sacramento, may work at the Capitol."

CHAPTER THREE

Dateline Fallbrook

"To those who love us!"

"And, here's to those who don't."

"To the dance of life!"

"Salute."

Two shot glasses clinked in midair before delivering a cargo of syrupy clear liquid to awaiting lips. The glasses landed back on the bar with unceremonious thuds.

"Damn good whiskey, Lindy."

The bartender laughed. "That wasn't whiskey shit head, that was schnapps. And the name's not Lindy. Now if you want whiskey, that will cost you. Anyway, it's Thursday, and you're not allowed to drink whiskey until the weekend, so just shut up and drink your beer."

Burt Reid was used to Lenny's abuse. It was an ongoing thing between the two friends. Reid dropped in almost every night, usually after eight, sometimes later. As editor of *The Fallbrook Newspress*, he worked most nights. *The Newspress* was published on Thursdays and Sundays to about 10,000 paid subscribers. It was the largest and oldest weekly newspaper in North San Diego County. And under Reid's direction it had become a publication of some stature, editorially speaking. *The Newspress* was a voice, and not always the voice of reason. It took a stand, sometimes an unpopular stand, but it reported the news as best it could from a weekly position. Sometimes it beat the big papers. Sometimes it cloned their stories. Most of the time they stuck to their own types of stories. Hard core news usually gave way to human interest.

Reid headed a team of three full-time news reporters who covered everything from the local school boards and planning committee to fires and crime. Once in a while, Reid's news team would get a timely lead or do a bit of extra investigative work that would lead to a breaking news story. _The Newspress_ and its editorial staff had won its share of awards over the years, but the real reward for Reid was in knowing they had beat the big boys and knowing that the big boys knew it, too.

Lenny and Reid shared idle thoughts and mundane conversation on most nights. Sports, women, places they'd been, places they were going. Lenny loved to talk about his travel trailer he had set up in a little fishing village down in Baja. It was on the gulf side, away from the lights of San Felipi. Lenny went down at least once a month and stayed for three or four days. He was not a sportsman, although he owned a couple of guns, two sets of golf clubs, several motorcycles, a duffle bag of scuba equipment, and numerous odds and ends that he had acquired through his second profession: informal banker. He went to Mexico to relax, which to Lenny meant sipping tall drinks and playing liar's poker in the local cantina. Of course, some of The Paddock regulars would argue that was what he did at work anyway, so why waste the gas.

The phone rang and Lenny answered with his gravelly southern drawl. "Yello, Paddock, Lenny speaking. Yep, hold on." He stretched the extra-long, coiled cord over to the bar. "It's for you, sounds like Pam."

Pam Molinski was one of Reid's reporters. Two years out of the Army, she was an aggressive young turk in the reporter ranks. A journalism graduate from a city college before she joined the service, she spoke four languages, including Russian. Type A, all the way. Liked to stay late in the newsroom so she could smoke while she wrote.

Reid took a long swig of his beer and swore under his breath before taking the receiver. "What's up, PM?"

The voice from the newsroom was excited, but then it didn't take much to get the young reporter excited. She had a love affair going with the police scanner, mostly because she could relate to all the code mumbo jumbo that was bantered on the air. Unfortunately, she couldn't afford one at home, so that was all the more reason she liked to camp after hours in the newsroom.

"Something is going on, Reid. They're calling downtown S.O. and using codes I've never heard. Something happened at Pete's junkyard. They called an ambulance . . ."

"Okay, okay, slow down. Start again. You heard something on the scanner, right?" Reid listened as his reporter repeated what she knew and what she had surmised. When she was done, he handed the phone back to Lenny and reached for his wallet.

"One for the road?" asked Lenny.

"Make it half coffee and half milk," replied Reid, throwing a five dollar bill on the bar. "I've got to go back up the hill."

Lenny got the coffee and set it in front of the newspaperman. He usually refrained from asking about the local news scene, but curiosity got the better of him this night.

"What's going on? 211? 1144? 5150?" Lenny only knew a few of the emergency codes: armed robbery, fatality, and crazy person causing a disturbance were among those that peaked his interest.

"I don't really know for sure, but it sounds like someone stole the car that was in the wreck today, from Pete's yard," said Reid. "And they conked Pete on the head pretty hard while they were at it."

"Is Pete okay?" Lenny knew Pete better than most and was one of his customers. Whenever Lenny needed a part for one of his project vehicles, he would check the junkyards first. And likewise, Pete knew Lenny as a wheeler dealer who knew where to find the best bargains on just about anything.

"He can't be doing too good, they called in LifeFlight. I gotta go," Reid pointed to the money on the counter. "Am I good?"

"Get outa here." Lenny picked up the empty beer bottle and shot glass with one hand as he wiped the counter with the other, casually sweeping the bill into the set-up counter that ran along the inside of the bar. His movements were almost ritualistic. Carefully measured actions that had been mastered from years behind the bar. Towel and glass removed, he scooped up the bill in his right hand and tapped the bar twice before turning to the cash register and ringing up the sale of one beer.

Reid was on his way up the hill, thinking about what Molinski had said. The fire department had rolled on a 9-1-1 call reporting a man down and requesting an ambulance. Had Pete called it in? When the EMTs arrived they found something that triggered an emergency call to the sheriff's office. When the deputies arrived they immediately called downtown, special investigations unit. That could mean just about anything, Reid thought, drugs, organized crime, homicide, or all of the above.

Driving up the hill, he felt a tinge of adrenaline. Something newsworthy was going on and it was happening in his backyard. He could visualize Sunday's lead story: "JUNKYARD OWNER DEAD, WRECK MISSING!" Wait a minute, Pete wasn't dead yet, and for all he really knew, the junk man had just been tapped unconscious. But they didn't roll LifeFlight for minor injuries. It must be fairly serious, he thought. It was a newsman's lot to think about such things. The more gross the scene, the better the story. Or at least that's the way it was perceived. And, like most perceptions, there was some truth in it.

Turning left at the first main intersection in town, Mission Road and Ammunition Avenue, Reid headed toward the back gate of the Marine base. The road fronting the junkyard was Alturas, the last turn before the gate. He turned left again and motored down the dimly lit road toward Pete's Towing Yard. Large eucalyptus trees bordered the road to the west, while industrial buildings and the occasional shanty lined the east side.

A sheriff's cruiser with its overhead lights flashing red and blue marked the entrance to the crime scene. Reid parked on the road behind Molinkski's car, a not-so-vintage Volvo sedan that was probably near-new when Nixon was president. She called it "Tank," and it definitely shared some of the same characteristics. It was loud, indestructible, and could go just about anywhere.

A midsize four-by-four truck with highbeams glaring pulled in behind Reid. He didn't have to look to know who it was. The sound of a police scanner scratching out a dispatch blasted from the cab as the driver jumped down. He was a big man who looked to be in his mid-fifties. He wore Levis and a flannel shirt and a bright yellow "turn-out" coat complete with florescent tape. Standard issue for most firefighters, but O'Malley was no firefighter, although he had seen his share of wrecks and fires. He was the staff "photog" for _The Newspress_. A more devoted employee would be hard to find anywhere.

By his own choosing, Mike O'Malley was on call twenty-four hours a day, seven days a week. Retired military, recovering alcoholic, empty nester, wife with a full-time job. O'Malley stayed busy living out a childhood ambition. He was half cop, half firefighter, and full-time press photographer, ready to go anywhere, anytime.

Not that O'Malley was alone in his tireless pursuit of police cars and fire trucks. News photographers, by nature, are a rare breed. Not really accepted by their journalistic brethren as "newsmen," nor as peers by the cops and firefighters they follow around. In fact, other professional photographers, those who work in studios and on location with creative directors and "talent," look upon news photographers with disdain. Blue-collar workers with a camera. In O'Malley's studio the "talent" is always real, and there's rarely time for a second take.

"What's up, boss? Didn't expect to see you up here," said the big man while putting on a khaki vest that held numerous rolls of film, lenses, and a battery pack. He grabbed his canvas camera bag from the seat of truck and took out a thirty-five-millimeter Nikon camera with no lens. Locking the truck, he threw the bag over his shoulder and started walking toward the junkyard. Two black camera bodies hung from his thick neck.

Reid walked with him, zipping up his windbreaker as he talked. "Molinski found me, said it was interesting, so I decided to come on up."

"Interesting, my ass, this could be the story of the year. They're calling in homicide. Who knows where it's going to go."

Reid was all ears. O'Malley spoke "scannerese" pretty well and surmised that someone had gone to quite a bit of trouble to remove the BMW from Pete's yard. For one, they had to get past Pete and his dog. Then they had to have towed the vehicle, which was pretty bazaar in itself.

"But that's only half of it," said O'Malley. "I've got it on good authority that when they ran the plates from the car in this afternoon's TC they didn't match the BMW."

"Interesting. The car was a stolen vehicle and the plates were switched with another stolen vehicle. Happens a lot," said Reid.

"Yeah, but get this. These plates were registered to a Mercedes owned by someone with a Sacramento address. A name that nobody will identify on the radio."

⌒⌒⌒⌒⌒

Two men watched the scene from a black van as San Diego PD interviewed the hooker. An ambulance had arrived shortly after the black and white, but no one had yet been taken to the hospital. The coroner's station wagon rolled up and parked alongside the ambulance.

"I knew it. This is not good. Why did you give the stuff to that asshole?" Ratface stared angrily across the van at the other man. "We're supposed to be giving it to the street people, so no one gives a shit. Now it's going to be a scene!"

"It just happened. He said he knew someone who would like to give it a try. Hell, I didn't know he was going to take it himself," said Lobo. "Hey, and we thought this stuff was the good shit."

Luis "Lobo" Lopez sat with his foot on the dashboard as he talked. He was solidly built at 210 pounds. With his "number two" buzz cut hairstyle and tattoo covered arms he looked to be the "A" typical Hispanic gangbanger prevalent in Southeast San Diego. He was. He had a wrap sheet that started when he was twelve with petty theft. Now, at twenty-six, he had been arrested no less than fifteen times for various crimes, including grand theft auto, assault with a deadly weapon, and armed robbery. He did three years of a six-year sentence for carjacking. One more felony, and he would do a stretch of hard time. That is If he got convicted.

The coroner's assistant rolled a gurney out of the back of the station wagon. A black zippered bag was folded neatly at one end like a pillow. He headed off down the alley as the flashing red lights from the police car cast an eerie montage of shadows on the side of a building.

Ratface sat behind the wheel sulking. They were given an easy assignment: Give away some dope, see how people liked it. They could give it to hookers or trade it to their hype friends for stereos. It didn't matter. It was a test. See what it does, the man said. See how people like it. They liked it all right. They liked it fine until they flipped out. A couple of junkies had overdosed and ended up dead, but that wasn't a big thing. A pimp had beaten up a couple of his women pretty bad after snorting some of the stuff. But shit happens on the streets.

Overall, most of the people who tried the new drug liked it. Anything can happen with street drugs, that's all there is to it, thought Ratface. But this guy—the guy in the alley that Lobo had given the stash—he was different. He could actually be missed by someone, and there would most assuredly be an investigation. Not that it couldn't be controlled. Still, they were in trouble.

"Let's go make the fucking call." Ratface started the engine and put the Econoline van in gear. He drove to the corner and made a left turn. "He's not going to like this."

CHAPTER FOUR

Moon Over Water

S enator David Dillard took a long drag of his cigarette. Exhaling, he watched the bluish smoke drift over his desk like a fast moving fog rolling in under the Golden Gate. He liked the smoke and the way it engulfed the telephone and Rolodex as it crept toward the edge of the desk. Smoking was one of his things. Few people knew he smoked. He hid it from the public as much as possible. Never allowed himself to be photographed with a cigarette. It would be political suicide.

The phone rang and he plucked the receiver from its cradle before the always-irritating tone was through. It was his personal line. The one that bypassed the receptionist and his secretary during working hours, and his voice mail after. Only he answered this line. Only a select few people had the number. It didn't ring very often.

"Dillard," he answered in a monotone. There was a pause and then a raspy voice from the other end acknowledged.

"We've got the car."

"Good work. How about the girl?" Dillard couldn't hide the sound of relief in his voice.

"She's a . . . disappeared."

"Disappeared? What in the hell do you think you're doing?" Anger quickly replaced relief. Dillard, as any who knew him soon found out, had a rather short fuse. Especially when he was out of the public eye. Something in his heritage maybe, the Sicilian, or Greek, or Irish.

"Right, sort of," said the hoarse voice. "There's cops all over the place. It wasn't easy getting the car, we had to improvise."

Dillard didn't like it when people improvised. In fact, most improvisations ended up with somebody, or something, getting hurt, or worse. Not that it mattered to Dillard that someone got hurt. It was the possibility of exposure.

"What the fuck happened?" Dillard didn't like what he was hearing.

"She got in a wreck. She crashed the car on the way out to the lake. We were waiting at the store like we planned and when she didn't show up, we started driving in. No way we could miss her unless she took a wrong turn. So we get all the way to Bonsall before we see the car as it's being loaded on to a wrecker." Rocco let the scene sink in before going on.

"There was a lot of commotion going on, but the car didn't look too bad. None of the doors were damaged. We saw the chick talking to the cops. Everything looked okay."

Rocco explained that he and Johnny followed the truck up to a wrecking yard. And then, listening on the scanner, they heard the cops tell the truck driver that they were sending a truck up in the morning to get the car.

Dillard thought about it for a second. Why would the sheriff's office be sending a truck to get the car? Maybe they were on to something. Or, maybe someone on the inside was trying to head off a bad situation before it started.

"I dropped Johnny off to case the place, and went back down to where the wreck was to get the chick. She was gone when I got there. I checked all the stores and places in the area. Then I noticed a couple of detectives cruising around so I took off."

The plan to retrieve the car unfolded quickly. Rocco bought some cough syrup and steak at the store. There were chain cutters in the truck. They drugged the dog, bopped the driver over the head, loaded up the car, and off they went. Rocco followed in the pickup and made sure they weren't being tailed. He was proud of their work and thought Dillard should be pleased that they had averted what could have been a disaster.

They had taken the car to an alternative destination, a backcountry-San Diego ranch where things got done. It was a safe place.

"What a fucking mess," said Dillard, who was now the one doing the improvisational thinking. "We need to get the stuff out of the car as soon as possible. Get your friend on it and start dismantling Asap."

"Johnny's gone, he's taking the wrecker to Tecate. I thought that's what we should do. Right?"

"Fine, but get the merchandise out of the car, I don't care how you do it. Call me back when it's done and I'll give you instructions."

Dillard wasn't pleased. He hated it when things went wrong. And things were going wrong fast. Snubbing his cigarette into the ashtray he swiveled in his chair and looked out over the city. The lights of Sacramento were not the brightest of cities but still a pleasant sight on a cold November evening. From his office he could see the light of a second quarter moon reflecting off the water of the Sacramento River. It's late, he thought, too late to be thinking about a bunch of imbeciles.

Detective Sergeant Manuel Cassio could also see the moon's reflection from his purchase overlooking San Diego Bay. He was sitting in his second favorite chair, the driver's seat of a Crown Vic sheriff's cruiser parked atop Point Loma. It was a good place to think, and tonight he was deep in thought about the events of the previous twelve hours. Something was going on. The car, the plates, the girl, and most of all, the finger of evidence pointing uncharacteristically at State Senator David Dillard, San Diego's pride and joy.

Senator Dillard was a wonder boy in a blue suit who was embraced by both the environmental front and the business community. He solved the Tijuana River sewage problem, and he developed an amazing bilateral agreement with Mexico to site a landfill and build a state-of-the-art recycling facility on Otay Mesa. If he could get his bi-national, international airport plan through the approval hoops, they would probably make him president. Former county supervisor and port commissioner, now chairing the state's Maquiliadora commission to promote trade and industry, David Dillard had forged a highly successful political career.

Dillard and drugs? It didn't add up. But something about him was different, Cassio had noticed.

If we could just talk to the girl, thought Cassio. Or search the car. Unfortunately, both were missing. He hated that. Nothing worse for a detective than letting important evidence slip away or get destroyed. Especially concerning a potentially big case. One with major political overtones. A bombshell case that could explode in any direction, at any time.

He started going back over the facts in his mind. A month ago, Narcotics had busted a meth lab out in the backcountry. Nothing big about that except that the perp, the son of a fairly prominent Point Loma family, claimed to have connections with the governor and threatened the arresting officers. Stephen Casey was stoned when they busted in on him at 4:30 a.m., loaded on crystal and booze. He boasted of selling dope to half the assemblymen in Sacramento, as well as to state officials in Baja. They couldn't bust him without major problems, he told the officers at the scene.

Casey denied everything later, after talking to his lawyer. Shut up like a clam. He had peaked the interest of the officers, though, and in a thorough search of the lab, they turned up some phone numbers and references that did indeed have Sacramento origins. Of the three Sacramento phone numbers, two were to private residences. The other was still being traced. Either that or it was just a wrong number, because it kept coming up as a number that had never been issued for service.

A week ago, San Diego Police had received an anonymous tip that a shipment of drugs would be heading north in a red BMW. The drugs, supposedly a new combination of synthetic morphine and methamphetamine, would be hidden in the side panels of the car. Such tips are not rare on the border. Most are bunk. Some turn out to be worth the effort. SDPD alerted the Border Patrol and other agencies, including San Diego Sheriff's Office. All would be on the lookout for the vehicle. None would make it a major priority. They all had plenty of those.

Yesterday, a car matching the description gets in a wreck in North San Diego County. Probably would have been overlooked completely if it hadn't of been for the plates. After the CHP had taken the reports, the officer had keyed the information into DMV's new automated information system. The system alerted the officer that the plate numbers did not match the vehicle. Unfortunately, this information arrived after the officer had excused the driver of the car. Further queries turned up the alert about a possible drug shipment and the registered owner name corresponding to the plates.

What a mess, thought Cassio. A hotshot drug dealer points the finger at a prominent politico and then evidence starts turning up to support it. Casey was probably selling drugs to parties unknown in the capitol area. The drugs could have seeped into the political arena. Cassio had heard stranger things about the Sacramento circus. But what about Dillard? Notes had been found at the drug lab with the Senator's initials, although David Dillard did not have an exclusive right to the initials DD. Then, license plates registered to a car owned by State Senator Dave Dillard show up on another car, the one that got in the wreck, that matched the description of a car that was supposed to be loaded with drugs. One that later disappeared along with the person driving it.

This was no ordinary case, thought Cassio. What was the thread that linked the parts together? It was late, he should be home in bed. He turned the key to the ignition and jerked the column gear shift into drive. There were few cars on the road as he drove back toward the city. Just one car far behind him, two dim headlights in his rearview mirror. A tail? Or just his imagination.

First thing he'd do in the morning would be to go over all the evidence found up at Pete's Towing. And then he'd go see if he could talk to Pete himself, if possible. Pete wasn't the most talkative person, even without having had his skull half crushed.

Cassio was about to take the 805 freeway home when he decided to take a swing by the office and glance at one more file. The records of drug-lab busts.

Within minutes of his arrival at his office, the phone rang. He recognized the voice immediately: Burt Reid, *The Fallbrook Newspress*.

"Kind of late for a big-city editor, isn't it?" Cassio jabbed. The two had always had a good rapport. Not too friendly, but not contentious. A relationship born of necessity and mutual respect. Good for a cop and newspaperman.

"Not any later than it is for a big-city detective," replied Reid. "Manny, what's the deal? They wouldn't let us in to the junkyard tonight. They said there would be a statement on the hotline in the morning. That's fine for the dailies, but we need an angle, it's our backyard."

"You know, Reid, I damn near don't know any more about this than you do. That's off the record," said Cassio. "On the record, we got an assault with a deadly weapon, possible attempted murder, or murder if Pete buys it, grand theft auto twice, removing evidence from a crime scene, and probably more by the time we catch up with these guys."

"So you think it was more than one guy? What did they hit Pete with?

"Can't say."

"Can't say or won't say?"

"Can't say."

"How did they get the car out of Pete's?"

"They took his truck, too."

"Manny, what about the high-heel footprints? Were they a woman's prints? Do you think it was the same woman that was in the wreck?"

Shit, Reid was being a reporter now, thought Cassio. How did he find out about the other footprints found at the junkyard. "I don't know anything about any high-heel footprints found at the scene."

"Come on, was the gal in the wreck wearing high heels? I'll find out from Chippies anyway."

"The CHP does not care what a person is wearing when he or she gets in an accident. And I don't have any information on what kind of footwear the driver in the wreck was wearing." Cassio was tired and Reid, as much as he liked him, was beginning to sound just like all reporters, which he didn't like.

"Okay, one more thing. Who phoned in the 9-1-1 about Pete?"

"I don't know."

"Was it from Pete's?"

"I can't tell you that."

"Can't or won't?"

"Can't."

"Was it a man or a woman?"

"Reid, it's late, I haven't been through the whole damn report, it isn't complete, and I don't like answering questions from the press when I don't have all the information. It makes for bad copy."

Cassio was squirming, Reid thought, he should go for the jugular now, but that wasn't his style. This would be the biggest story in years, he would milk it. Stay in good with his sources. And Cassio was a good guy under all the crap.

"All right, sergeant. Sorry to jump on you this late, but this thing has really got me going."

Cassio sighed. "Me, too."

High on a hill overlooking a moonlit Ensenada Bay, another set of eyes reflected on the events of the day while watching the moonlight dance on water. Carlos Sobrano wished desperately for the phone to ring, a voice of assurance on the other end of the line. He took another sip of his VSOP and puffed at the Macanudo cigar in his left hand. Damn gringos, can't do anything right. So easy, just get the car to the ranch. The hard part had been accomplished easily; the inspectors at the Tijuana border had waved the car through without a second glance.

Sobrano wasn't a man to worry, but he knew if the car fell into the wrong set of hands there would be hell to pay. Years of carefully planned infiltration erased with a crunch of metal. The risks, the money, the time, all for nothing. And, much worse, a scandal that would surely ruin many lives and shake the foundation of an agreement between two countries. But what else could he have done?

High on a hill overlooking a moonlit Ensenada Bay, another set of eyes reflected on the events of the day while watching the moonlight dance on water.

Out at sea, beyond the lights of Ensenada Bay, a commercial fishing boat was plying its trade. The *Linda Marie* was trolling for selective varieties of fish: swordfish, dorado, wahoo, yellow tail. The fish that brought the high dollar. She would circle the Coronado Islands heading south from San Diego Bay to Ensenada and then back again through the early morning hours. Sometime in the night, hopefully, one or two of the lines would go taut and a long pole would bend like the stick of a pole vaulter. A fish, two fish, a school, the jackpot!

The throb of the diesel and sounds of the sea at night were suddenly interrupted by the frenzied whine of a fishing reel spinning off at high speed. The music of fishing. The alarm that brought crew members to their feet with anticipation. Somewhere behind the boat one of the imitation squid or herring had attracted the attention of a sea creature. Maybe more. The captain of the *Linda Marie* cut the engines as a deckhand ran to tend the line.

Looking down from his perch above the deck, the captain watched as the line was reeled in. Big fish by the looks of the pole and the effort of the deckhand. The captain turned and flicked a toggle switch on the control panel. Light illuminated the water behind the boat. Eyes anxiously scanned for that telltale sign. The jump of a swordfish, the explosion of a yellowfin tuna. But this time there was no such action. Instead, the line was sluggish with dead weight.

"Feels like a log or something. No fish here," the crew member stopped reeling and looked up at the captain. "Want to back us up?"

The captain let out a sigh and turned to put the screws in reverse. They would back up after the other hands had secured all the other trolling lines. They could cut the line and move on, but they would lose a jig. Jigs, especially good ones, cost money. And the captain liked his jigs. He made many of them himself. Within minutes the *Linda Marie* was bobbing backwards in the swells following a rigid line that led off into the moonlight. The lights of the coastline danced on the water as three of the six men on board returned to the card game they were playing in the cabin.

"Oh, noooo." The deckhand reeling in the line stopped. "Look at that." He pointed in the direction of the line.

The captain knew by the tone of the deckhand's voice it wasn't going to be good news. He strained his eyes to see, following the line out into the dark water. There, about fifty feet away, he could just barely make out what was at the end of the line. It was wearing a white coat.

CHAPTER FIVE

Long Ball

A whoosh of air followed by a crisp hard knock. The solid sound of hardwood hitting rubberized plastic. It was the morning serenade at the Bonsall Downs Driving Range, on a cool, sunny November morning in Southern California. Music to a snowbird's ears.

Logan Mullhaney looked up in time to see the ball he had just struck start to tail off to the right. It was a long ball, and hit high above most of the trees that lined the fairway, but it was curving to the right. Ever so slightly at first, and then more pronounced with each foot of dissension as it returned to terra firma.

"It's back . . . . Damn it!" He spoke to no one in particular. In fact, no one else on the driving range was within hearing distance. Big Mike was at the other end of the range pitching balls at the 100-yard flag. There were three other golfers hitting balls. Snowbirds most likely, thought Logan. They were strangers, with strange swings, and, for that matter, strange clothes. Snowbirds always had strange clothes. Something about the scarcity of sunlight in Canada that made them go crazy when they hit Southern California. Other than the clothes, and the fact that they didn't tip very well, it was hard to tell a snowbird. No accent, other than the occasional "ey" or "oot," and "aboot."

Using the club in his hand, a classic persimmon three-wood, he nudged another range ball from the bucket lying on its side in the grass. He tapped it into place in his stance and then set the polished wooden club directly behind the ball. With his right hand he turned the shaft of the club counterclockwise about one sixteenth of a turn, closing the club face ever so slightly, which had the effect of aiming it about ten degrees left of the target. Placing his left hand on the club, he adjusted his grip and settled into his stance. He looked at the ball first, then at the target, and then back to the ball. An unconscious ritual, he repeated it three times before starting his swing. After each look back at the ball, he lifted the club about an inch off the turf and took it back a foot or so using only his wrists. He had read where this "waggle," as it was called, was one of Ben Hogan's swing keys.

On his third look at the target, and following his third waggle, Logan's right knee moved about two inches toward the ball, which initiated a whole chain of events that would eventually launch a nondescript golf ball on a trajectory toward a randomly selected target some 220 yards away.

"Damn," he let go with a breath. "Not now, not before tomorrow." The slice that plagued his game from time to time was creeping back into his swing. It had a way of rearing its head at the most inopportune times.

"Inside ooot, man, that's the only way to cure the slice."

The voice startled Logan. He turned to see one of the strangers from down the range watching him from behind. He hadn't seen the guy come over.

"It's not really a slice, it's a fade. And I'll work it out," shot back Logan.

"Fine, but the only way it will go away is by swinging inside ooot," said the man in white and blue plaid pants. He gave up and walked back toward his golf bag, which was lying three places over. Logan hadn't really noticed the man hitting balls, mostly because he was intent on working on his own game and because snowbirds in plaid pants and funny hats usually all looked and played alike. Logan noticed the hat as the man was walking away. It was a classic Tam O'Shanter. Maybe the guy did have some Scottish blood in him, Logan thought. Still there was something odd about him, and familiar. He was tall and thin with dark hair and a moustache. His eyes had deep dark circles under them. He was either a worrier or an insomniac or a drug addict. Had he seen him before?

Logan had a smooth swing. Not textbook, but good enough to earn him occasional prize money in the Bonsall Downs Mens Club weekly tournaments and respect as a "player" at the club. Which really meant he played golf and would usually pay his bets off when he lost, and buy drinks when he won. On the next swing, Logan left the club face square to the target as he set up and took the club back a little more to the inside, turning a bit more in the shoulder. When the clubhead struck the ball, he could feel the solid contact. The ball exploded off the clubface and cut through the morning sky like a tiny white meteor. This time the ball's trajectory took it dead straight in the direction Logan was aiming, slightly left of the flag. It came to rest about 220 yards away, a good twenty five feet left of the target.

"All right," muttered Logan.

He quickly reloaded a ball into his stance and fired off another round. The ball traced the trajectory of his last ball. Logan was pleased. The clatter of spikes on an asphalt cart path turned his attention to the hill. The man with the funny hat was on his way back up to the clubhouse. Logan watched as the snowbird passed another golfer making his way down to the range. It was Burt Reid.

Reid stopped to put a couple of tokens in the ball machine that was housed by a small gazebo at the end of the range. The machine made a distinctive racket when it dropped its load of range balls in the bucket, sounding like a berserk drummer in a frenzied drum roll that began with a wild flurry of beats and tapered off sporadically as the last few balls fell.

Reid retrieved a bucket of balls and walked over to where Logan was diligently launching balls into the ionosphere courtesy of his classic persimmon 3-wood and revamped "inside ooot" swing.

"All right, looks like you're in the groove for the match," commented Reid as he dropped his bag next to Logan's.

"Yeah, just a little something I've been working on," said Logan.

Gripping a club at opposite ends, Reid held it over his head and began a series of warm-up twists and turns.

"Logan, have you seen that blonde since yesterday?"

"No, should I have?"

"I don't know, you seem to get around a lot, and I thought you might have run in to her at the club, or Ringers," said Reid.

"Nope, haven't seen her. Never saw her before yesterday, probably never will." Logan recalled the intensity of the two detectives the night before. "Why?"

"Seems like you're the only one who talked to her, and then she just vanished into the blue," said Reid.

"She had a drink and left, I really didn't talk to her." Although there was some sort of communication between them, thought Logan. The way she looked at him. Her movements, the tone of her voice. He felt as if he knew her a little, at least he knew he would recognize her if he saw her again, and he was confident that she would remember him.

Logan tapped a couple more balls out of the bucket and went about the routine of gripping the club, setting up, aiming, waggling, and hitting the ball. Reid was finishing his warm-ups by swinging two clubs together back and forth in the approximate arc of a full swing. The morning sun was well up over the hills to the east. The early morning dew had all but evaporated from the fairways, leaving only a trace of dampness. High up on a hill to the south, overlooking the golf course and country club, a set of binoculars focused on the two golfers as they talked.

"This whole thing is pretty bazaar," explained Reid. "I've been hearing all sorts of rumors. The car is tied to the Mexican Mafia, part of a big drug operation, the girl was a runner, there was a couple of million stashed in the car and the crooks want it back . . . any of it could be true."

Most of it, of course, was newsroom conjecture. O'Mally, the photographer, had most of the theories. At times, O'Mally had tabloid potential as a reporter. He definitely had a vent toward the extreme and was fairly quick to voice his opinions.

Molinski had been poking around and had her own ideas. And then there was a call Reid had received from a reporter in Sacramento. He was working on a story about the car involved in the crash being connected to someone in the state government. In typical reporter fashion, he tried to get as much information as possible without divulging too much about what he was doing. In typical editor style, Reid had given him as little as possible while scrutinizing the requests for possible leads of his own.

Reid recounted what he knew about the case to Logan. The car had been stolen out of Pete's junkyard, along with Pete's truck. And that Pete had been hit over the head and was taken to Palomar Trauma Center by LifeFlight helicopter. "People and things just keep disappearing. It makes for pretty interesting stuff."

Reid knocked over the bucket of balls at his feet with the 7-iron. The balls spilled out on the grass. After a couple of full practice swings, he tapped one over and began his pre-swing routine, which was much the same as Logan's with a few variations. His waggle was much slower and more pronounced. His knee twitched oddly before he started the final swing. Reid clipped the ball with the 7-iron, catching it right in the center of the club. It sailed through the morning air heading straight for a flag that marked 150 yards.

The conversation switched to golf and the upcoming match. The two were regular partners in the Saturday morning Men's Club. They played against other twosomes, most often Big Mike and Spike. The Saturday golf match was a ritual. Like a job.

Logan finished hitting the last of his balls, said good-bye to Reid, and headed back up the hill to go to work. It was Friday. Always a good day, he thought. The binoculars followed him uphill and to the parking lot, where he threw his clubs in the back of his truck and changed shoes. The Paddock was just down the hill from the club, "a drive and a 9-iron." Easy walk or short drive. Logan never walked where he could drive.

He drove down the hill, past the 100-year-old schoolhouse and past the re-locatable building that served as the fire station. He pulled routinely into the back lot of the Paddock. A car pulled in next to him as he was opening the door to get out. It was a new Toyota that had rent-a-car written all over it. He glanced at the driver. It was her.

Logan opened his door and let it hang open for a moment while he gathered his clipboard and some papers off the front seat. A controlled stall, in the words of an old surfer. Moving in slow motion, he gathered his thoughts and got out of the truck. He glanced again at the car, half expecting it not to be there. It was.

The door opened and he watched as she stepped out of the car. One long tan leg at a time. She was wearing a white flower-print, knee-length sundress and white pumps that were somehow out of place for a fall day in Bonsall. A blue wool shawl was draped around her shoulders, and she pulled it together tucking the left side under the right, which was long enough to toss over her shoulder. Turning around after she stood up, she leaned over and reached back in across the seats to get her purse. Logan couldn't help but notice the dress ride up the back of her legs, revealing rather well-toned muscles.

He cleared his throat but was at a loss for words. He looked away as she moved out of the car and turned around. When he glanced back, she was looking directly at him. She was beautiful, he thought, blonde, wavy, shoulder-length hair, a face with thin features but soft and tan. Very tan. She was wearing rose-colored sunglasses that revealed a hint of her almond-shaped eyes. He guessed they were blue. She was tall, probably about five-foot eight, thin, and not without shape.

"You're Logan, the bartender?" she asked, opening her purse and pulling out a light green pack of Bensen and Hedges. There was an edge to the voice. Stress will do that, hard living, late nights, or any of life's other sidebars.

"I'm Logan, and I do tend bar here, so I guess that would make me Logan-the-Bartender," he said, smiling. "And you're the mystery lady from the crash."

Logan thought he noticed a twinge when he said the word "mystery." He was just making conversation. Nervous conversation, at that. She looked innocent in the morning light, not the kind of person the cops would be after. Maybe they were wrong about her. He reached in his jacket for a match, but she had already found her lighter. He asked how she was feeling after the ordeal.

"Thanks, my back is still a little sore and my neck, but I didn't get hurt. I need to talk to you for a minute. Can we go inside?"

She followed him in through the back door, glancing more than once at the highway and surrounding area. She smelled of gardenias, or jasmine, or both. It was a thick sensual smell that evoked visions of tropical islands and jungle forests.

Logan followed the sweet scent and talked as he led her through the kitchen. Tony and Carlos were busy chopping fresh vegetables for the day's offerings. Tomatoes, onions, lettuce, an assortment of chili peppers, avocado, and cilantro were the mainstay. He told her he didn't know the driver of the other car. He didn't mention the cops.

She listened to the mundane account of the previous day's mishap as Logan led her to the bar area.

"You'll have to talk while I set up," Logan said as they walked out the door to the dining room. Logan pointed the way for her around the cocktail waitress station and into the bar. He went back through the kitchen and through the arched open doorway that led behind the bar. He tossed the bag and keys on the sink board and turned on the hot water. With no wasted moves, he started a pot of coffee, tuned-in the jazz station on the radio, filled the two ice bins with ice, filled the sinks with water, one with soap, one with rinse water, set up his garnish tray rubber catch-all, and put out clean white folded towels.

Each move was made with unconscious effort. He was on automatic pilot, a magic bartender's dance that prepared him for the onslaught of the day. The positioning of the tip jar, the tuning of the radio, everything in its place. Routine.

She began with her name, Janine.

"Would you like a cup of coffee?" he asked, reaching for two mugs.

"Thanks, but I'd rather have a drink. Stoly with a splash of soda, please, and a twist," she said.

She talked calmly as he made her drink. She wanted to know everything that happened after she left the bar the day of the accident. He told her about the detectives coming to The Club. She was very interested in what the cops had asked and didn't appear surprised when he told her they were from downtown.

"How could you tell they were from San Diego?"

"The suits were a tip off. We've got all uniforms up here," Logan took a towel and started wiping down the bar, not that it needed it. "And, I know one of them. Cassio. Used to work up here. He's a good guy."

"Were they asking about me?" She watched Logan nod. "By name?"

"Nope, but they were also very interested in the car." He thought she jumped a little when he said "car."

She looked away. "They towed it away. Do you know where it is?"

"From what I hear, it was stolen from the junkyard. They are definitely looking for it, and definitely looking for you."

She wanted to know if anyone other than the police had been asking any questions. Logan hadn't heard of anyone asking about it other than Reid and that pesky reporter from _The Blade_. Logan thought she seemed relieved with that bit of information.

"Look, I'm just a bartender. I don't know everything that goes on around here. I don't want to know. If you're in some kind of trouble, I'd just come clean with it and get it over. There are better things in life."

Finishing her drink, she reached in her purse and pulled out a twenty-dollar bill. Logan continued his bartender set-up dance by counting his bank for the cash register. He made neat stacks of quarters, dimes, and nickels on the bar. He had already counted the bills and put them in the cash drawer.

"Want me to freshen that up for you?" he asked. He looked into her eyes. Trouble, no doubt. His little voice told him to back away from it. Stay out of it. He didn't need the pain. But then, he always had a soft spot. Especially for pretty blondes with troubled pasts. "Look, why don't you tell me a little more about what's going on and maybe I can be of more help." He knew better than to ask specific questions, but maybe given the opportunity she would open up.

It was a stupid thing to say, he thought. But, he was curious and couldn't help wanting to know more about her. Damn that voice. Yet, there was some natural chemistry here gaining momentum in the moment. Attraction, infatuation, intrigue, they were all at work. And, there was another emotion brewing. She was a dangerous woman.

"From where I stand, this thing is all about drugs and gangsters and bullshit that I don't want to get involved with," said Logan. "But I admit I'm curious, and if I can help, without getting myself involved, I will." There, he said it, and knew as soon as he did that it was a ridiculous statement.

The last thing Logan wanted in life was to get in to the fast lane. He didn't have much to show for his 40-odd years. He didn't own anything that couldn't be packed up and thrown in the back of a car in less than ten minutes. Nothing permanent like a house or a condo. Hell, he didn't even own a car. He drove Mori's truck. But he was happy and free, and he had friends.

She watched him with an aloof sort of stare, like she didn't really give a damn about anything. "Give me another, easy on the Stoly. I'll be right back," she said, picking up her purse. He watched as she walked through the dining room to the ladies rest room. Long tan legs and all.

Logan switched the radio back to AM and tuned in the all sports station. He glanced at his watch. It was almost eleven o'clock, time to open the front doors. He could hear the chatter of the two lunch waitresses, Tracy and Dorothy, setting up in the back. They were talking away as usual about everything and nothing. He poured Janine's drink and went back to his routine, which also involved going next door to get the morning paper and the _Racing Form_.

When he returned, Janine was still not back from the rest room. Her drink sat untouched on the counter. The $20 was where she had left it. Vaguely familiar, he thought. He went around behind the bar again. The side door to the bar rattled open with a scraping, clanking sound, and the morning sun poured through the door, silhouetting a short, stocky body. Detective Cassio was paying a morning visit.

"Morning Logan." It was the good cop's voice again, but it could still send chills down an innocent man's neck. "Need to ask you a few more questions."

Cassio's eyes didn't miss the drink and twenty dollar bill on the bar.

Reid had just about finished hitting his bucket when something caught his eye. Big Mike and a man wearing a funny-looking hat were deep in conversation near the gazebo. The man handed Mike a small folded paper packet. Reid hit another ball, keeping an eye on the two by the gazebo. He liked Mike, but he also knew his potential for trouble. The big man could have been much more successful in life and in business if he could just stay away from the booze and other distractions. What he was witnessing looked for all the world like a drug deal.

He waited a minute and then sneaked another glance. Sure enough, Mike was taking a sniff of something from the packet. Reid looked away. This was none of his business. What people did with their lives was their own doing, as long as it didn't hurt someone or infringe on someone else's life. Live and let live. Unless, of course, it was a news story. This wasn't. He went back to hitting balls and concentrating on his game.

The tall snowbird with the funny hat walked up the asphalt path to the clubhouse, leaving Big Mike sitting on a bench in front of the gazebo, staring off into space. When Reid walked by ten minutes later, Mike hadn't moved except to blink his eyes. Reid said hello, but there was no answer. It was as if he didn't exist.

CHAPTER SIX

Ranches And Branches

Rocco checked the garage door one more time to make sure it was locked. He hated leaving the ranch alone when there was stash there. But there was no phone and he needed to report back to Dillard. It wouldn't be a good news report.

He had no luck getting the cargo from the BMW. He was not a welder, nor a mechanic, and he really didn't want to blow himself up trying to cut through some panel with an acetylene torch. There were some things that he was good at; this was not one of them.

Dillard would be hot. But then Rocco had never seen any other side of the strange politician. It had been a little more than a year since Michael "The Marlin" Marleano had introduced Rocco to Dillard. A year of running errands, counting money, driving loads of drugs from stash houses to customers. Marlin was Rocco's only real friend. Rocco was Marlin's number-one gopher.

It was Marlin who had put Sobrano in touch with Dillard, a brilliant introduction that netted all three of them hundreds of thousands of dollars in the past year. Dillard and Marlin controlled the "El Norte" operations with ranches in the backcountry of Riverside and San Diego counties. They used them as holding areas for various illicit commodities. Dillard controlled the Riverside facility, while Marlin managed the one in San Diego. It was a nice arrangement that gave them a lot of options in dispersing their wares.

Marlin's eleven-plus acre spread was located in the extreme northeastern reaches of San Diego County overlooking the Anza Borrego Desert. It was a dry yet alpine setting, desert-hot in the summer, mountain-cold in the winter. A unique microclimate tucked away in the calico hills of inland California.

Rocco stepped up into the cab of the pickup and cranked the ignition key. The starter motor groaned with the unmistakable sound of a Dodge. After a prolonged whine, the big motor fired up with a roar. He let it warm up a bit while he made sure he had everything. His small notebook and bank bag full of quarters were on the seat. He used a lot of pay phones.

Opening the book, he went over his notes, which were more like two and three-word reminders. It wasn't good to ramble when you were talking to Dillard, he was a stickler for efficiency. He demanded that Rocco keep a notepad with him all the time so he wouldn't forget anything. Make a list, do the things on the list, burn the list. That was the code.

With his right foot on the brake pedal, Rocco wrenched the column-shift into drive and released the emergency brake. The truck lurched, then started its tractor-like roll down the dirt driveway toward a row of medium-size pine trees leading out to the gate. Rocco felt like blasting through the locked gate, the frustration of dealing with the BMW was building inside him. Now he would have to tell Dillard about his failure to complete the orders. Dillard would not be pleased.

He always felt like someone was watching him whenever he got out to open the gate. Worse, when he was alone, he had to get out a second time to lock the gate behind him. It was a hassle just to drive down the road and make a phone call.

The ranch was about a half-mile from the highway. There were at least three phone booths within a thirty-minute drive and he was instructed to never use the same booth twice in a row. That was another of the rules Rocco didn't like.

There was a bar and country store down the road with a phone he hadn't used in a while. The place was supposed to have been an old stage stop on the Butterfield Overland Trail, but then just about every store in the backcountry claimed to be a stop on the Overland Trail.

The day was cold and gray. Rain was on the wind or maybe even snow. It could snow at the ranch, at least that's what Rocco had been told. He was usually only there in the summer or fall.

Arriving at the Old Stage Stop Bar and Grill, he angled the truck into the parking lot. A woman was using the phone in front of the old log building that was the bar. He turned off the truck and debated going in for a cup of coffee. That would be breaking another of the rules. No contact. He watched as the woman hung up the receiver and left the booth. She had dull blonde hair and a plain face with thin lips. Her faded jeans fit tight and she was not unshapely, Rocco noticed.

Rocco grabbed a roll of quarters and his notepad and walked to the phone booth. He closed the door, dialed the number, and waited for the computer voice to tell him how much he needed to insert. The line made some funny noises and then started ringing. Something seemed different about the sound. Maybe it was his imagination.

The phone rang, no answer. He dialed again. Same result. Again he felt the pangs of frustration building within him. It was tough being out here alone, he thought. Dillard needed to know he hadn't got the stash to Anza yet, and he would need some help.

Rocco flipped his notebook to the inside back cover, where he kept his emergency numbers. He dialed a number and waited as the phone shifted through its automated series of tones and clicks. More quarters, more little bell sounds. The ring, if you could call it that, sounded distant and under water.

"Hello," a man with a very horse voice answered.

"Bobo, it's me Rocco. What's happening, man? You sound wasted." Bobo, which was a nickname for Bob, and Bob was known to have a few drinks. In fact, he was known to have a few drinks and a few of whatever else he could get his hands on to insulate himself from whatever reality was serving up. When he was sober, he was a brilliant mechanic, locksmith, handyman, and jack-of-all. When he was twisted, he could be worthless.

"Hey, Roc. I'm just working on some stuff here, what's up? Where are you?"

"I'm in Tim-fuckin'-buck-tu, now listen. I may need your help, but I need to get it okayed first. Are you ready to leave for a couple of days and give me a hand?"

There was a pause on the other end and some muffled sounds Rocco couldn't make out.

"Sure man, I can help," said Bobo. "You know me. Just as long as I ain't going to get in any trouble."

Another pause, then Bobo continued with more of a hushed tone to his voice. "Hey Roc, this won't have anything to do with this shit that's been in the papers would it?"

Rocco's stomach twinged. "What's happening? I haven't seen any papers."

"Well . . . you might want to look at yesterday's _Times_. There was a story in there about some new drug that's hit the streets in San Diego. People are dying and shit. Then there was an article about a car registered to some state senator guy named Dillard getting stolen and connected to a drug ring . . . it's bazaar, man."

Bobo was half-laughing as he talked. Rocco was not amused. He knew Ratface and Lobo had been giving test batches to people for several months with mixed results. The last thing they needed was for the media to get the cops worked up about a new drug. That would bring heat. He wished Marlin was around, he would know how to handle this. Rocco always did what Marlin told him to do. His last instructions were to work with Dillard and see that he gets whatever he needs.

Dillard was a strange duck, thought Rocco. Most knew him as an important politician who had a lot of connections. But there was the other side of Dillard, the side his constituents didn't know. The Dillard that craved drugs, money, women, and power. Rocco also knew Dillard, the complete asshole, the stoned idiot. The stories were horrendous, but only a few knew them.

He said good-bye to Bobo, without inviting him out to the ranch. There was an impending sense of danger now and he needed to think very carefully before doing anything stupid. He needed to see what was in the _Times_, then speak to Marlin. There was a bubble-top newspaper rack in front of the store. He went over, but before putting his quarter in the slot he looked at the date. It was today's. Where could he find yesterday's edition of the _Times_? His eyes fixed on the door to the bar. It was against the rules to go in any establishment within the area of the ranch. But it was time to bend the rules. He could feel his hands shaking, and there were butterflies in his stomach. His forehead was hot. This was an emergency.

Walking through the door, his eyes had to make an adjustment to the dark room. The walls were natural wood and covered with old beer signs, tack and harness equipment, and assorted farm implements. The term "rustic" didn't do this decor justice, Rocco thought. There were four or five customers lounging in the bar, one of whom was the girl with the tight jeans. She was sitting at the end of the bar drinking what appeared to be a shot and a beer. She was smoking a cigarette, as were several of the other patrons in the dingy room. The stench of stale beer and cigarette smoke enveloped his senses.

"I'll have a Lite beer," he said. The bartender was a woman. Short, squatty, with fleshy white cheeks and dull brown hair worn in a thick braided ponytail. She had a hard look to her that came from too many late Saturday nights in a backcountry bar. She'd likely broken up her share of fights, Rocco thought. He wouldn't want to mess with her. She set down a smallish bar napkin without a word and proceeded to dig through the reach-in for a bottle of Lite.

She came back with the beer and a glass that could have used another run through the hot water.

"Buck seventy five," she said in a flat tone. Rocco put out a five and she snatched it off the bar like a bear grabbing a drumstick off of a picnic table. As she ambled over to the cash register, Rocco could feel the eyes in the room watching him. He needed to be low key, but how could he blend in a place like this?

"Excuse me. You wouldn't happen to have yesterday's _Los Angeles Times_ behind the bar, would you?"

"Why? Something special in there you want to read?" shot back the bartender. The way she answered startled Rocco. It was like she knew exactly what he was looking for.

"No . . . ," Rocco fumbled with his words. "I just like to keep up and I missed yesterday's paper."

"Got today's out in the rack, that's better than yesterday's. But I don't read no _Los Angeles Times_ anyway. Only reason they have that damn thing out here is because of all them people from L.A. movin' in."

Rocco forgot he was in San Diego County, worse, he was in the backcountry of San Diego County, and people here especially didn't like urbanites from Orange County or L.A. Rocco decided to drop the matter. Maybe there would be a follow-up in today's edition. He took a sip from his beer.

"I think I still have some of it." The voice was deep but feminine. A voice that had maybe yelled a lot, talked too loud and said too much. Rocco looked up at the blonde at the end of the bar. "It's on the table." She exhaled smoke and pointed to a table in the corner.

She slid back the bar stool, went over to the table, and returned with parts of a disheveled paper. Rocco thanked her.

"I'm Sally," she said. "What are you looking for, maybe I can help?" She wasn't going back to her seat.

Rocco took a long drink of beer. Another time he might have been interested in talking to her. Today he was beginning to get annoyed.

"Just wanted to check a couple of things," he replied. "Don't need any help . . . but thanks."

He continued trying to fold the paper back into its original order, or as close to it as possible. He had the front section, Metro, and the classifieds. Sports and the Feature section were missing. He started scanning the front page. On the fourth page under State, he saw the headline: "State Senator Questioned." He looked up. Sally was still standing there. She was looking at him, sort of dazed, with a half smile on her face. It was a smile he recognized.

"You're kind of cute," she said, the booze clearly having its effect.

Cute? He'd been called a lot of things but "cute" was not one of them. His mother had told him he was handsome, but that was a long time ago. Before he'd gone to Viet Nam. Now he was just an average guy with a receding hairline, an average build, and sad brown eyes that had seen too much. Rocco put down the paper. He wished she would go away.

"Look, I gotta go," he said, folding the State section into quarters. He picked up the change from his five, leaving a dollar and a couple of quarters on the bar along with the rest of the paper. Sally looked disappointed. He walked out into the gray mid-day light and dug into his jacket for his sunglasses.

He'd left the truck unlocked, another rule broken. The door from the bar opened and Sally appeared. She headed straight for the truck.

"Hey, can you help me out and give me a lift? My car's broke, and I need to get back home and wait for my mechanic to come out and fix it."

Rocco thought for a second. No way out, it would be more of a scene not to take her, unless he could think of an excuse fast.

"Where you going?" he asked. She indicated that it was just "down the road a bit" and wouldn't take him out of his way at all. She got in, and he started the truck. "Which way?"

She took a cigarette from her purse and lit it. She set the purse on the floor, then turned so that her back was in the corner of the truck between the seat and the door. She lifted her left leg up on to the seat.

"Where we goin'?" he asked, feeling a little tingle between his legs. This is ridiculous, he thought. He could see the booze in her eyes, smell it in pores, and she was coming on to him. A shadow of lust lingered in the moment. There was no way he was going to let this happen. He had enough troubles.

"Turn right," she said. "It's just down the road a bit."

They drove down the highway for about a mile to a defunct old motel, where she told him to pull in and park. It was a spooky old place. A place where tramps and druggies were likely to hang out. A forgotten place, on a backcountry highway. A destination, for some.

"Would you mind coming in with me for a second? Just to make sure there's nobody here. A girl can't be too careful nowadays." She looked at him with apprehension in her eyes. He had to say no.

She led him across the broken asphalt parking lot to one of the rooms. The motel had obviously been abandoned for some time from its appearance, but the buildings were made of solid adobe brick and still very much intact. Probably built in the '20s. The room was dark and had a musty smell. There was a bed with a bare mattress in the corner. She closed the door behind them and let her purse slide off her shoulder. In one swift motion she was kissing him and pressing herself against him.

Rocco tried to stop but found himself giving in. Subtle at first, then harder. Too late. He danced her back toward the bed. No stopping.

Her hands found his belt buckle and in a second his pants were at his ankles. He felt her hands on him, and then he felt the touch of her naked skin. They hit the bed with a bounce and he fell into her. The bed squeaked with the motion. Her breathing was loud. Too loud. He could see her eyes were slightly open in the dim light. Two slits staring off at some unknown mantra. Her mouth was slightly open and smiling. He could see her yellowing front teeth. He was pounding now, an uneven sprint to some imaginary finish line.

It was over in a flurry. They lay still for what seemed like a long time. The room was ghostly silent, except for their breathing. A truck passing on the highway interrupted Rocco's thoughts and brought him crashing back to reality. He felt a twinge of panic. Guilt. He had broken all the rules. He had gone to the bar, he talked to people, hell, he had sex in an abandoned motel. All in the course of about two hours.

It would have been funny, except that now a feeling of impending doom swept over him. Dillard might be under investigation and might come unglued at any moment. This was a disaster. He had a car full of dope at the ranch and a stolen tow truck that, hopefully, was far below the border by now and still heading south. Things were not going well. He needed to read the article again and hopefully find out what kind of investigation was going on.

Rocco stood and pulled his pants back up. He had never even taken his shoes off. Sally remained on the bed, sitting up after he stood. She dressed without saying anything. Finally Rocco broke the silence.

"I've got to go, I'm late for an appointment," he said.

"I know," she said, not looking at him. "Can you drop me off? I'll just go back to the Stage Stop. I can get a ride from there," she said, a note of despair in her hoarse voice.

Rocco felt sorry for her. And, he had the feeling, he wasn't the first suitor she had taken to this unsavory boudoir. Among other things, he thought, she was desperately lonely.

Sally lit up a smoke and they left as unceremoniously as they had arrived. Rocco started the truck and pointed it back down the highway toward the Stage Stop. Nothing was said until they pulled into the dirt and gravel lot of the shaded little country complex.

"I don't know why I did that. I'm sorry," said Rocco feeling he needed to say something.

"You don't have to apologize. It's just something people do. You know. It's fine." There was something in her voice that made him feel better. Less guilty.

"So you hang out here often?" he asked.

"Mostly on weekends. I live down in San Diego now. I used to live up here, then my family split up. It's a long story."

Rocco nodded. "We've all got stories. Most aren't worth telling." He caught a glance at her looking out the window. Sad eyes. "Maybe, I'll see you around. Maybe we'll both be in a better place then."

"Maybe. Hey what's your name?"

"Roger. Roger Green."

"Okay, Roger Green. Be safe."

He took one last look at her before pulling out. What a waste. She wasn't bad looking, plain maybe, but she had something. She could have made somebody a good woman, but probably not now. It was obvious she had some problems. The thought came to him that Sally hooked in San Diego, and that he was a freebie. He hadn't noticed that there were two less rolls of quarters in his bank bag.

On the way back to the ranch, he stopped under a stand of oaks and rummaged through the paper until he found the article. He noted that it had a Sacramento dateline.

"Police in San Diego are investigating a bazaar string of events involving a hit-and-run accident, an attempted murder, and a possible link to a Sacramento legislator."

Rocco's eyes widened as he read the words "attempted murder." Shit, I didn't hit him that hard, he thought. That guy must have had a soft head. He read on. The story said that allegations linking the senator to a car and unidentified driver had surfaced in an article that appeared in a Fallbrook paper. It gave an account of the disappearance of the car from the junkyard and the assault on the owner. Nothing linking anyone with those crimes. He read on. The plates on the wrecked car were registered to David F. Dillard. "Damn, who in the hell did that? Idiots," Rocco said aloud. "How in the hell could they do something so stupid!"

He turned the page. In a separate incident, a drug bust in the east county area a month before had turned up leads linking Senator David F. Dillard to a meth lab and dealing operation. The senator called the allegations preposterous and blamed the whole thing on a conspiracy to unseat him from the state Senate.

The senator did have a drug problem, thought Rocco. It was his weak point. He loved the speed, and it made him irrational at times and extremely hard to deal with. Even though Rocco knew the two events were unrelated, the article made a good case for making the senator look pretty bad. A drug test on the senator, although not proposed in the article, would probably show that he was a regular user. The wreck and the plates were two unfortunate mistakes.

He turned the big Dodge back on to the highway and drove toward the ranch. Why were the senator's plates on the Beemer? Whoever loaded the car must have put them on for a reason. The Mexicans probably just switched them out of habit. And what happened to the driver? The whole thing was getting out of hand, maybe he should just pack up his shit and head south. It wasn't a bad idea, he thought.

He drove down the dirt road to the ranch, thinking about Mexico. He was oblivious in thought until he came to an automatic stop at the front gate. It took a second for it to register, then his jaw dropped, and he stared in disbelief. The gate was standing wide open.

CHAPTER SEVEN

Pink Polly

Rocco's heart was pounding. Why was the gate open? Cops? He tried to calm himself and think. He could turn the truck around and take off, but where would he go? He could drive on up and just meet the situation head-on. Or, he could park the truck by the back gate and sneak around by the stable. If it was really bad, he could run. One thing was for sure, whoever was up there and why they were there, it couldn't be good.

Rocco eased the truck back out and up the road to the back gate, less than a half mile away. Parking the truck at the back gate would look funny to the neighbors, but there wasn't much else he could do.

He climbed over the gate and made for the house through clumps of scrub oak and sumac surrounding the ranch. Nearing the house, he heard voices but couldn't make out the words. It took him a minute to figure out they were speaking Spanish. He crept in closer and saw a dark green Mercedes sedan parked in the driveway. The license plates were Mexican and had B.C. Front at the top, which meant they were from Baja California.

Two men were standing in front of the car. They were dressed in expensive casual clothes. Designer label shirts, creased slacks, Italian loafers with tassels, and an assortment of gold accessories from watches to chains and bracelets. Decked out.

He was about to move closer when he felt the cold steel barrel of a gun touch his right ear.

"Easy, mi amigo, raise your hands and stand up slowly and I won't shoot you," the voice was smooth with a Mexican accent. Rocco complied. The man with the gun motioned Rocco to walk out of the brush slowly and toward the others. Rocco didn't have to look to know that the gun was now pointed at the small of his back.

The men by the Mercedes looked up but expressed little surprise. Some words were exchanged in Spanish and they laughed. Rocco was directed by the man with the gun to stand by the car. He kept his hands over his head as instructed.

"It's okay now, Senor Rocco, you can relax. Put your hands down." The voice had a Spanish accent, but the English was clear and concise. Rocco put his hands down and turned. The man was Latino, like the others, and dressed in a lightweight white suit and dark dress shirt with open collar revealing several thick gold chains.

"I am Carlos Sobrano, and I believe you have my car."

Rocco didn't know what to say. He wished Marlin were here and said as much. Sobrano laughed and said that they would have some company soon enough. In the meantime, Rocco was to cooperate fully so that they could finish the business as smoothly as possible.

Sobrano spoke in Spanish to one of his men, then asked Rocco for the keys to the truck. Rocco complied, and the man went down the road toward the back gate. Rocco's head was beginning to ache, the stress of the morning and the beer was having an effect.

"Where's the car? We need to get working on it before the others arrive," said Sobrano.

Rocco walked to the side of the large barn and lifted a small wood cover from the wall near the corner. It was almost unnoticeable. He punched a four-digit pin code, which unlocked several master deadbolts throughout the structure and disarmed the alarm. Closing the hidden cover, he moved to the front of the building.

The large barn doors moved easily on their hinges despite the fact that they were twice as thick as a normal barn door and had been reinforced with a metal inside panel. In fact, the whole barn was like a fortress with walls of concrete and steel. Only the outside was aged barnwood, a skeleton of the original barn. Sobrano's eyes widened when he saw the BMW.

"So, you brought the car here after the wreck?" It was a rhetorical question, and Rocco shrugged.

"I did what I thought Dillard and Marlin would want. Otherwise, the cops get it. Right?"

"It's all right senior. Just a little inconvenient. That's all. Have you talked to Dillard?"

"I tried to call just now, but there was something wrong with the number."

"Si, there's something wrong all right." Sobrano took a cigar out of his pocket and clipped the end with a shiny gold cigar cutter. "This fucking Dillard is a bust. But, that's another story." He struck a wooden match on his heel and puffed the cigar.

Sobrano asked Rocco a couple of more idle questions about getting the car, studying the man's face as he answered. With a look to his men, they went to the Mercedes and retrieved a couple of duffel bags. Rocco watched them take out some coveralls and boots.

"You do have some tools out here, si? Bodyshop tools, I think."

Rocco directed Sobrano's men to where the tools were kept, including the acetylene torch. This was not the first time a car had been worked on in the barn.

"You want me to help?" asked Rocco.

"That won't be necessary." Sobrano seemed at ease.

His men went to work on the car like a team of IndyCar mechanics. Using an array of tools, both from the ranch and some they had brought with them, they located and opened a series of well-hidden compartments. Sobrano watched intently directing them in Spanish. After the first compartment was opened and before the contents was removed, Sobrano asked Rocco to make sure everything was secure outside and check and close all the gates.

It was mid-afternoon before Rocco got to take a shower. Sobrano and his men had remained in the barn. From the sounds they were making, Rocco surmised that they were repairing the damaged front end of the car. Rocco was exhausted, but there was no time to rest. There was work to be done and Marlin would be showing up soon, according to Sobrano. The shower helped restore some energy and Rocco went back out to the barn to see what was going on.

The large doors were closed but not locked, and he pulled one open causing a draft in the room. The men inside moved all at once in a programmed motion. In an instant they all had guns in their hands pointed at Rocco. It happened so fast Rocco couldn't believe his eyes, it was almost as if they were expecting it, or they were very well trained.

"Whoa now, it's just me, take it easy," said Rocco instinctively, putting his hands above his head. The room was silent and Rocco could feel the tension. There was a warm sensation in the back of his neck, like he was about to pass out.

Sobrano stood in the rear of the barn at the workbench. He, too, had his pistol drawn but was the first to lower it out of the firing position. "You should always knock before entering a room, senior," said Sobrano in a cold steady voice. "A man could easily get killed."

He put the gun down on a bench, and the other three men followed suit and holstered their guns turning back to resume work on the car. Rocco noticed they had replaced all the panels and were making repairs to the front end so the car could be driven.

"Actually, I'm glad you came in," said Sobrano. "I have something I'd like you to try."

He motioned Rocco over to the area where he appeared to be working. On the bench next to his gun were several plastic bags of pink, crystalline powder, some test tubes, and a small metal attache case.

"What is it?" asked Rocco.

"That's what we want you to tell us," said Sobrano. He took a small knife from his pocket, opened it, and handed it to Rocco.

What the hell, thought Rocco, after a day like this, he could use a little buzz, and it was probably good cocaine from the looks of it. Except that it was sort of pinkish in color. He took the knife and, using the tip of the blade, he scooped up a little pile and took two small knife-tip snorts. One for each nostril. The crystals stung his nostrils fiercely and his eyes began to water.

His first thought was that this was really strong cocaine, because he could feel a sensation run through his body immediately. Suddenly, the conversation with Bobo the mechanic came back. Bad dope. People flipping out. This was it, the shit from the car. Those assholes, he thought. Blood seemed to be rushing to all parts of his body at once. His mouth was suddenly dry. It struck him that whatever this drug was, it was not cocaine. There was a throbbing in his head that beat along with his heart, except faster. He couldn't tell if the sound was real or imaginary. Then he realized he was staring at his feet, and the cowboy boots he wore had turned grotesquely red. And they were melting. He looked up and the room started spinning. He thought he could hear a phone ringing, but he couldn't answer it. He knew the call was from Sobrano, but he couldn't get himself to answer the phone. It was as if his hands were tied. It rang and rang. Finally, the sound faded away. His mind slipped passed it and moved on. He saw fireworks and felt the breeze from the ocean.

"Rocco, are you okay? Rocco, Rocco." Sobrano gave up and watched as Rocco swayed back and forth, eyes blinking wildly.

Rocco would not remember what happened next, but the rest of the men in the room surely would. They would remember Rocco breaking out in a cold sweat, staring unconsciously into space, and then going into what appeared to be a mild seizure. They watched as the drug took control, transforming Rocco's mellow demeanor to that of a mad man. And they ran for cover as he grabbed a gun on the counter and started shooting wildly and randomly at objects in the room.

Rocco blinked and looked around. It was hot and humid and he could smell the stench of the jungle. He could hear popping sounds. Fireworks? No, he was in a firefight. Charlie was here, he knew it. He had to be careful. Suddenly they were there, Viet Cong. Four of them. He shot and ran.

The gun had sixteen bullets in its clip and all sixteen were fired in less than a minute. The BMW, the attaché case, and several of the lights in the room were among Rocco's victims in the wild shooting spree. When the gun was empty, Rocco threw it down and ran out the door. Two of Sobrano's men tried to stop him, but it was no use. He seemed to have the strength of ten men and he was beyond all reasoning. All they could do was to try to herd him away from areas where he might get hurt. His rage lasted almost twenty minutes and then he sat down, unassisted, on one of the patio lounges under the large oak tree. He seemed for all the world like he was asleep, except his eyes were open.

In his mind, Rocco had broken away from his captors and run through the jungle to the beach. He loved the beach. It was safe. He found a hammock. A cool breeze blew in off the ocean. He could feel the eyes of the enemy staring at him, but he didn't care. Maybe he was dying. He was staring off into the South China Sea. And the waves were breaking white over the reef.

⁓⁓⁓

Rocco was still staring off into space four hours later when a black Lincoln pulled up the drive. The senator was alone in the car and talking on his car-phone as he stopped. He got out, wearing a dark, European-cut business suit and a hand-painted silk tie. Sobrano greeted him and the two went immediately into the house, leaving Rocco tended by the three men.

"What did you do to him? Is he drunk or asleep, or what?"

Sobrano laughed. "He wanted to try some of the new product, thought it was coke, so we gave him some. He's been on his ass ever since. It is much improved since the last batch, but it's still strong medicine. He got a little more than he needed."

Sobrano went to the pantry and retrieved a 1978 Paulliac, one of several classic French wines Marlin stocked at the ranch. Sobrano popped the cork and poured two glasses half full. They sipped the wine as Sobrano continued on about the latest version of their product. Dillard was always anxious to learn, especially when it came to potential profits or power. It had been more than nine months since Sobrano had come up with the idea of a synthetic drug. At first it sounded like an exceptional idea. Dillard remembered Sobrano's description.

"It's a powerful hallucinogen that can be used like coke or crystal, It has some side effects, but we should be able to work them out with more testing. It will have the profile of a recreational drug, non-addictive, easy to use, with a medium to short duration."

Sobrano went on about the economics of manufacturing the drug and the logistics of putting a lab and a team of chemists together to mass produce it.

"It is simple. This is a synthetic drug that will have mass appeal, once we have worked out the right dosage. It is incredibly cheap to manufacture and most of the chemicals needed are readily available in Mexico," said Sobrano.

Dillard was immediately intrigued. The idea of controlling the whole distribution chain was appealing. His job would be to provide a little protection, establish some safe warehouses in strategic locations, and make sure everything went smoothly and uninterrupted on the California side of the border. Not hard for a man with his power. On the other side of the table, Sobrano would manufacture the product and ship it north in much larger quantities than the load in the BMW, and with much less trouble.

But it wasn't so simple. They had tested the prototypes of the drug on various animals, vagrants, and drunks in Tijuana. It produced the desired effect, but it was fickle. For some it was a mild high with few side effects. For others, it was a powerful speed–like narcotic that turned them into raving maniacs.

A known Tijuana prostitute had driven a car over the guard rail of the Coronado Bridge in a spectacular suicide. Another had burned herself to death in a hotel room. In all, about a dozen people, all of some ill repute, were thought to have committed suicide in unusual or bizarre ways.

And that was not the only problem. Their lucrative cocaine and marijuana business had been put on the back burner in an effort to develop the new drug. Profits were down and tensions were up.

The two men had never been friends, but they had made some exceptional profits. That seemed to be changing. Sobrano's call to Dillard this morning was not the usual stock report. He had demanded that Dillard meet him at Marleano's ranch; Dillard suspected it was about the stories in the newspaper and the death of his aide Dawson.

"So why am I getting all this heat? I'm being hounded by cops and reporters . . . everything was going so well," said Dillard.

"Well?" replied Sobrano with a hint of agitation. "You've obviously made a few mistakes. You're being investigated for using drugs. You've made some bad friends. And you think everything is going *well*?"

Dillard winced but remained calm. He didn't have a drug problem, and he would get past the stories in the papers. It would be all right.

There were just a few loose ends to tie up. He sat back in his chair and sipped the wine. He admitted that he had made some mistakes, been in a couple of the wrong places, but was sure the press would drop the story. And there was no real evidence, especially if he could tie up a few loose ends.

"What about this damn drug of yours?" Dillard changed the subject. "According to your projections it should have been producing for us by now. We've still got people jumping out of windows and bashing their heads against the pavement. What in the hell is the problem?"

Now it was Sobrano's turn to twist. He related how their chemist, Walter, had started getting a little weird. With each new batch he kept requesting more and more equipment. Things that didn't seem to be needed. Then when he heard about the suicides, he would go through periods of depression. Marleano, who was living with Walter's sister, was the only one who could talk to him.

Dillard listened to Sobrano's explanation. He was happy to be off the hot seat for now but concerned about the future of their project.

It got worse. Walter's work continued to stagnate. They finally resorted to threatening Walter with the fact that if he didn't finish the formula they might have to harm his sister. Sobrano admitted that it was a desperate ploy. Walter flipped out and tried to destroy the lab. From then on they had to keep him restrained hoping that he would come back to his senses. Three weeks ago, he escaped.

Marleano was sent to look for him. There were sightings, but no one knew where Walter was hiding. He was seen in Tijuana, Ensenada. Never across the border.

"About a week ago, we heard he was in Cabo. Marleano went down there. Now we haven't heard from him," said Sobrano. "It makes me worry a little that we are not the only ones playing this game. Do you have any ideas about that?"

Dillard shrugged. All his problems, and now this. The last thing they needed was a third party stirring up the mix. Maybe he could take care of it.

"So this latest shipment was the last batch that Walter made before he flipped?"

Sobrano nodded. "We think it is very close to being right. It needs to be cut, of course."

"What about this latest mishap? How did the shipment get derailed?" asked Dillard with a note of sarcasm.

"My shipment got derailed because of an accident, but you may not of heard the worst part. It seems that the license plates on the car were off of one of your cars. The 350 SL at your condo in Coronado, I would imagine. I'm surprised they haven't tried to question you about that."

"They probably will. You've obviously read yesterday's papers," said Dillard. "Some little weasel out in the desert got busted and is spilling his guts about me buying coke from him. And, if that's not enough, somebody is sending anonymous faxes to various agencies linking us and a number of others. I've got my moles going over the details, and will have my staff build a response."

The room fell silent for a moment as both men looked into their wine. Then Dillard stood up abruptly.

"So who in the hell put those damn plates on the car? That's the question I want answered," said Dillard.

Sobrano shrugged. "It's a good question. And, right now, I don't have the answer. But we're working on it."

Dillard finished his wine in one swallow and reached for the bottle. He went over in more detail what he knew so far about the inquiries. A detective in San Diego, a Sergeant Cassio, had been snooping around and was probably following up on those plates right now. Stephen Casey, the "rat in the desert" who started the investigation would not be a problem. Orders had already been given for his removal. Ultimately Dillard's reputation would mend. He could go on to his continued political successes such as the improved trade relations with Mexico and a booming Mexican economy. Dillard the good.

"What about your aide, Mr. Dawson?" asked Sobrano. "He seems to have killed himself in the Gaslamp Quarter the other night. Snorted some of the straight stuff, I suppose. How did he get it?"

Dillard looked embarrassed. "It was those idiots you and Marleano sent me. They were supposed to be giving samples away and testing it on their friends. Somehow Dawson got a packet from them. Actually, it probably worked out for the better that he is dead. Dawson was getting too into drugs, and he knew too much."

"How about the police?"

Dillard set his wine down on the table and stood up. "I have some contacts, and let's just say it's being handled with discretion. I must say, however, that I am getting tired of the inconsistencies with this product. Sooner or later it is going to be trouble."

The two men looked at each other in silence. Dillard lit a cigarette and sat quietly reflecting. How could so many things be going wrong so fast? This was supposed to be an easy deal. Maybe there were too many power trips going on. Sobrano and his connections; Marleano thought he was some kind of kingpin. These guys were all just a bunch of punks, thought Dillard. Was there anybody else involved? If there was, it was this Mexican's fault. It worried him, but he concealed his troubles.

"So where are we now? Dillard asked. "You have some of the product and the formula . . . right?

"Yes. We were lucky to have taken Walter's notebook and made copies before he flipped out. Also, we recovered several kilos of what we think is the finished product, which is now here," said Sobrano. "We are putting together a team of chemists from Mexico City that will build a facility at one of our ranches in Baja. We should be operational in about a week."

There was one problem that Sobrano didn't share with his colleague. There was a good chance the notebook didn't contain the finished version of the formula. Hopefully, his new men could figure it out. But more disconcerting was the fact that Walter may have been putting together a dossier on the operation. Maybe it was to be his insurance. Maybe he would try to blackmail them. Either way, Walter was going to be dead when Marleano found him. The key to resolving the situation now was getting the girl, Janine. She could help them solve a lot of problems, thought Sobrano. That would be his focus as soon as he was done with his business with Dillard.

Sobrano outlined his plans for the warehouse facilities, as Dillard listened. He needed an American with Dillard's power and resources. Yet he wished it wasn't Dillard. The senator was ultimately a liability. A weak sister. Worse, he was a man without character, thought Sobrano. Someday he would do without him.

Dillard filled the two glasses again with the last of the Bordeaux. A thick, oily, red wine that left a residue at the bottom of each glass. He raised his glass in a toast.

"Here's to resolving our little challenges and bringing our new product to market. What shall we name it?"

"We're calling the shit Pink Polly, and it's some bad stuff, man," Big Mike looked up from the urinal at his buddy, Spike, who was about to take a sniff of the pink powder. "Easy, there, Ace. This is not coke. It's way stronger than any whiff you've ever had."

Spike emptied the pile on the match cover back into the paper bindle. Then, in a well practiced move, he dipped back into the paper with the corner of the match cover and came out with a slightly smaller pile. He put it to his nose and inhaled. The pile disappeared like it had been sucked up by a vacuum cleaner. After repeating the process for the other nostril, he folded the paper and handed it back to Big Mike.

"Rightous, now I'm ready for Tootsie and Morticians," said Spike with a smile.

They walked out to the bar and returned to their places on the corner. Tootsie and the Morticians were tuning up. That was not the real name of the band, in fact they were the Ray Williams Swing Band featuring Thelma White. But everybody called them Tootsie and the Morticians because they were old people playing old music for more old people. In another era, they would have been considered quite good. But for the regulars on the corner, they were simply something to talk over.

A half-hour later, Spike was staring at the bandstand. He had a tall collins glass in front of him, but he wasn't drinking with his usual gusto.

Big Mike smiled. "Pretty weird stuff, huh?"

Spike nodded. "I'm seeing trails . . . It's really far out."

"Wait until the band starts playing. You're going to really dig them tonight," said Big Mike.

"I thought they were playing."

"Oh yeah, I guess I wasn't paying attention." They both laughed.

The door next to the bandstand opened with a scraping sound. Big Mike looked up instinctively and saw his new friend John, the Canadian, come in. He was wearing his golf hat as usual. He walked down to the end of the bar and took a seat near the corner.

After ordering a Corona and a shot of 1200 Tequila, he turned his attention to Mike and Spike.

"What's going on, boys? Into some of the gump tonight?"

Big Mike nodded and smiled.

John moved over next to them. He took a long sip of beer, then leaned close so no one else could hear. "How is it?"

"That is the best dope I've ever had," replied Big Mike. "It gets you way out there for about ten minutes, then you just mellow into a groove. It lasts for about an hour, then you're okay to do whatever."

The Canadian looked pleased. He took a drink of his beer.

"So you could sell it for $100 a gram without much of a problem?"

Mike smiled again and said he, or someone he knew, probably could. John told him to pass the stuff around to get people familiar with it, and then he would contact him next week and bring him a supply. Mike agreed. It would be pretty easy money, he thought to himself.

The door opened again and a group of seedy looking people walked in. Two guys and a girl. All in their late twenties or early thirties. Meth heads by the look of them, thought Mike. John finished his beer and left by the side door as the three took a table in the corner. Mike thought the girl looked familiar. She had short black hair and dark eyes. The page-boy look gone bad. He watched them take off their jackets and sit down.

The cocktail waitress went over and took their order. Spike had said virtually nothing for about a half hour. Mike took a long sip from his tall glass, thinking about what John had proposed. He was a salesman, but not a dope salesman. He liked to do his coke and pot and would go in with others to share the expense, but selling it had just never materialized for him. Now there was an opportunity. He would have to think it over. In the meantime, maybe he might go in the bathroom and take one more little taste of the Pink Polly.

Tootsie and the Morticians were into a groove of some sort. People were dancing anyway. Spike was into the band, or the people dancing, Mike couldn't tell which. Mike walked down the bar to the bathroom. He went in and took out the packet, carefully unfolding it. He had a little pocket knife that he used to snort coke. He took it out and started poking through the pink crystalline powder.

He had a small pile on the end of the knife and was about to inhale it when the door to the bathroom opened. Mike took a big sniff, then jerked the knife down by his side. He tried to hide the bindle in his left hand as best he could. Looking in the mirror he saw one of the three people he had watched come in earlier. It was the tall, thin guy. He looked like he hadn't shaved or taken a bath in about three days. His eyes had deep dark circles under them. All the signs of a meth head.

The newcomer's eyes lit up when he saw what Mike had just done. "Go ahead, man, I don't give a shit," he said, walking over to one of the urinals.

Mike smiled slightly and nodded. He stuck the knife back into the packet and dealt out another small pile. He snorted it, then looked in the mirror to make sure there was no residue on his nose. Out of the corner of his eye, he could feel the guy staring at him.

"You want to try some? It's a designer drug," he said, holding up the bindle.

"Sure, I'll take a little." The guy flushed the toilet and zipped up his pants.

Mike handed him the bindle and his knife. He suggested that the guy take very small portions.

The guy loaded up the tip of the knife and inhaled like he was taking his last breath. He repeated the process on the other nostril and handed the packet back to Mike.

"Thanks, man. I'll let you try some of our stuff later."

The door opened and an older gentleman walked in. They exited quickly and Mike resumed his position at the corner of the bar. He watched the guy from the bathroom weave his way through the tables and thought about what he must be going through. Probably hallucinating by now. He would be tripping out for a while, Mike thought. In typical fashion, the guy had not heeded Mike's advice and had taken a larger dosage than recommended.

Mike, himself, was experiencing the rush of the synthetic narcotic but to a lesser degree. Still, it was enough to send him off to his thoughts and far away from the corner of the bar at Bonsall Downs.

CHAPTER EIGHT

Choices

S unday mornings were usually a time of reconstruction for
Logan. A good time to kick back at the Blue Doors, which
was what everyone called the apartment complex he lived in near The
Club. A time to sleep in and dream the good dreams. Rest the good
rest. Gray moments of recuperation after a possibly damaging Saturday
night. The morning would begin with a flick of the remote control for
the pregame shows and a repositioning of pillows. Half awake and half
asleep, he could still absorb any important information and blow by all
the hype. The coffee maker was set for 10 a.m. It would automatically
shut off at 11 a.m., if he didn't get up. Hobie, his cat, would usually try
to wake him before then. Either way, sometime between the kickoff and
the first quarter, he would get out of bed, put his robe on, and walk to
the kitchen for a cup of coffee. Sometimes he would forget to retrieve
the Sunday paper from the front door until halftime. His subscription
was for Sundays only. *The Union.* There wasn't enough sports news in
The Newspress. Sunday mornings were a set routine.

Something was different this Sunday. He sensed the welcoming
smell of coffee, eggs, and toast. And there was the sound of a television
emulating from the front room. It wasn't a football game. Where was
Hobie? He hadn't recalled any of the cat's insistent requests for breakfast.
Logan looked at the clock. Just after 8 a.m. Rolling over under the
covers, he pulled his pillow over his head and tried to dive back into
his dreams. And then, like every Sunday morning, Saturday night started

playing back in his mind. A montage of visions and sound bites. Pleasant. Obnoxious. Alarming. Disarming. Saturday night mysteries in a Sunday morning fog.

The smell of bacon seeped in under the pillow and with it another smell, not of food. It was the fragrance of a woman. Perfume. The mystery started to unfold. She had been waiting outside of the club. When she approached him, his heart had skipped a beat. She was attractive. Very attractive. They talked. Decided on a drink, then ended up driving to a small out-of-the-way restaurant in the country, The Lazy H. The dinner special was coconut shrimp. Damn good, too. The juke box played schmaltzy, big band music. In the mood. When they returned to Bonsall, it was to his apartment and the pool. And the Jazuzzi. He sat up in bed. She was still here! Janine the beautiful. Janine the passionate. Janine the fugitive. She was still here, and she was making him breakfast.

"How about some coffee?" She was in the doorway, wearing one of his T-shirts and holding a steamy mug. Logan smelled the coffee, but all he could see were her long tan legs.

Logan managed a smile. "Thanks, that would be great." He could barely get the words out. His voice was hoarse from talking and the booze. "It's early, how can you get up and make breakfast after staying up so late?"

"I've got a lot of energy," said Janine with a smile as she handed him the mug. She turned and walked back to the kitchen. Logan's eyes followed her and he remembered the night before. She did have a lot of energy. And it was good. Very good. He sipped the coffee and turned on the television in his room with the remote control. It was still chilly, and it had rained a little the night before. He wondered how Janine could walk around with almost nothing on. And the thought stayed with him.

She returned, along with a plate of bacon and eggs, sourdough toast, and slices of peach for a garnish. What a concept.

"I know this might sound a little strange," he said, "but I feel like I know you. It's like we've been together, or something."

She smiled. "Deja vu? Another lifetime?" They laughed and she took his hand. "You're a nice man." She let him go back to his eating.

After breakfast, he showered. She stayed in the living room with the TV, giving him his space. Logan liked that. He dressed in some jeans, a golf shirt, and a white San Diego State sweatshirt. He never went to State, but he had planned to. Mesa Junior College was as far as he got before he took off and went to Hawaii, on the advice of friends. She showered and came out wrapped in a towel and asked for a hair dryer. Logan didn't have one. Janine took her keys out of her purse and tossed them on the bed next to him.

"Would you go out to my car and bring me my small suitcase out of the backseat . . . please?" The scratchiness in her voice that he had noticed before was absent. Standing there with her hair wet, wrapped in a towel, she looked like a girl just out of high school. The morning light was kind to her. It accented her naturally beautiful features: High cheekbones, almond eyes, a large mouth, but not too large, with rich, luscious lips. She had such a radiant complexion; Logan wondered why she even bothered with makeup. She reminded him of the girls he had met when he had first gone to Maui. Young, fresh, lean tan bodies and clean white smiles. Girls that make butterflies in blue skies.

He took the keys and went out to get the suitcase. It was the smaller of a set of two. Cloth-woven designer luggage by French, a distinguished luggage company Logan had heard about. He brought the bag back to the room and set it outside the bathroom door, knocking to let her know it was there. The Chargers were on television, playing in Cleveland. Trailing, of course, by three points, midway through the first quarter. He decided to watch the game in the front room on the large TV.

By halftime the Chargers were down by ten, and Janine came out of the bedroom. She was dressed in tight-fitting jeans and a sweatshirt with a light blue floral pattern.

"Do you have any plans today?" she asked, again in the sweet tone. "I was going to take a drive in the country, and I'd love some company."

Plans? Logan's Sunday routine was to wake up late, watch football, and then do whatever came natural. Usually take a nap, or go to the club for an afternoon between the driving range, putting green, and bar. Cards, sports, and war stories. If it was raining or cloudy, he would forgo the club to stay home and loaf around the house. If he had the energy, he would go to the store and buy groceries. On sunny days, he liked to get out. It was a natural thing. Nine holes of golf was nice, too, given the inclination.

"Sure," he said, not giving it much of a thought. He didn't have to think. Janine was nice . . . very nice, even if she was a bit mysterious and, in a way, a bit scary. She was a lady with contrasting personalities. Soft and vulnerable, hard and aloof. A sort of desperado complex, Logan thought, yet like the song, she could be kind and compassionate. He had a feeling he wanted to know her better. "The backcountry sounds great. We can take the truck."

"Let's take my car, but you drive." It was settled, and without bothering to catch the halftime show, they gathered what they needed and went to the car. Logan couldn't help notice the sticker on the rear bumper. It was a rent-a-car, but not the economy model.

They headed out east on Highway 76. Janine's directions. It was a winding but beautiful road that led away from the urban sprawl through the Indian reservations to Lake Henshaw. There was an optional route, even more scenic, that went over Mt. Palomar.

"We don't know much about each other do we?" Janine's voice was calm, almost removed. Just making conversation.

Logan smiled. He knew all he wanted to know about this woman. At least for now. "We know that we like the same kinds of food, and that we like to dance and have fun." He couldn't help a mental flashback to the candlelit bedroom, the sound of smooth jazz on the stereo. There was a pause, and then Logan said, "So where did you grow up?"

She was born in Orange, grew up in Newport Beach, went to private schools mostly, and dropped out of the University of Hawaii in her sophomore year.

"I've been traveling ever since."

"That's nice, how does that work? I mean, how do you support yourself?" he asked.

"It just works. How about you? What's your story, Logan the Bartender?" She smiled a smile that not only changed the subject but ignited another candlelit flashback. It took him a moment to get back to her question.

"I was born in Tom's River, New Jersey. My dad was a Naval aviator, and we moved around a lot. Once he got transferred to Miramar, we never left." Logan looked out the window. "He was shot down in Korea. I don't really remember him very much."

Logan was still a baby when his dad was killed in action flying a combat mission in enemy territory. His mother had remarried and the family stayed together in San Diego. Logan was the second child of three. His two sisters also still lived in San Diego. A teacher and a quarterhorse trainer, both successful in their respective fields.

"We're still close. My dad, Harry, was one of my real dad's best friends and he's been really great to us."

"What did you do for fun when you were a kid?" Janine seemed to want the conversation to stay focused on him.

"I surfed. That's about it. Went to college for a year, but then dropped out and went to Maui."

"Were you any good? I mean at surfing." Again the smile.

"Surfing is like an art form. I can't say I was any good. I never got paid for it. But, there were a couple of pictures of me at Sunset Beach and Honolua Bay in the magazines. I guess I was okay."

He had made his living in the restaurant and bar business. It was a natural for him, work nights and play in the days. He'd been at it for more than twenty years.

"I started as a pearl diver and worked my way up," he said.

Janine had been daydreaming a little and the words pearl diver brought her back. "You dove for pearls?"

Logan laughed. "No, a pearl diver is what they call the dishwasher in the restaurant business. You know, you dive and dive and never know what you'll find. Then one day, you find a pearl." Janine didn't get it. Logan liked to spin off metaphorically, often not knowing where it might lead. Some of the best things happen that way, he thought.

State Highway 76 wound its way around mountains, hugging the San Luis Rey River up through the Pala Valley. The tailings of old mines could be seen on the steep sides of hills bordering the reservation. Tourmaline mines mostly, but there were a few gold and silver mines, too. The hills were covered with the greens and browns of California chaparral, a wondrous mixture of sage, scrub oak, sumac, and manzanita. Green in the spring, brown in the fall. There were ancient California

Live Oaks and willows along the river, and here and there an Elepo pine. A unique mixture of mountain and desert.

Logan tried the radio, but there was no reception. They drove past the turnoff for the Palomar Observatory and continued on over the pass to the La Jolla Indian Reservation. The road and river ran closer together here as the canyon of the San Luis Rey narrowed. In the springtime the stream took on river-like proportions, flowing wildly over the rocks and gushing with whitewater. On this winter's day it was merely a stream meandering through large boulders. Most of the willows had lost their leaves, allowing the dark green pine trees to stand out.

"Do you want to stop at Henshaw and walk around the lake?" Logan asked. "Or we could drive up to Julian. It might not be too crowded up there now."

Janine was looking out the window like she was miles away. She hadn't said anything for a while. She seemed deep in thought, perhaps coming to some sort of decision.

"Logan, I need you to help me." She turned to look at him, and, as their eyes met, he caught a look of despair. "You know I'm in trouble, but you don't know what it is and you don't know how bad it is."

He kept his eyes focused on the road, both hands on the wheel. "I don't like to pry. I figured you'd tell me if it was important. Anyway, I think it's healthier to stay out of other people's business. Especially if it's, well . . ."

He meant to say monkey business but stopped. Janine looked back out the window across the river at the hillside. She knew what he meant. "It's more than monkey business, Logan. It may have started out that way, but it got bigger. Now it's about life and death and a lot of money. The people involved are very scary, and I can't lie to you, it's very dangerous."

"Janine, I've seen a lot of good people go bad when they got into the drug scene. A lot of lives ruined forever because of some fast money and fast times. I promised myself I wouldn't get involved. I have my vices, but I don't want to have anything to do with dealers and dealer money. Not today and not ever."

He slowed down, unconsciously, and the car rattled over a cattle guard that stretched across the road marking the border of the reservation. The ripple-like sound machine-gunned through the car, two split second bursts, and then gone.

"You're right, I'm sorry, let's turn around. I've got to get back." She reached in her purse for a cigarette. It was the first one she had smoked since the night before. Logan hadn't smoked either, and now he, too, retrieved a pack from his pocket and lit one up.

He kept his eyes on the road and drove. There was no immediate place to pull over and turn around. He had a feeling from the first time he saw Janine that it might come to this. He knew she was involved in something illegal. It was written all over her the day of the wreck. Still, he was attracted. Like a moth to a flame. A dangerous woman living on the edge. To his dismay, he had an inherent feeling that he had to help. It wasn't just Janine, but all women living on the edge. He felt sorry for them. Little sheep who'd been led astray. It was his duty to bring them back, help them lead a better life. White knight syndrome. But then there was reality.

"You know, I read a saying somewhere: 'Change occurs, but only when the soul is willing.' All the help in the world is useless unless your mind is made up to change." Maybe he was talking to himself, it was hard to tell. He took another drag of his Marlboro and snubbed it out in the ashtray.

The Lake Henshaw coffee shop and store were just ahead, and he pulled in to the parking lot. This was it, he would turn around and drive back to Bonsall, there would be few words said. Janine would go on her way to whatever destiny lay ahead. He barely knew her. He had talked to her twice, briefly, before last night. But, it was night to remember: the Jacuzzi, the candlelight and the lovemaking. Soft noises in the dark. But the reality of it was she was involved in something of which he wanted no part. Best to cut the ties now, before he knew anything more and before he was involved at all.

"I'm sorry, Janine," he said after stopping the car. The parking lot was a large asphalt and Macadam strip that paralleled the highway. He had pulled in and swung a U-turn so that now the car was perpendicular to the highway and heading toward the large, half-empty lake. He looked out on the water. There were ducks and a few fishermen bobbing about in boats. A woman on the dock was basking in the early afternoon sun.

He felt suspended by the lake. As long as he looked out upon its waters, he was safe. He didn't have to make a decision of whether to hurt and disappoint someone, or to pursue something he knew would be trouble, and likely dangerous. Janine had gotten herself into whatever it was, and it was her responsibility to get herself out. Karma.

He shifted the car from park into drive and cranked the wheel to the right. They headed back to the highway in the direction they had been traveling. Farther into the backcountry, farther away from Bonsall, and farther away from the safer road.

"So what's going on?" he asked without looking at her. "I have to know more about it if I'm going to help you."

"My brother was a chemist with a major bio-tech firm in San Diego. He's a genius, in certain areas. My ex-boyfriend is in the drug business. Through me, they got together."

The explanation had been brief, but it had shattered a somewhat fragile image he'd been conjuring. He could guess what was coming and he felt his temper rise.

"How could you get involved with a sleazeball drug dealer?" He couldn't help asking the question.

"It's not that hard," she said, gazing out the passenger's window. "You make a few choices, take the easy way out of making decisions, and you're on your way. Money and drugs have a way of padding over reality. You think everyone else is stupid for not seeing what you see."

She had met Michael at a party in Lahaina, Maui. He was handsome, dashing and obviously well supplied with means.

"I went to Hawaii to get out from underneath my mom. She was suffocating me with her attention. Always introducing me to her friends' sons. Trying to set me up with the right kind of person. She was so Newport Beach, I couldn't stand it. I met Michael at a party in Lahania. They call him The Marlin because he's a big fish. I found out later what that meant. He was good looking and had a lot of money. It wasn't hard to become interested. We went out to dinner every night, and it just became one big celebration."

Logan listened and thought about her as the party girl. He could see it, although he didn't want to. Michael provided her with everything she wanted. Shopping and the beach during the day and a party every night.

The world rolled by for her, and she never thought about where she was going, or where she had been. Life in the fast lane.

Logan listened, bristling at times with an emotion that was half jealousy and half animosity. He didn't much care for the flamboyant lifestyle. The fast-money people. They were in the bars, on the golf course, at the beach. Flashing easy smiles, flaunting quick money. Quick because it would be gone quick. All part of the mystique of the fast lane. But, sooner or later, they all crashed.

"So you couldn't get away from it?" Logan let his emotions flow. "You're a smart girl; didn't it occur to you that there would be an end? That you might end up in jail?"

"People who live that lifestyle never think about jail. They never think beyond what they are doing at the time. Day to day."

Janine said she stayed with Michael for more than a year. Long enough to become dependent on the money and chemically enhanced lifestyle. Cocaine was her best friend. It got her through the times when Michael went away, sometimes for a week at a time. And it bought her friends wherever she went. Her little bottle of joy. A bottle of parties.

"When my brother Walter came to Maui everything sort of changed. My mom sent him to help, but if she could have known what was going to happen, she . . ." her voice trailed off lost in thought. She took Logan's hand in hers and looked into his eyes. He could feel the tears coming.

"What was so bad? Sounds like Walter came to Maui to save you. What happened?

"He changed." Her voice was softer now, a confessional voice. "Walter and Michael were complete opposites in a lot of ways. He's a chemist, a brilliant chemist who had worked for a large pharmaceutical firm in San Diego. I'll never forget when he showed up at our door in Kehei."

She explained how Michael answered the door and, at first, was a little miffed at the intrusion. Although Michael and Walter were from different worlds, there was some sort of instant acknowledgement of friendship and a potentially beneficial relationship. The one thing they had in common was a passion for money. Michael spent his like he had an endless supply, while Walter hoarded every dollar like it was the only one he would ever have.

"Walter stayed on Maui for a couple of weeks, and the more they saw of each other the more they talked. I wasn't involved; in fact, I was sort of relieved they were getting along. What I should have known from the beginning was that Michael had a plan."

The plan, according to Janine, was to create a new kind of speed and to control the entire production and distribution of it. They did it and had instant success. Demand outstripped supply despite ever increasing production and price adjustments. Michael established clandestine labs for Walter in California, including a production lab operated by hired flunkies and a personal lab for Walter's experiments. Walter took an extended leave of absence from the pharmaceutical firm, and the illicit business venture blossomed.

"It was the big fish's partners who changed things," Janine sounded resentful. Logan tried to gather the story in, but still felt little compassion for any of them, except maybe Janine. "They pressed Walter for a new, more powerful, drug. One that couldn't be copied and that only they could provide.

"They moved the operations south of the border and outfitted Walter with a huge laboratory. He had unlimited access to all the chemicals needed, and ultimately he could control production without being interrupted. Smuggling it back was no problem for these guys. They had a lot of the right resources."

According to Janine, their routes included air, sea, and land transportation, paid and unpaid entry. They even had a sophisticated series of tunnels linking warehouses on the Mexican side of the border to warehouses on the American side. Michael's partners were, however, very demanding.

"How did you find out about all of this?" he pushed. "I thought you were just the party girl."

Janine shot him a quick look, and took her hand away. He'd touched a nerve.

Logan turned off the road at Warner Springs and parked in the lot of a glider port. "Let's take a break and get out of the car for awhile."

There was some relief in the fresh air. It was strange hearing so much about someone in such a few hours. Maybe it wasn't good.

"So you became concerned?" Logan brought them back to Janine's story.

"Of course I was concerned. All of the sudden Michael's business was becoming my business, because my only brother was involved. And I could tell he wasn't happy."

Janine explained that after about six months in Mexico, Walter became despondent with the new product's failures and wanted to return to his old job. The partners refused. They needed him to finish the new drug. The last time Janine had heard from Walter, he wanted her to help him leave. She pleaded with Michael to let Walter return to his normal life.

"Michael told me that Walter could return to his old company, only first he had to finish the project that he was working on. Some sort of synthetic coke, I think. I blew up at him and told him to get out of my life."

A sailplane was skimming in over the runway for a landing, touching down softly like a water bird setting down on a glassy lake.

"Then Michael went down to the lab in Baja and I haven't seen or heard from him since."

"That's quite a story. I mean, you've really been through a lot." Logan felt himself being torn between feeling sorry for Janine and feeling like getting out of the situation all together. He didn't need this much excitement. "You know, I think we should start heading back soon. Maybe we can have dinner in Temecula."

Logan studied the sky. He was looking for a good way out.

Janine walked up behind and put her arm around him. "Logan, I'm scared. If you don't want to help, I understand. I'll be fine."

He looked into her blue-green eyes. There were tears there, and pain. He felt his heart pound a little harder. "I don't know what to do," he said, "but if it helps telling me the story, then go ahead."

She explained that one of Marlin's Latin American associates had called a few days after their fight and told her that Michael wanted her to pick up a car in TJ and drive it to a ranch in North County. No big deal, they just needed to store it there. Michael and Walter would be coming up to meet her there. She received the keys and directions from a courier a few days later.

"Then things began to get strange. I kept getting phone calls, but there would be no one there, just static. Then Walter called. I could barely hear him because of the connection, but he sounded bad. Like he was scared, or really stoned or something. He told me to go to a bar in Tijuana that night, The Hotel Nelson, and ask for a bartender named Marco. He would have something for me. I found the place and managed to even find Marco. He gave me a large envelope and said to keep it in a safe place. He said it was Walter's life insurance policy."

She said that she had returned to Michael's condo in Carlsbad and took care to keep the envelope in a good hiding place. Michael's associate called her the next day with more instructions. She picked the Beamer up on a Thursday and was driving to the ranch when she got in the accident.

"Where was this place that you were supposed to be going to?" asked Logan.

"Out here somewhere. I was supposed to pull into that store back at Henshaw and call this number."

She produced a small notebook from her purse. Logan didn't recognize the prefix, but there was no area code so he assumed it was from somewhere in the near vicinity. He wondered out loud if they should try to call it.

"I called as soon as I could after the crash. The guy who answered was not happy. He told me to wait at The Paddock and he would come by to get me. I didn't like the sound of his voice, so I called a friend from the coast and she came up and got me. Sorry I didn't finish my drink."

"That's okay, you left a nice tip." They laughed.

"I've still got the envelope."

She pulled a legal-size manila envelope from her purse. She opened it and held the pages in her hand. It looked like a small manuscript of some sort. No more than thirty pages, it consisted of both handwritten and typed pages of formulas, notes, code-like numbers and paragraphs describing various procedures. There were also some photocopies of photographs. Pictures of Michael Marleano, Carlos Sobrano, and Senator David Dillard.

"What's he got to do with this?" asked Logan, looking at the picture of Dillard.

"I don't really know, but I have a feeling he is one of the partners."

"Shit. This is getting a little heavy. I can't believe it." Logan snatched his cigarettes off the dashboard. "Janine, I'm a bartender. You need a lawyer. Or a bodyguard." He lit his smoke and inhaled deeply. This was not good.

"What can I do? All I care about is getting my brother out of trouble."

It was an admirable objective, thought Logan. But what was it worth? Something very valuable must have been hidden in the car. Whether it was drugs, a secret formula, or both, she didn't know. Whatever it was, it was missing. Michael's associates wanted to see her. Michael himself never called.

"I think I've got what they want," she said, putting the contents back in the envelope. "But I'm not going to give it to them until I know that Walter is safe."

A tractor-like tow plane out on the tarmac started its engine with a roar, ready to pull another silver ship skyward to soar with the thunderbirds and Indian spirits that watched over Warner Mountain. A dark-colored van passed on the road, then slowed as it went around the corner.

∼⚮∽

Cassio sat in his office in front of his familiar board. Sundays were nice days to work. Everybody was doing something else. Football, family get-togethers, matinees, relaxing, all great Sunday pastimes that got people out of his way. He took a sip from his coffee. The phone rang and broke the silence.

"Okay, we've got preliminary information. You want to come down?"

"Give it to me over the phone. I might stop by later you have anything," said Cassio.

The assistant coroner was not one to mince words, but then most in his profession weren't. He reported about the body that had been brought in from Fallbrook the night before. A tall, thin, Caucasian male. Shot once through the back of the head with a large caliber hand gun found at the scene of the shooting: an avocado grove in the southeastern area of town.

"We ran his fingerprints. His name is Stephen Casey, he is a resident of San Diego. Has a record."

Cassio stopped him. "Yeah, I know who he is. Have ballistics run the bullet, and I'll talk to you later."

Cassio hung up the phone and went to the large white dry-erase board on the wall. He picked up a red pen and drew a line through one of the dozen or so names. Stephen Casey. He wrote yesterday's date, then a couple of notes beside Casey's name. He used a blue pen for the notes.

Casey dead. Who did it? Why? Could it be because he talked too much? Taking another pen, he drew a yellow line from Casey's name to Dillard's. What was going on in Fallbrook last night? He picked up the phone and called the Fallbrook substation. The voice of one of the dispatchers answered. Cassio asked if last night's log had been posted on the network. He went to the computer terminal that sat on a separate desk. He logged on the S.O Network and typed the command for the reports.

The entries from Fallbrook scrolled up.

"Is there anything in particular you are looking for, Manuel?" Doris had been answering the phones and handling local dispatch duties at the Fallbrook substation for almost twenty years. She knew every road and back road, every nosey neighbor, and every bit of gossip in the town. She also knew every cop who had ever worked the substation, and Manuel Cassio was one of her favorites.

Cassio's eyes scanned down the log entries.

"What was this 2120 at The Downs?"

"That was Brown and Garcia. They responded to a 9-1-1, 2120 in progress. Lot's of screaming. Sounded like a guy beating up a girl, according to the RP."

"Who was the reporting party?"

"Room next door. Snowbirds down for some relaxation. By the time the officers arrived, the guy had split. The girl was still there. No visible marks. They found some pot and some sort of crank or speed.

She was way out, couldn't talk. They took her to Fallbrook Hospital for observation."

Doris knew everything. She was better than any computer when it came to dispersing information. Fast, simple, and extremely intuitive.

"Looks like there were three people in the room when all the commotion started. The room was registered to a Casey. Stephen Casey. No I.D. on anyone else."

Cassio thanked Doris and hung up. He went back to the board. With the blue pen, he added some more facts next to the name with the red slash through it. Was Casey the guy making the disturbance? Who was the girl? Maybe she could help. Who else was at The Downs?

CHAPTER NINE

Thunder Mountain

The early afternoon sun warmed the meadows below Hot Springs Mountain. There was wind, but it was not the wind and showers that had threatened the night before. In the summer, the mountain was the source of great thunderclouds. On hot days, the clouds would start to form in the late morning. Small and innocent at first, light and wispy. Then, as the sun rose in the sky, they would expand to gargantuan proportions and surround Hot Springs Peak. Cloud spirits that towered skyward and stretched over the valley until they exploded with violent authority. They would produce rain, yet by late afternoon, the showers would dissipate and the clouds would clear.

Logan watched as Janine fumbled with the contents of the envelope. It looked like a mishmash of information. Complex formulas, a log of dates and times written with some sort of code for reference. And pictures. He saw one of Dillard snorting something through a straw, and another of him with what appeared to be two rather plump Mexican whores. Another showed a dapper Mexican looking guy and Dillard together in what appeared to be a laboratory. The log of dates could be associated with the photos, or not, thought Logan. Either way, this was a lot of incriminating information that could ruin a budding political career.

"I can't believe it's come to this. Walter had such a good career ahead of him. I guess I'm to blame." Janine was crying.

"You can't put it all on yourself. People make their own beds." Logan tried to sound convincing. But Walter sounded odd. All the makings of a mad scientist. Extremely bright but lacking in social skills. A loner. The type only a sister could understand.

"I hope he's okay. I have a strange feeling that I'm never going to see him again." Her eyes started to well up. A tear formed and ran quickly down her cheek.

Logan took her hand. What a twenty-four hours this had been. His emotions had gone up and down like one of the gliders they were watching. First in love, then wanting to escape a bad dream. If he was smart, he wouldn't become any more involved with this flaky woman and her loser brother, he thought. Yesterday, he barely knew her. Today, he was her only friend. He held her hand for a minute, then reached up and turned the key to ignition.

"Let's head back. Maybe get some dinner in Temecula," he said. What the hell else was there to do? He turned the wheel and pointed the car west on the two-lane highway 79. There was a long stretch of straight road running parallel to the runway. The road was almost perfectly flat, probably the bottom of an ancient lake. Traffic was light for a Sunday. Logan put his foot into the accelerator and headed for the inevitable curve about a mile ahead. They were closing in on the curve when he noticed the van approaching from behind. It was moving fast. He looked at his speed. Sixty-five. This guy must be doing eighty. It was a dark-colored van with tinted windows.

The first of many curves was coming up. The road twisted and turned its way through the foothills from Warner to Temecula. It was about twenty miles, yet it could take up to an hour to drive depending on the traffic. Locals out here always drove fast. They knew the road and tried to own it, thought Logan. He slowed to let the van pass. Instead the van pulled right up on his tail, almost tapping the rear bumper.

"What the hell is this guy's problem?" Logan looked in the rearview mirror and thought about pulling over. They were approaching the curve. Not a good place. He rounded the curve with the van closely behind. The rent-a-car tires protested the speed of the turn, but there was nothing Logan could do. If he hit the brakes, it was a sure accident.

There was another straight section of road after the curve. An easy place for the asshole to pass.

"Pass me, you son of a bitch!"

The van stayed behind them. Logan took his foot off the accelerator and the van bumped them from behind. The Toyota swerved with the impact. Logan fought the wheel and managed to keep the car on the road, but the van was coming again. The impact was harder this time. A taillight shattered and the tires squealed as the rear end of the Toyota reeled with the force of the hit from behind. Again the car almost skidded off the road as Logan struggled to correct the drift.

Logan didn't bother to look in the rearview mirror anymore. The intent of the van was obvious. The straightaway was coming to an end. Beyond was nothing but winding curves. He stepped on the gas and made a run for the curve. Janine grappled with the envelope, tucking it under the seat before letting out a shriek.

The van was setting up for another charge from behind. If Logan could make it around the first turn without being hit, they might be able to find a way to escape. He shifted the car from drive to second and steered into the oncoming lane to get a better angle at the turn. The advisory speed sign read thirty-five. Logan was going to double that, although he didn't have time to look at the speedometer. All his attention was focused on the turn. If there were any cars coming the other way, it would all be over.

The Toyota approached the curve in the left lane. Logan would ease into the turn, gently at first, then turning harder as necessary to maintain a safe line through. That was the plan. A high-line power-glide with a minimum reduction in speed. A bottom turn on a big wave. Any quick movement or overreaction and the whole thing would blow up. He'd lose control and go spinning off toward oblivion. The engine was wound up well above redline, not good for a motor, but he would need the resistance of the lower gear to slow the car naturally through the curve. He took his foot off of the gas pedal and turned the wheel ever so slightly to the right. The tires began a high-pitched whine as the weight began to shift to the outside.

It was a blind curve. No way of telling what was on the other side. They had crossed the centerline and were headed into the turn when a large pickup truck towing a horse trailer appeared. The truck swerved and missed them by inches. A blaring horn trailed off behind the truck and trailer as they passed. Logan had swerved, too. Just in time. A natural reflex, done before he had a chance to think about it. The result was instantaneous, too. The tires and shocks of the rent-a-car were not designed to hold a turn of this magnitude. Logan's right foot jammed down on the accelerator as the car pitched hard to the left. He could feel the car start to float. The tires screamed. The burst of acceleration helped stabilize the moment. And then there was a loud pop and the car began to spin. For a second he could see the van through the windshield and then it was gone in a blur. Janine screamed as the car left the road.

It was over as fast as it had begun. The driver of the van slowed as the Toyota lost control. He smiled as he watched it spin wildly across the road, sliding off on the dirt shoulder. Rocks flew and dust rose as the car went broadside into a stand of brush. Then it flipped and disappeared from view down an embankment.

"Whoa, mother fucker bought the farm!"

"Maybe, we got to check it out."

The Toyota came to rest on four flat tires. Steam rising from under the hood, engine dead, water from the shallow creek flowing around a new obstacle in its path. Nothing moved inside of the car.

The van skidded to a stop. Two figures in dark blue coveralls emerged slowly, assessing the situation. One was wearing a cap, the other a dark bandanna tied around his forehead. Both had dark glasses. Ratface and Lobo were in their element. In a minute they were scrambling down the embankment toward the car.

Logan was in a state of half consciousness, like a dream. He tried to focus his eyes. At first he thought he was parked on a narrow road. Except there was water in the road. Then the sounds of the pop and the screams came back to him. A wreck! They had spun out and rolled. He looked next to him. Janine was there. Her head was down, held above her lap only by the seatbelt. He unbuckled his and reached out to touch her. She was unconscious.

A ripping sound broke the brief silence. The door flung open and a hand grabbed Logan's shoulder. He turned his head to see a black hole staring him in the face. It was the barrel of a gun less than a foot from his face. He gasped. The gun went up.

"Out of the car."

Logan thought he detected a slight accent in the voice. He acknowledged the command and stepped out. He was dizzy, and everything seemed slightly askew. His legs were shaking, and it was hard to stand. He wobbled when he got to his feet. He took a step and fell to the ground. He heard muffled voices, then felt a sharp pain in his ribs. Another sharp jolt of pain sprang from the back of his head, then everything went black.

He was on Maui. Sitting on a cliff overlooking the ocean. The late afternoon sun reflected like a million diamonds off the moving swells. Tradewinds blew spray from tops of lime-green walls of water. Surfers jockeyed for position as a set of large winter waves rolled out of a sea framed by two mountainous islands. Long lines of energy rising skyward as they danced closer to land. The surfers paddled outward furiously, then spun their boards toward the beach. There were at least a half dozen paddling for the first wave. It grew higher than a three-story building. Wind rushing up the face. Spray blowing off the top and out to sea. A giant green movie screen. Then there were three paddlers scratching to catch the energy. A gust of wind rippled the water in front as the top of the wave pitched out toward the shore. A lone surfer dropped in under the top of the curl. A blazing white trail followed him down the face. Down and down as the wave turned inside out. Time froze as the frothy white lip of the wave seemed suspended in midair by the wind. The white trail of a streaking rocket turned abruptly at the bottom and shot skyward in a path that ran parallel to the beach. Surfer and board were flying away from the tons of water exploding on impact as the thick ledge of the wave collided with the flat, stretched-out surface below. A thundering sound, like no other, echoed off the cliffs and through the air.

There was an explosion, and he lost his balance. He was falling, loose and easy through space. He felt the warm breath of stale air. It smelled empty. He was spinning. Was he underwater? He held his breath, but he couldn't hold it long. He breathed in slowly. He was breathing water. Then he was falling again. In the darkness. Falling toward a light. Stale air. It reminded him of the air inside an amusement park ride on a hot summer day. Stuffy. The tunnel of love. The House of Mirrors. The tunnel from hell. Sticky. He felt pain. In his head, in his legs, and in his stomach. He was sick. And falling. He struggled to regain his balance but it was no use. He was spinning out of control. Breathing thick air. Or water. He gave up and let go of his thoughts.

A light beamed through the darkness. A tiny pin of a light, piercing the void of blackness. He closed his eyes, and it was still there. Open or closed, it was there. He watched it for a while, then fell back asleep.

Pain brought Logan back. A throbbing in his head, his wrist, and his right leg. There was a cold, hard feeling running the length of his body, from his heels to the back of his head. He was lying on a cold hard cement floor. That was a bit of reality, he thought. There was life. He tried to wake up and gather his composure. How long had he been out? Where was he?

He was in darkness. His hands and feet were tied. The air was cold, like he was outside. There was a sound of wind in the trees. Yet he was in a building with a cement floor. A cold cement floor. He struggled to roll over. It was a chore, but after a few tries he was on his side. His back felt better, but now the cold was on his side. So much pain, he thought. How the hell did this happen? The events came back slowly. The drive to the country. The talk with Janine. The van. The wreck. Why had the car spun out? What happened next?

It was night, perhaps the middle of the night. He could hear the wind in the trees. Pine trees no doubt, and lots of them. That was a sound he knew: wind in the pines. It was a comforting sound, if there was such a thing. A sound of the mountains, a warm fire, and hot chocolate. What he would give just to have a few of those simple pleasures now.

His whole body ached. The jarring from the tumble over the side of the road must have got to him. But, he couldn't remember being hurt in the car. Seemed like they were protected by the seatbelts. There was no breaking glass that he could remember. But his ribs ached. And the back of his head. Then he felt the stabbing pain in his side. Somebody had kicked him.

He wanted to yell for help, then thought again. He was tied up on a cold cement floor. There was probably no help around. He rolled over on to his stomach. He could bend his legs. He hunched his back and pushed with his shoulders. If he could just get into a position where he could sit up, the world would be better.

It took the better part of an hour, and several different methods of struggling, but Logan managed to scoot himself over to a corner and get into a sitting position. It was a great relief. But he was still hurting. And it was cold. He decided to yell for help. It couldn't get much worse. Any change would be a change for the better.

"Hey, anybody out there?" The sound of his voice was foreign to his ears. It was hoarse, and not as strong as he anticipated. He tried again. Then he whistled. He had a good loud whistle. One his dad had taught him. They used to call their dogs by whistling. He could hear his dad's whistle from blocks away. It always meant the same thing. Come home. He whistled again.

He heard footsteps on a cement walk. More than one person. The murmur of voices. Logan yelled again. He heard keys jingling and the sound of a padlock, then the scraping of a door being pulled open. Light shot in through the open door. Two figures were outlined in the doorway. They didn't speak. A beam of light probed around the room until it found him. It fixed on Logan's eyes and blinded him. Footsteps came toward him. It was quick. A hurried motion, then pain. Bolts of lightning in his head. Muffled voices he couldn't understand. Then he just let go again and lost consciousness.

The light shown on Logan's slumping form. A trickle of blood ran down the side of his face. It looked almost black in the harsh light of the flashlight.

"You hit him hard, man. Broke his fuckin' head."

Ratface grunted. It was a big flashlight. The kind the police use as nightsticks. A weapon and a light. Convenient, quick, and easy to use. Light up rooms and bash in heads with just a flick of the wrist. Ratface had found it in the cupboard, now it was his. They pulled the door shut and put the padlock back in place.

"He ain't going nowhere," said Ratface. "Sweet dreams."

Janine heard them coming. Their footsteps crunched in the gravel as they crossed the driveway to the house. Heavy, foreboding steps in the dark of night. She kept her head down on the table. Maybe they would believe she was asleep. Just as long as they didn't hit her anymore.

"Looks like we'll have to carry her to the bedroom," said Ratface with a leer in his eyes. Lobo knew the look, and he didn't like it. They were supposed to get information from her, not kill her. Not that Ratface would kill her on purpose. But it could happen.

The phone rang and the leer quickly evaporated. Ratface answered on one ring and stepped into the other room. Janine could hear enough to determine that the voice on the other end was angry.

"Find out what she knows," said Dillard. "See if she has anything that could be used against us as evidence. She may be in contact with her brother. Find out!"

"I will. But it won't be tonight. She's finished. She needs some rest or medication. Something."

Dillard didn't like these two at his ranch. He also didn't like to make calls to the ranch. The phone there was strictly for emergencies. Maybe he should have taken Marleano's advice about no phones. Too late now. He didn't trust Ratface or his partner. They were unpredictable. They should have followed the girl, found out where she was staying, and then a plan of action could have been made. Instead, these idiots had almost killed the girl, and then taken her to his ranch.

"All right, make sure they're secure and not going anywhere. I'll send somebody out to take care of the situation," said Dillard. "You two stay there until I call."

Dillard hung up. He should call Sobrano and tell him they had the girl. But maybe he would wait. Information like this could be valuable. He might be able to use it to gain some power. Sleep on it and call in the morning. That was the plan.

Janine looked up from the table. She had been beaten, but she had let them think they were hurting her more than they actually were. They weren't too smart. Hadn't bothered to search her. For all they knew she could have a gun. That would be nice, she thought. Still, it was going to be a long cold night.

CHAPTER TEN

Smoke Signals

At first the staffers didn't know what to think of it. A grainy photograph of two men in business suits carefully inspecting a plastic bag containing a powder-like substance. The strange thing was that the men looked for all the world like Senator Dave Dillard and his colleague from Mexico, Carlos Sobrano. It was a joke. But not that funny, considering the type of press the senator was getting lately. There were a few chuckles around the coffee machine before any decisions were made about how to deal with it. The senator should know about it, they decided. With that they left it in his in-basket with a note that read "what will they think of next?"

It wasn't funny. Dillard fumed when he saw it. He swore. He crumpled it up and threw it in the trash. He called in the staff and demanded to know who sent it and when. It had come in the early morning, no cover sheet and no coded numbers from the sending fax machine. No way to tell who sent it. Dillard sent the staff out, shut the door to his office, and lit a cigarette. Walter, he thought. Walter was the only one who could have taken that picture. He was there with them when they were looking at the materials. Walter must have had some kind of micro camera. What other pictures did he have? It had to be Walter. Otherwise he would have appeared in the photographs, too.

It had been a couple of days since Dillard had been out at the ranch with Sobrano. At least they had most of what they needed to move forward with the plan. It would be much harder without Walter to set the production facility up. If they could have just kept him for another couple of weeks, it would have all been done. Then they wouldn't have needed the beady-eyed geek. He could have kept his date with the fish. Maybe, he already had. Marlin was tracking him down. They would have him back again to set up the lab. All the pieces were going to come together. Once they got Walter.

But who in the hell was playing games with this photograph? Was it Walter? Had to be. Dillard puffed on his cigarette. There was a vial of Peruvian cocaine in the secret drawer in his desk. He needed a little boost now, he thought. He opened the drawer and dumped a small pile on the glass desktop. He chopped it up finely with a credit card, formed it into a small line, then inhaled some in each nostril using a cut off straw. He felt the blood rush to his head. Now he would get something done.

The phone rang snapping him back from a moment away. He pushed the speakerphone button. His secretary sounded perturbed. "It's a man on the phone. Won't give me a name, but he says he must talk to you. He said it was about this morning's fax."

Dillard's heart jumped. "Put him through." Dillard waited until he heard the sound of an outside line over the speaker and then he pressed a button to record the call. Lifting the receiver, he answered, "This is Senator Dillard."

"How do you like the picture, asshole?" The voice was deep and rather hoarse but educated.

"Walter? What in the hell are you doing? Where are you?" Dillard wished that he could trace the call, but that would be too risky.

"I want you to listen and listen good. You let my sister go. Give her a car and don't follow her. If she is harmed in any way, I am not only going to ruin you, I will personally see that you are so publicly humiliated that you will wish that I had killed you."

"Walter, I don't have your . . ."

There was a disconnecting click, then a dial tone. Dillard hung up the receiver. Damn, how in the hell did Walter know that his sister was being held? He was a smart bastard, that was a given. But he was also a little crazy, and that made for a bad combination. The tone of Walter's voice left no room for second guessing.

Dillard reached for the phone, his private line. He dialed the international number. It, too, was a private direct line. He hoped Sobrano would be in. He looked at his watch. 9 a.m.

"Yes . . ." The voice was heavy yet smooth. Like honey on toast. A rich, deep voice, even toned, no hint of stress or paranoia. Dillard was relieved.

"It's me. Walter is alive, and he's playing games. I don't like it." Dillard described the fax and the phone call.

Sobrano listened. The strain in Dillard's voice was evident, as was the fact that he was chemically impaired. Of course, it didn't take much to set him off. He was strung a little tight, thought Sobrano.

"I got the same fax here."

"What? That son-of-a-bitch. He's going to try to blackmail us. Or play us against each other. We've got to stop him." Now Dillard had something to really set him off.

"That's not all. They fished Marlin out of the channel last Friday. Didn't identify him until yesterday. He'd been shot and dumped out of a boat. Nothing on him. Ensenada police are investigating. They've contacted San Diego to see if they can find out who he is. It won't take them long."

"Shit." Dillard had heard enough. He reached into his inside coat pocket for the vile. He held it in his hand while he talked. "I never thought Walter had this in him. That pencil-necked geek of a prick. Makes a clean getaway with a complete set of records. Including surveillance pictures. Kills Marlin. What the hell is going to happen next?"

"Next? Next, my friend, you will do as he asks and let his sister go. Then, who knows. Someone is holding some trump cards, and they are going to play them."

In San Diego, Manuel Cassio sat staring at his white priority board. He liked his board. It was an extension of his thought process. He used it to sort out and track the pieces of a puzzle. Put things together. Connect the lines. The board was taking on monstrous proportions in this case. There were names and places and events. All with corresponding, cryptic information and arranged in a loose circle. In the upper left-hand corner were the words "TC Bonsall, Car/Truck stolen, Assault, Footprints." Next to this entry was another group of clues: "Anonymous tip, Plates registered to Senator, possible drugs or contraband, pay phone." On the far right side of the board were the words "Meth lab bust, Desconso, Dillard." On the bottom left: "Janine Anderson, Michael Marleano, Walter Anderson, Parks Institute." The right corner of the board bore a single word followed by a question mark: "Sobrano?"

These were the pieces of the puzzle. Somehow at least three of them were connected. And the connection was going to reveal significant criminal activity. Possibly linking some very prominent figures to some rather illicit dealings.

Brado walked into the room and threw a stack of reports down on his desk. He looked over at Cassio and the board.

"How's the map coming? I only see a couple of lines."

Cassio would eventually start drawing lines that connected circles drawn around various pieces of the puzzle. It was his method. He used different colors for different connections. Not that there was any connection in the colors. But then maybe there was. It was mostly just for clarification. Red was not hot. Blue was not cold. But they could be. Sometimes he would add plus signs or minus signs. Sometimes he would put a star by a word. It was an arbitrary method changing as it needed to change. When the case was over, the board would be wiped clean. Ready for the next case. Or maybe just a list of things to do over the weekend.

"You can cross another one of those names off," Brado said as he settled into his government-issue posture chair. "I just came from the morgue. The 1144 was Michael Marleano. A commercial boat snagged him out around the Coronados."

"Did you I.D. him?"

"Yeah. Unless I'm mistaken, it's him. Had a tattoo of a devil on his right calf. I remember it being listed in one of the DEA briefs. And the body fits his description. And the DEA guys that have been watching him haven't seen him in a couple of weeks. It's him."

Damn, Brado was meticulous, thought Cassio. He'd know what color underwear a perp wore if he could. A detailed son of a bitch. Marleano dead. What did that mean? Did it have anything to do with the case, or did he just run into the wrong connection. Hard to tell with drug dealers.

"Anybody claim the body?" Cassio asked as he picked up a red-colored felt pen from his desk.

Brado said that the coroner's office was still in the process of identifying the corpse through dental records. Once the I.D. was positive, they would notify family. If they could find any. Marleano was known to have a brother, Cassio thought. He drew a blue line through Marleano's name. He never erased anything until the case was over. Dead or alive, hot or cold, the clues all stayed on the board until he handed the case over to the D.A.

On the driving range at Bonsall Downs, Burt Reid was beginning to worry. No one had seen Logan since Saturday night. It was now Tuesday morning. Logan took Sundays and Mondays off. He could have gone up the coast. He'd done that without telling anyone before. A mid-life crisis thing. Went to Ojai for a week one time. His fortieth birthday. The guys at the club were going to throw him a party. Strippers and the whole thing. But Logan took off the night before. Just threw some clothes and his golf bag in the truck and took off. He was like that. With the natural skills of a bartender, Logan made friends easily. Too easily perhaps, thought Reid.

The sun was warm for winter as Reid tapped another golf ball over to a small piece of turf that allowed the ball to sit up a little higher than the surrounding grass. He took his stance, waggled his club, and took a nice smooth swipe at the ball. He was hitting his 4-wood. It was his thinking club. It was a club he could hit without using a tee. And he could hit it a good distance without a lot of effort. Reid liked his 4-wood.

Logan was usually on the driving range at this time. Part of his routine. Tuesday morning at the range. The last time he had seen Logan was Saturday afternoon, after the match. He had left the club after the minimum issue of drinks. Said he was going to take a shower and come back to the club for dinner. Reid wondered. Maybe Logan had run into one of his long lost loves. He was always rediscovering some lady from his past.

Reid pounded out the rest of the bucket of balls unceremoniously. Time to get up to the office and see what was on the wire. He picked up the clubs he had carried down to the range, a 6-iron, a 4-iron, and the 4-wood, and started to head up the hill to the parking lot. Big Mike was on his way down the asphalt-paved cart path that led down from the first tee, past the entrance to the driving range. Mike's spikes clicked on the pavement as he walked. His golf bag was slung over his right shoulder, a cigarette dangling from the corner of his mouth.

"Hey Burtie., what's up?" The big man was usually always jovial. Mr. Humor. The life of any party. A natural salesman, he made his living on the road selling photovoltaic cells for industrial use. Solar energy. Big Mike was the industry's preeminent spokesperson. But today, for some reason, the quick smile was not there. It was replaced by wide, saggy eyes punctuated with dark circles.

"Not on the road today?" Reid asked. Mike said that he had some local appointments and thought he'd hit a few balls first. Reid knew better. Mike either had a game set up with someone who he thought he could take for more than he could make on the road, or he was so hungover that he would rather just hang out. From what Reid could tell, it was the latter.

Mike carried a seven handicap but could shoot par golf when he needed to. Golf could get serious at The Downs. And Big Mike was a serious golfer. Reid asked if he'd seen Logan. He hadn't.

"What's up with you? You don't look so good," asked Reid.

"Some weird stuff has been happening around here."

Reid was curious. He hadn't checked his messages or stopped by the office. In fact, he had taken the entire day off Sunday and spent it in San Diego doing some research for his book. Mike told him about the cops coming up to one of the rooms and taking a girl away. Someone had said that there was a fight there and that someone had been kidnapped by two guys in a plainclothes-type car. But that had not been confirmed by anyone but Headband Dave. And he may have been seeing things. Big Mike said that he and Spike had gotten pretty ripped Saturday night.

They had crashed up the hill at Spike's and hung out there recuperating until yesterday.

"Man, I still feel shitty," said Mike. "I don't remember what happened after about eight on Saturday. Neither does Spike. All we know is we made it to his house somehow."

"Were you guys into some of the stuff I saw you get from that Canadian guy?" asked Reid.

Mike shot back a glance. "Is that a personal question from a friend, or a question from a reporter?"

"Friend."

Mike acknowledged that they had snorted some lines and had shared a few with some other people at the bar. They had also been drinking, of course.

"Not a good combination," said Mike. "I have this bad feeling that something happened that night. Something I don't want to remember."

Reid listened and then, after it was apparent that he had heard all there was to hear, he left Big Mike to the practice range. He needed to get to the office and see what was going on. After stowing his clubs in the trunk of his Buick Regal, a golfer's car if there ever was one, he drove down the hill from the club. The short drive took him over the bridge that spanned the San Luis Rey River and through the infamous intersection of West Lilac and 76. Kelly's Corner. The scene of many a wreck. Reid thought about the last wreck there. Probably the strangest aftermath of any wreck he could remember. Car gets stolen from the junkyard. Along with a tow truck. Junkyard guy gets conked on the head. Attractive and mysterious blonde on the scene and then gone. Detectives from downtown on the case.

He was ready for something to happen that would break the case wide open. A newsman's wish. He glanced at the parking lot of The Paddock as he turned the corner on to the highway. A couple of cars at Mori's store. No truck. No Logan. He was usually there by now. Or at least on his way from The Club. On an impulse, Reid pulled into the lot. He cruised by the store and the group of migrants that seemed to always be out front. Years ago there had been a store and gas station on the adjacent corner. Perry's. In the late sixties and through a good part of the seventies, the vacant lot next to Perry's had been an unofficial campground for hippies, migrants, and travelers of the road. There were lots of stories about Perry's.

Reid parked the Regal behind the restaurant, next to where Logan usually parked the truck. He walked to the back door that led to the kitchen. Tony and the workers were busy preparing the day's salsa and other fresh elements that made The Paddock one of the best restaurants in the area. Authentic Californian Cuisine was what the sign said, and it was true. Tony just shrugged his shoulders when Reid asked about Logan. There was a sound of clinking glasses coming from the bar.

Mori was setting up. A tray of glasses sat on top of the bar, along with two buckets of ice and an assortment of bottles and other bar room staples. This was not organization in action. Mori was a small statured man, balding, with thick horn-rimmed glasses. Always wore a hat. When he talked to restaurant patrons, he had the spiel of a jazz musician. Unless he was talking to one of the ranchers, then he sounded like any other transplanted Southern Californian. He was a character from a Woody Allen story. He and his wife owned The Paddock and the adjacent store on the corner. They should call it Mori's Corner, he always said jokingly. The corner was Mori's world. He spent most of his waking hours there, minding his interests.

He looked up as Reid walked in.

"Hey, Mori. Where's Logan?"

"I only wish I knew. Haven't seen or heard from him since Saturday night. The truck is parked up at the Blue Doors, but he's not there. The landlady let me in. So I checked, but he's gone. The cat was so hungry it almost attacked me. I'm sort of worried."

Reid agreed. It was like Logan to take off on the spur of the moment. But it was not like him to leave people hanging. He would always call, if only to say he was having a great time, or needed more money, or had just found the girl of his dreams. Logan was a fun hog. Mori had decided to come in and set up the bar and see if he could get Jim, "the weekend bartender," to come in. Jim tended bar in the daytime at The Paddock on Sundays and Mondays. And at Ringers, a bar that was down the road a ways from The Paddock, a couple of other days. He also tended a bar in Vista several nights a week. He was Jim, the relief guy. Reid poured himself a cup of coffee and took a seat at one of the squeaky bar stools. Mori went on about how this wasn't like Logan. Reid listened and tried to imagine where his friend might have gotten to. Hawaii? No, Logan wouldn't go anywhere like that unless he made a big thing out of it. A two-to three-week buildup, countdown, with a gala going-away celebration. That was Logan's style. Not disappearing. Without even feeding his cat.

"Did you feed the cat?" Reid asked Mori.

"Of course, I fed the cat. He was going to eat me if I didn't."

"See anything that might give us a clue to where he went? Did it look like he left in a hurry. Was there a struggle?"

Reid's detective mind started kicking in. Years of news reporting gave him a certain amount of curiosity and skepticism. Mori said he didn't notice any signs of a struggle. The apartment was relatively clean. There were dishes in the sink, like someone had made breakfast before they had left. All the lights were turned off.

Must have taken off Sunday morning, Reid thought. But where? And with who?

"Dishes in the sink? As in more than one plate?" asked Reid.

"Two plates, I think. Two cups. Also, there were women's clothes in the bathroom. Probably had a guest, I figure."

Mori was good, thought Reid. He had definitely snooped a little beyond checking on his friend. Snooping was good, sometimes. Reid asked if he could use the phone. He called the office to check on things. Molinski was working on a couple of stories. Whenever Reid was absent he could count on her jumping right in and taking the initiative. Sort of a self-appointed assistant editor. There had been a break-in at the old Walker house, some things missing. There were a couple of vehicle "TCs." One was a car over the side. A drunk had driven off Mission Road into a ditch. The other was a vehicle versus fire hydrant. A front-page picture for sure. O'Malley was on that one. In a heartbeat.

"Anything on the sheriff's line?" The line was a recorded message, updated as news happened, for the media. It gave the basic facts of a news event. Major accidents, robberies, homicides, a daily ration of bad news. Reid hoped there would be no bad news about Logan.

"Nothing in our area, but I'm still checking with Fallbrook S.O. on things around here over the weekend. They've been a bit slow getting back to me."

Reid wondered about what Mike had said about cops being called up to The Downs. Maybe he was just hallucinating. He told Molinski he'd be in shortly and hung up. Mori had the bar nearly set up and was unlocking the doors. He told Reid that Jim was coming in around noon. Within minutes of unlocking the doors, the regulars started walking in. Little Jerry was first, followed shortly by Chicago Bob, and Gary Scott. They went straight to the bar. Three beers and three shots of peppermint schnapps. Like a job.

Reid glanced at his watch. 10:42 a.m. He poured himself a little more coffee and walked over to the rowdy group of horse folk. It was afternoon for them. They weren't much to look at: dirty boots and jeans, sweat-stained caps, unshaven all. To an untrained eye they might have looked like street people. Yet these were no jobless wretches. The sweat and dirt came from hard work. Half of their day was over before the sun came up. Rain or shine. Summer or winter. And they were skilled. They worked with the world's best Thoroughbred trainers and they rode and cared for the world's fastest, and most expensive, horses. Derby winners.

"Have any of you guys seen Logan?" Reid asked.

Little Jerry looked up from his beer. "Shit, he's a dog in a man's body. Probably run off with some rich chippy and got married."

They all laughed. It didn't seem all that strange for Logan to be taking a leave of absence. He was always talking to these guys about getting on a sailboat and heading south. Or about the rich lady that was going to take him away. Maybe he'd done it. Reid didn't think so. He asked some more questions. No one had seen Logan since Friday except Headband Dave, who was in the process of maintaining his regular bar-to-bar schedule. He related how he'd pulled into The Club about 4:30 Saturday afternoon and saw Logan talking to a girl in the parking lot. A blonde.

"I didn't really notice her much. They were pretty far away. I knew it was Logan though, talking to a blonde with nice legs." Headband was nearsighted, and at that time of day he was usually more than nearsighted.

"Shit. Maybe we should launch a search party or somethin'," offered Little Jerry. They laughed.

"Launch a search party? You don't launch a search party, stupid. You launch a ship, or a rocket, or a glider," said Scott. "You form a search party, and then you ride out and search."

The argument was enough to keep them all busy for awhile. Reid left and walked over to the store. Ed would be in the back. He was always a voice of reason. Ed saw and knew a lot more than he let on. Reid liked Ed. He was quiet. Steady. Had that dependable quality that came with twenty years in the Corps. If you were in trouble, Ed was a good guy to have on your side. He ran the store for Mori. The store, like the bar next to it, were great sources for information. Nearly everyone in Bonsall came into the store at one time or another to pick up something. There was no other market in Bonsall. Little bits of information would pass over the counter, along with the dry goods and liquor. Ed had a talent for putting them together into a cohesive story. He would make a good newspaper man, Reid thought. Trouble was, Ed liked to keep his thoughts and opinion to himself. Stories usually had to be coaxed out of him. But he liked Reid and the way he treated the news. Reid was a fair editor and avoided taking sides whenever possible. He often defied the publisher and nearly paid the price a couple of times. Respect was a word both Reid and Ed understood.

Reid walked to the back of the store and found Ed doing the books in a small closet-like room.

"Hey, Reid. What you doing around here this time of day. Come to take my picture?

Reid managed a thin smile. "Have you seen or heard anything from Logan?"

Ed thought for a second and said no. Then he added that someone had mentioned that he was out at The Lazy H Saturday night.

"Did they say who he was with?"

"He had a date, according to the Fergusons. Said she looked nice, and they were relieved because they always thought Logan was gay. That was the only reason Mrs. Ferguson even noticed, I think," said Ed.

Reid pondered the information. Out at The Lazy H for dinner on Saturday night. Disappeared Sunday. He thanked Ed and left.

The drive up the hill to Fallbrook was a pleasant one at this time of the morning. He glanced at his watch. It was getting on noon.

When Reid finally arrived in the newsroom, the deadline panic had hit. There were stories to edit and approve, messages to answer, calls to return. It was not a slow-paced job that you could ease into. Being late didn't help. Molinski was at Reid's desk, hovering as usual. Asking too many questions. She had pictures of the two TCs.

"Shall we go with the shot that shows Harrison's in the background, or should we go with the bank?" Molinski held both shots up. "The bank does more advertising, but Ron is such good friends with Harrison, and he's on the Fire District Board and the School Board."

Ron Taylor was publisher of _The Newspress_. He had more than forty years in the newspaper business and loved every minute of it. He knew everyone in town, and knew where all the bones were buried. He was a good man, but Reid thought he leaned a little too far to the advertising side of the desk. But then, that's what paid the bills.

"Screw the politics. The shot with Harrison's is the better angle. Run with it. Three-column, left," Reid was good at making decisions. "What else?"

Molinski held up a picture of the car over the side. It was a late model import that had rolled down an embankment. Molinski gave him the details as he looked at the shot. The car was pretty caved in. It was a good wreck shot.

"Where did it happen, what were the injuries?"

Molinski ran out the details like a verbal newswire. "Vehicle over the side, sometime Sunday afternoon, Highway 79 near Warner Springs. Occupants left the scene. Blood found in the car. At least two injured. Car was a rent-a-car from Oceanside. CHP is checking hospitals for the driver."

"How in the hell did we get this picture? Warner Springs is out of our territory." Reid didn't have time for this.

"O'Malley was out taking pictures of the lake and heard it on the scanner. Maybe _The Cal-Ranch News_ could use it."

Reid thought about it. Probably too late for their deadline, but what the hell. He called the editor of their sister paper in Temecula. Louie was a no-nonsense editor from the old school. Past deadline. Send it up with the courier. Reid held the halftone picture in his hand, looking at it. The car had rolled several times. Hell, maybe there was a good story here. Why had the people left the scene? He looked closer. The driver's side door was open and he could see a bit of the interior. There was a visor on the dashboard. He took out a large magnifying glass from his desk drawer. He looked at the hat. It had an insignia on it. A logo. Bonsall Downs.

CHAPTER ELEVEN

A Drive To Survive

The air was cold. A single sliver of sunlight sliced the darkness through a tiny rent between the door and the door jam. Particles of dust hung like stars in the air over the hard concrete floor. Morning sounds on the other side of the thin walls stirred Logan's conscious. Birds squabbled as a rooster crowed one last late-morning greeting. The whinny of a horse. An eighteen-wheeler's Jacob's braking system popped like so many firecrackers. It was miles away.

Logan managed the first movement of the day: a roll to his side. The army cot he had somehow found in the dark was the most uncomfortable excuse for a bed that he had ever experienced. But it was a step up from the cold concrete floor. He was stiff and felt bruised all over. The blows had been brutal. His hands were tied behind his back, and he was already hurting from the wreck. Bruises, lacerations, contusions: he was a mess. Worst of all, he had cracked a rib, and pain came with every breath. It had been a long night, or couple of nights. He couldn't remember.

They had come early in the morning. Was it yesterday? Two men, one slightly larger than the other. They had set him up in a straight chair and threw water on his face. It was cold water, and it dripped down the front of his chest as they drilled him with questions. At first he didn't answer. They hit him. Then he had cursed them. They hit him more, and threw more water in his face. They got mad when he wouldn't answer. They wanted to know what he knew about the formula, and about Walter. Finally Logan gave in and told them that all he knew about

Walter was he was Janine's brother and he was in trouble. Hell, he barely even knew Janine.

He thought he had heard her voice the night before. Yelling at the top of her lungs, until they shut her up. Or was it a dream? Was it last night? Time seemed to register only in pain, and sleep.

He moved his hands. They were still tied behind him, but the rope had loosened a little during the night. Either that or his wrists had shrunk. His feet were tied, too. He moved his hands. The rope cut into his wrists, but it was definitely getting looser. This could be his only chance, he thought. He worked through the pain. Dust danced in the spotlight of the sun that was shining through the crack in the door. He concentrated on the rope, trying to think it looser.

What if the two who had beaten him came back? There was no telling how much time he had, he just needed to take each moment as it came. Thinking about what might come next made him work his wrists harder. There was a bit more slack now. Something about a constant motion that loosened the ropes. A relentless attack. Little by little he gained more movement in his wrists. If his hands were just a little smaller he would be free. He tried to think them smaller. Small hands. Contracted hands. Hands in ice cold water. Little hands.

He was careful to listen as he worked. No people sounds, and that was good. He thought about the two men who had beaten him. It would be nice to turn the tables on them, but then again he thought about the reality of it all. They seemed like hardcore criminal punks, and even if he did beat them with his fists, they would likely come back with a gun or a knife. The reality of it was, he never wanted to see them again.

What about Janine? Was she okay? It was still quiet; they might have taken her away. But why leave him? At this point, he could only hope and keep working at the rope that bound his hands. He let his mind drift as he worked. Trade winds, warm water, hard sand beneath his feet. Walking on a pristine beach. Standing on a cliff overlooking a small inlet. The images kept changing: clouds over the mountains, slopes to the sea, rocky coastlines with the sound of waves pounding against a cliff. Voices in the distance, and laughter.

His wrists were red and nearly raw when his left hand finally slipped through the rope. He quickly slid the rope off of his wrists and went about untying the knot at his feet. His body ached, but slowly he worked his muscles into a responsive mode. Who knew what was beyond the door. He would be no match for the two assholes. Not today.

On instinct, he tried the door. To his amazement, it was open. Stepping into the sunlight, he saw that a dirt yard separated the shed from an old house. The main house, no doubt. No sign of activity from the house, or from anywhere in the yard.

The sun was high in the sky. Where was Janine? The spread was some kind of working ranch. There was a complex of buildings constructed in a loose semicircle. It was at the foot of small hill covered with chaparral. A dirt road led from the complex through a row of pine trees and disappeared. This was high desert. Logan could feel the dryness in the air and smell pine and sage.

He listened for any signs of life from the house or garage. Still nothing. Slowly, he crept to the outbuilding next to the shed. It was some type of bunkhouse, or guest house. He looked in through the dirty windows but couldn't see much. He moved to the door and turned the handle, but it was locked.

He decided to check the garage. If there were no vehicles, then he could assume he was alone. Except for Janine, who he hoped would be in the main house. Crossing the yard in even strides, he moved to a window on the side of the large wooden building. His heart was pounding and he could feel beads of sweat forming at the temple. His mouth went dry when he peered through the window. The sinister-looking black van that had run them off the road was there.

He quickly retreated to the opposite side of the building and listened. Still no sounds. Where were they? He felt like running down the dirt driveway and making a clean break. There had to be a road somewhere, and he could flag down a ride. But what about Janine? His adrenaline was pumping and it was hard to think straight. His body wanted to react. To run, or punch, or something. Anything. He took a deep breath and tried to slow his heart.

A small insect buzzed by his ear and he slapped at it with his hand. He had to do something, and he knew he couldn't live with himself if he left without checking for Janine. Maybe the two goons had gone. Maybe not.

With no further thought he stepped around the garage and went alongside of the house. Should he open a door and just walk in? He listened. There was no sound. He tried a side door. Locked. He walked around the house cautiously. There was a front entrance, although it was obviously not the most used. Weeds were growing through the Spanish paving stones, and the planters in the entranceway were overgrown with native bushes and weeds. He knew this door would be locked and it was. He went to what was the back side of the house. A large Elepo Pine shaded the entire length of the building. There was an old swimming pool. Dry as a bone with caked dirt in the bottom. It was a homemade effort.

The rooms all had windows facing the pool. He looked in through the first window. It was a bedroom. He removed the screen and tried the window. Locked, of course. A rock would do the trick. If there was anyone inside this would bring them running, and so be it.

He broke a pane with a single, well aimed blow. The sound of glass breaking was louder than he had expected, but no one came. He crouched below the window, ready to run, or to fight, another rock in his hand for good measure. He found the latch and opened the window. Once he was in he shut the window and closed the curtain. The room was cold. The musty smell of an old house permeated the air. He walked past the fireplace and the large bed. The room seemed to be in use. Down the hall there was another room. Another smaller bedroom with a smaller fireplace. There were four bedrooms in all. Two of them had been used recently. There was dried blood on one of the pillows. Logan tried not to speculate and kept checking for other clues as to what may have happened.

The rooms were in disarray. There was no woman's touch here. People had been using the place to sleep and that was about it. A door creaked from a room down the hall, and Logan felt his heart pump. Was he alone? Surely if the goons were around, they would have made a move by now. Maybe not.

He went down the hall to find out. The sound had come from the end of the hall, probably the master bedroom. He picked up his pace as he approached the open door and squeezed the rock in his hand like a baseball.

He sprang into the room anticipating a confrontation. It was empty except for an unmade queen-size bed and an overstuffed chair. Wind blew down the chimney making an eerie wailing sound. The door to the closet creaked again. Only the wind, thought Logan.

No Janine. No goons. No time to wait around. He let out the breath he had been holding. He left the room and headed back up the hall to the kitchen. There were signs of a scuffle there. A chair was knocked over and there were some blood spots on the table and floor. He found the refrigerator and checked for food. There was some sandwich meat that looked edible, slices of cheese, and wheat bread. He thought about making a sandwich, a good idea if he had the time. But not now. He needed to finish checking the place and then hit the road. Hopefully he could find a phone and call Reid.

The closet door creaked again, but he paid no attention. He was sure he was alone now. Then he heard a noise from behind. It was a soft, shuffling noise. The sound of footsteps on a cement floor.

"Logan?"

He whirled around to see a disheveled-looking woman in a bloodstained dress holding a fireplace poker. It took him a second to realize it was Janine. She looked all but done in. Her eyes had dark circles, and her face was bruised. She dropped the poker and threw her arms around him.

"I'm so glad to see you . . ." she cried, sobbing on his shoulder. He could feel warm wet tears through his shirt. "They hit me. I thought they had killed you, or left you at the accident. They wanted to know about Walter, about his formula. I don't know what's going on."

He held her close and she felt good. "Where are they?"

"I heard the phone ring, and there was a lot of cursing. Then they just left. Got in a truck or something and drove off. I couldn't believe it. That was this morning. I was so tired and relieved; I guess I just passed out. Then I heard the glass breaking, and I thought they had come back. But it was you. I'm so glad it was you."

Logan held her close and let her babble like a lost child who had just been found. He tried to put the pieces together. They had interrogated Janine until late last night. They left hurriedly after receiving a call. Why hadn't he heard them? It didn't matter. What mattered was that they were probably going to come back just as fast.

"We need to get out of here. Those guys will be back," said Logan. "I was going to put some things together in case we need to hide out. But maybe we should just go out to the road and try to hitch a ride. We need to call the cops."

"No. We can't call the cops. I have a bad feeling about that. They will arrest me," Janine looked forlorn. "If I go to the cops, they will ask me questions I don't want to answer. People will find out, they always do. And my life won't be worth living."

Logan looked at her and thought for a moment. Maybe life wasn't going to be worth living anyway. This whole thing was a meatball of catastrophic proportions. He had been sailing along in life, not really going anywhere but living a lifestyle that suited him. And then came the wreck at Kelly's Corner, and this lady had stepped into his life. A meatball. Have to watch out for the meatballs in life, he thought. There would always be meatballs flying around. A person needed to know when to duck. This one had hit him square in the face, and the sauce was dripping down his chin.

"Wait a minute. I saw their van in the garage, they must have had another car or something." Logan walked nervously to the window. "Maybe we could just drive their van out of here and make it back to my place."

She didn't approve, but there was not much else they could do. They went to the large garage and found it wasn't locked. Better yet, the keys were in the van. What luck, Logan thought. He turned the key in the ignition. It was a Ford Econoline and it seemed fairly new. Except that it smelled of rotting food and stale cigarette smoke. There was half a tank of gas. In a minute, they were rolling down the dirt driveway to a touch of freedom. At least for the moment. They went through an open ranch-style gate and Logan slowed down a little to get his bearings.

"I'm not sure where we are, but it looks sort of familiar. I know there's a paved road around here somewhere. I heard the trucks."

A range of foothills rose from the desert floor to their right. Logan's instinct told him that was north. A couple of minutes more of bouncing down the dirt road and they came to an intersection. Logan followed the road to the left. A gut feeling. Hopefully he would find a highway soon. Just a matter of time, he thought, and luck.

Suddenly, in the rearview mirror, he saw a cloud of dust kicking up from the road behind. Another vehicle was coming, and it looked to be in a hurry.

He jammed down on the accelerator and took off down the road. There were no houses of any kind. A remote area, thought Logan. The road had huge ruts and they were playing hell with the steering wheel. They came to another junction and this time the intersection had some mailboxes. This new road was more traveled. But still dirt. Logan checked for the plume of dust. It was still coming. Again, Logan turned in the general direction of the hills and put his foot to the floor, hoping to find some blacktop somewhere and a road that would lead them back to Bonsall.

He looked over at Janine. She was crying again. Softly. Tears running down her cheeks. He took her hand.

"I'm sorry," she said. "I didn't mean for this to happen. I never wanted you to get involved. It's so out of control. Everything is screwed up."

Logan looked at her. She was right. Everything was definitely screwed up. They had been run off the road, beaten, held captive, and were now driving what amounted to be a stolen vehicle. Probably was stolen before they had borrowed it, he thought. There was also the possibility that they were being chased, and to boot, they were basically lost.

Logan tried to sound calm. "Yeah, well we just have to take it a step at a time and see if we can get things a little less screwed up. Hopefully, with a little luck, we can get out of this mess in one piece."

He said it with a laugh and a smile, but inside he was scared. This had become a deadly game. Those two guys back at the ranch would not have had any trouble if he had cashed in. Something about them told him they had seen death before. And it didn't upset them much. They were hard and cold with flat-line emotions.

"Janine, I think we need to get back to Bonsall and talk to Reid. He's the only one I know that might be able to help. At least, I know he will have some ideas."

She nodded. "Maybe you're right. I need to do something. Running away is not going to do anybody any good."

The dirt road came to an end at a paved road. Logan could tell it was one of the major backcountry highways, but he wasn't sure which one. Right or left? He instinctively turned left. Something inside told him this was the way to the coast. He took the road at a good pace and wondered if the other vehicle was still in pursuit. A car passed from the opposite direction and it was followed by a truck. The road curved around small hills and eventually came into what amounted to civilization.

"I know where we are now," said Logan. "This is Anza. We can be home in an hour or so."

They drove through the small, stretched-out town of Anza. A series of stores and country strip centers. It looked like it could be the modular-building capital of California, thought Logan. Temporary as opposed to contemporary. It was a high-desert town. Dry. And crusty. Hard people with weathered skin, wearing Levi's and workboots. And seed hats. This was a farming area.

"They grow a lot of pot around here, and mix up speed like it's moonshine. You have to be careful where you go. You never know what you're going to find." Logan headed the van in the direction of Temecula. For some reason, he felt talkative. "This has always been a wild sort of area. In the old days, this road was the Butterfield Stage Route from Tipton Missouri to San Francisco. And the Pony Express used it to for a short time," Logan fancied himself a historian and felt compelled to tell Janine about their route. "Juaquin Murietta, the famed bandito, used to hold up the stage in these hills. Made a lot of money, until they hanged him. That's the trouble with breaking the law, there's always that price to pay."

Janine was miles away. Alone in her thoughts as Logan talked on. Then an on-coming car caught both their attention. It was a black and white Riverside County Sheriffs cruiser. At first Logan was glad to see some law out here. He wished they had been around the day before. The black-and-white passed and he commented on it to Janine. She didn't respond, but she watched it pass and continued to look out the rear window.

"They're turning around, Logan. I think they're going to pull us over."

Logan looked in the side mirror. Sure enough, the sheriffs car had spun a U-turn, kicking up a puff of dirt and dust in its wake. The cruiser closed on them fast and pulled in right behind the van.

"Logan. They've got their red lights on."

CHAPTER TWELVE

Rocco's World Rocks

Rocco sat staring at the oak tree. A giant green world of its own. Birds chirped nervously, darting in and out of hundred-year-old branches. No grass grew in the world of permanent shade. Instead the ground was covered with layers upon layers of multi-colored leaves. The gophers that made their homes at the base of the tree did not eat the roots, preferring instead the roots of younger plants. These roots were very old. Reaching deep below the surface and extending out beyond the parameter of the complex of buildings. A squirrel stopped his fidgeting to steal a glance at the man sitting in the lounge chair. Neither moved for a second, then the squirrel climbed down the trunk and scampered off to a nearby bush. The man remained still, void of motion.

Inside the main house, Ratface and Lobo sat at a small round table in the kitchen. They, too, were staring at the tree. Although not with the intensity of Rocco. It had been two days since Rocco had tried the new drug. Sobrano and Dillard had left him at Marleano's ranch to sleep it off. But Rocco didn't sleep.

"I kind of don't get this," said Lobo, "We find the chick they been looking for, then they tell us to split and let them get away. What the fuck?"

"None of our fucking business, that's what. We do what they tell us to do and that's it. Anyway, those two will be so freaked out. Probably split the country. Especially the chick. Like Sobrano said, let them be and everything will take care of itself."

"What about that asshole?" said Lobo looking out at Rocco. Sobrano had directed them back to Marleano's to check on Rocco. When they arrived from the other ranch shortly after 8 a.m., they found Rocco still under the tree. Comatose.

"I don't think this Pink Polly shit was a good idea," said Lobo still looking out at Rocco. "They should stick to the stuff they know. This is trouble."

Ratface took a sip from his cup, and nodded agreement. He didn't really care.

Lobo fidgeted in his chair. He looked at the pockmarked face across the table. The small, pale blue eyes. The sharp, pointed nose. The yellow teeth. The receding hairline. Ratface was a perfect name for this guy, he thought. Lobo was an up and coming criminal with an up and coming mentality. He used drugs occasionally. Not like Ratface. He'd shot a couple of guys along the way. Hadn't killed anybody that he could remember.

"I think we should call Carlos and tell him he was right. Rocco is out of it," said Lobo. "Let him decide what we should do, then go back to finding this guy Walter."

"I think we should stick a gun in Rocco's mouth and see what he does," said Ratface. "If he wakes up, we call. If he just sits there, we off him and dump him somewhere and make it look like a suicide."

They both laughed. Then Lobo actually thought about it for a minute, like it was a serious plan, and then opted again to call Sobrano before taking any action. He was in charge here. At least he thought so.

"We should call. Nothing is happening here."

Lobo asked about the bag of quarters. Ratface shrugged his shoulders.

"It's in the van. I told you we shouldn't have taken the other car."

They had taken a sedan that Dillard left at his ranch. It was Lobo's call. "Been using the van too much," he had said. "I just have a feeling about these things."

He took the keys to Rocco's truck and scooped some quarters from a bowl of change on the counter. The ranch had a well-maintained bowl of change—nickels, dimes, and quarters only. No pennies. It was for making use of the pay phones in the area. At least a drive would get him away from Ratface, he thought. He had been seeing a little too much of that ugly mug lately.

"I still don't get it. We should have dropped those two off in the bushes somewhere instead of leaving them at Dillard's," said Lobo. "He's going to be pissed. They might tell the cops."

"No way," said Ratface, "she's on the run herself. Anyway, I heard Dillard owns the cops out here. You know what I mean. They start singing, and he'll have them capped for sure. No witnesses. No case."

Lobo shrugged, "whatever, I'm going to call Carlos. I want to get the fuck out of here. Back to the city."

Ratface sipped his coffee and watched as Lobo got into the truck and drove off toward the front gate. He waited until he heard the truck pull away from the gate, after stopping to lock it. Without hesitation he went to the cupboard above the counter with the bowl of change and took down a chrome-plated revolver from the top shelf. It was a large gun. About as large as revolvers get. A magnum 357. Ratface loved to have this gun near him. It was a good feeling. Power. Surety. Authority. No one could give him any shit when he had his "Chromie."

He detached Chromie's revolving cylinder and spun it to make sure all the bullets where there. Time for a smoke, he thought. He went to the cupboard where the gun had been and took down a wooden tray. In it there was a plastic bag half full of marijuana. With a Zig-Zag paper, he twisted a mixture of the weed into a tightly-rolled cigarette. It was not even a third as large in diameter as the Marlboros or Camels he smoked. But it was ten times more effective.

With a wooden stick match he lit the freshly rolled joint and inhaled deeply. He held the smoke in his lungs for an inordinate amount of time. He felt his lungs scream to let the gaseous mixture out, yet he held it in, almost gagging himself. Finally he let it out, then broke into a fit of coughing. It was deep coughing, from the bottom of his lungs. He felt the blood rush to his head. The veins on the side of his face were pumping. His eyes watered. He heard a high-pitched whine ringing in his ears. He put his head down on the table and let the drool run out of his mouth on to the Formica finish. His eyes were closed. He saw red. There was a land beyond the red with flowing vines like strands of kelp growing from the bottom of the sea. Flowing back and forth with the currents. Long vines of leaves and bulbs, swaying in the wind. It was a warm place, but there was something out there that scared him.

⚘

Lobo didn't like the feel of Rocco's truck. The steering had a little play in it, and the brakes went down a tad too close to the floorboard before there was any action. He turned on the radio. It was a country station. Willie Nelson's twangy voice floated out of the static. "Mama, don't let your babies grow up to be cowboys . . ."

The road curved through a countryside of centuries-old California Live Oaks. The Lusiano and their predecessors had used the trees for food and shelter. The Anza expedition had no doubt used some of these same oaks for shade in the seventeenth century. Bootleggers had set up stills here during prohibition. Today many of the trees were dying. Cut back to make way for the road. Ridden with disease and petulance brought here by civilization. The new residents had brought their own trees. Fruit trees from other climate zones. Apricot and apple to feed the birds. Conifers to line driveways and highways. Maple trees that turned yellow in the fall. The deciduous trees had all lost their leaves with the coming of the first winter nights. The majestic oaks remained unchanged against the weather.

Lobo drove to the intersection of two backcountry highways and turned left toward The Old Stage Stop. There was a phone there he could use. He drove the three or four miles in a mental fog. He was hoping he could talk to Carlos and that Carlos would have a plan. Ratface was not good company. All he wanted to do was get loaded. And his stories were grotesque. His life was grotesque. Maybe they should put Rocco behind the wheel of this shitty truck and drive it off a cliff into the desert, Lobo thought. He knew a good spot for it. Right down the road. Straight off a sheer cliff into thin air. A thousand-foot vertical drop into a remote canyon with huge granite boulders. It would be years before anyone found the body, and when they did there would be nothing left to investigate.

Highway 246 led up over a small pass, then began its long descent into the Anza Borrego Desert. This was the old route down the grade.

The one the Spaniards had taken. Lobo pulled the truck into the parking lot of The Old Stage Stop. There was a girl in tight jeans talking on the phone. He started to get out and then hesitated. He could go into the bar, or he could get something at the store next to the bar. He sat with his hand on the door handle. Maybe she would be off soon.

A green-and-white sheriff four-wheel-drive unit pulled in and parked in front of the store. The unmistakable scratch of the radio dispatch sent a chill down Lobo's back. He hated that sound. He looked nervously at the girl and avoided the direction of the annoying sound. She hung up the phone and stood for a second lighting a cigarette. When it was lit, she turned. Her eyes raked over the truck, then focused directly at Lobo. She started to move toward him and then stopped. There seemed to be some sort of acknowledgement by her expression. She looked again at the truck, then turned and walked to the bar. Lobo had a strange feeling about the look. It was like she knew the truck and was going to come over, until she saw him.

The sheriff's deputy had gone into the store. Lobo went for the phone. He was nervous, but he tried not to let it show. He hated making these calls from a pay phone. It was a stupid rule, he thought. Why couldn't they just have a phone at the ranch. Hell, they had machines that could tell if the line was tapped. And there were scramblers. All the calls from here were long distance, and that meant lots of dialing and lots of waiting for the lines to connect, and the whole time he would be standing out in the open. Exposed. Parked in plain sight. He didn't like it.

Calling Carlos Sobrano was even worse. It was an international number. Mexico. A call back to the fifties. At least now he could dial direct without the assistance of an operator. The phone rang. Sobrano answered.

"Hola?"

"He's just sitting there under that tree. Shit, he'll probably die of starvation before he comes out of it. I tell you boss, that shit is bad news."

Sobrano listened. Yes it was more bad news. Delivered because of bad decisions and now more decisions needed to be made.

"Listen my friend. I want you guys to grab the rest of that shit from the garage and get it back to San Diego tonight. We're going to end this business once and for all. Comprende aqmigo?"

"Si, comprende. We'll take care of it boss."

Sobrano told him to ditch the BMW in the desert. "You know the spot. Put Rocco in it and send it over," he said.

"Sure, I got it. No problem, we'll take care of everything and be back on the coast this evening," said Lobo.

Lobo hung up the phone and looked around. The girl was standing about ten feet away and looking straight at him. Could she have heard anything? He wondered. She didn't look right. Crazy. Or drunk. Both maybe.

"Where's Roger?" she asked. Her voice took him by surprise. Low, throaty, a whisper with volume, void of emotion.

"I don't know any Roger. You got me mixed up with someone else."

He walked to truck without looking back. The sheriff was nowhere to be seen. The girl with whispery voice watched as the truck rolled out of the lot. Another day.

Lobo had just finished pulling onto the highway when the deputy walked out of the general store. He took a small notepad from the inside pocket of his jacket and took down Lobo's license number. Lobo drove down the highway to the turnoff. He kept glancing in his rearview mirror expecting to see the green-and-white. He didn't.

The gate to the ranch was locked. Just like he had left it. He went through the routine of getting out and unlocking the gate, stopping again and locking it. Always a hassle when there was only one person. He wished he were somewhere else, doing something different. But what? He drove up the dirt drive past the row of blue spruce. A gust of wind blew through the tops of the trees, ruffling the needles and disturbing a curious blue jay.

He parked the truck under the large Live Oak and turned the engine off. It was always so quiet out here once the sound of the motor died. He got out and walked obliviously to the ranch house. He smelled something as he got to the door. Marijuana smoke, and something else. A sulphurlike smell. He opened the door and his nostrils filled with the smell of gunpowder, and death.

Ratface lay facedown on the table in a dark, translucent pool of blood. The back of his head was exposed like a big chunk of raw meat. His blood-splattered arms lay outstretched across the table. His fingers grasping for something to hold on to. Crimson red drops were everywhere. On the white refrigerator. The sink. All over the floor. On the ceiling. His forehead seemed smashed into the table. Almost flat, like a Frankenstein forehead.

Lobo gagged. He felt the fluids in his stomach start to rise. He ran out of the door into the yard and heaved. Nothing came out. He heaved again and fell to his knees. He tried to yell, but nothing came out. He was screaming inside. What happened here? Why? Suddenly, he remembered Rocco. Where was Rocco? He looked up to where he had been stationed on the patio. He was gone.

Panic. He needed to get out of there quick. Whatever happened to Ratface was not self inflicted. He had been shot at close range from behind. Someone was watching. Lobo could feel it. He ran to the truck parked under the oak. No keys. He shoved his hands in his coat and felt his pants pockets. No keys. Maybe he dropped them. He looked back to where Rocco had been sitting. Still not there. What happened to Rocco?

Lobo made his way back to the kitchen, half running, eyes on the ground, looking for the keys. No keys. He didn't want to open the door and go in, but he needed the keys. He needed to get the hell out of there. Someone was watching. He opened the screen door and heard it squeak ominously. It seemed louder than before. In fact, he had never really heard it before. The door was ajar. He pushed it and went in. Ratface was sprawled across the table as before. Blood draining from his body. The stench of death hung in the air. Lobo winced. He'd never seen, or smelled, death this close. His eyes searched the room for the keys to the truck. Where had he put them? Maybe they were in the ignition and he just hadn't seen them in his state of mind. It was possible. The keys to the car he and Ratface had driven were somewhere. He would take that car. A Ford Grand Torino. It would take him out of there. Where were they? He searched the counter where they usually were. Not there. No key anywhere. Maybe they were on the bureau in the bedroom.

He left the kitchen and went through the Spanish arched doorway to the long living room, and then down a dimly-lit corridor with three bedrooms. There was nothing in the first room. That's where Rocco had slept. He went to the second bedroom and hurried to the bureau.

Some change, a watch, a pencil, and a pad of paper with some notes. No keys. He glanced around the room. He was on his way to the closet when he heard the squeak of the spring from the screen door. It was opening slowly. He froze. There was another way out through the master bedroom that led to the patio facing the oak. He could make it. He wished he had Ratface's gun. He needed a gun. There were a couple of rifles in the room off of the kitchen. No way to get to them. He had a blade. He took it out and opened it. A long, ugly, cheap-looking copy of a stiletto that he had picked up in Tijuana. It wasn't much of a knife. It was intended to scare, not to protect. Not to kill. Too flimsy. He went to the master bedroom.

The door to the patio was locked and bolted. Lobo tried to be as quiet as possible. He slipped the dead bolt and turned the doorknob. It was old. The door was old, but it had been opened over the summer and wasn't stuck. He pulled it open. The screen door was latched. He opened it. It squeaked like the kitchen door. But not as loud. He closed the doors carefully behind him, not making any noise, and started to run across the patio. He held his cheap knife in his hand. Stupid knife, he thought. He needed a real knife. Instinct led him to the truck, and he crouched behind the passenger's side, away from the main house.

Slowly he gathered his thoughts. He would look one more time for the keys. Maybe they were in the ignition. Maybe he had dropped them on the floor. That was it! He had dropped them on the floor. He carefully opened the door. They were there, right where he had left them when he pulled in. He crawled behind the wheel and put the keys in the ignition. He would run the gate. Hell, he didn't care now. He was getting out of there. His right hand turned the key to the ignition. Beads of sweat trickled down the side of his face. The starter motor turned, but the engine didn't start. Lobo pumped the gas frantically. The starter motor slowed. He stopped and tried again.

Lobo remotely felt the driver's side door begin to open and then he was flying. There was a falling sensation as he was dragged violently from the seat. An arm of steel grabbed him from behind pulling him backwards on to hot coals. There were hot coals on his back. On his stomach. And in his throat. Suddenly, he was warm all over.

The jail in Temecula consisted of a windowless room in an industrial building with a fortified door. It was what was referred to as a tank. A built-in bench lined two of the four walls. It was just about square, ten by ten. The once white walls were smudged with dirty finger and hand prints. A few names and choice bits of information were scratched into the surface. Mostly illegible, for all the effort. A poor excuse for gang graffiti.

Logan sat alone on the bench, staring at the walls, wondering how he got to this lifeless room. The officers didn't say much when they pulled the van over. They had asked for I.D., but Logan and Janine's identification and other personal belongings were lost during or after the rent-a-car had gone off the embankment. The two Riverside County sheriff's deputies had handcuffed them and put them in the back of the patrol car. They were brought to the sheriff substation in Temecula and put in separate holding cells. Strange, thought Logan.

The cell was quiet. He could hear the blood throbbing inside of his head. It had been a long day, or couple of days, it was hard to remember. He thought about the two guys who had run them off the road. Never did get a good look at them. Were they wearing masks? Not that he could remember. It was dark in the little shed with the cold cement floor. That was torture. But it could have been worse. They could have killed him. He had heard Janine screaming, not frantically but definitely in pain. They had knocked her around, too. But why?

The flat air in the room suddenly moved as the door to the cell opened. One of the two officers who had taken them in motioned to Logan and told him to get on his feet. Logan stood. He was very sore. And very tired. The cop handcuffed Logan and led him down a well-lit hall to another door. Logan was stationed, toes and nose against the wall, while the cop unlocked and opened the door.

"Logan?"

It was Janine. Her voice was hoarse, but it sounded good. Why? She was the one who got him in this mess. He should have shut her down the first time she had asked him to talk. Hell, that was only a few days ago. It seemed like years. He gave Janine a smile and shrugged.

"What's going on, officer? Why are we being held?" It was about the tenth time Logan had asked the question and for the tenth time there was no answer. In fact, the two officers had not talked to them at all. And they didn't talk on their radio. There was no communication with a dispatcher or, for that matter, between the two of them. They hadn't really said anything other than giving Logan and Janine a few commands as they were being detained.

They were led down the hall to another door and told them to sit down. Janine had been handcuffed like Logan. At least their hands were not behind their back, thought Logan. This was nuts. They were being treated like convicted criminals.

After the door closed, Logan looked at Janine. She was a sad sight but somehow still beautiful. She had the eyes of a small animal that had been mistreated. Sad eyes.

"Are you okay?" Logan would have taken her in his arms if he could. In a nightmare of pain and agony, she was the one positive note.

"Yes. I just don't understand why this is all happening. It doesn't make sense." Her eyes began to well up with tears again.

Logan took her hand. It felt good in his. Solid. He couldn't help feeling sorry for her. He always had a soft spot in his heart for life's mistreated. Janine was a victim, yet at the same time he knew that she had made all the choices that had led to this point. When the cop returned, Logan would demand to know the charges. He would demand to make a call. What was this anyway? The cops hadn't said two words to either of them since they had been stopped on the highway.

"Don't worry. We'll figure something out," said Logan. "Something weird is going on here, and I think that we've sort of landed in it. Janine, what about the envelope? What happened to it?"

"I put it under the seat after we left that airport. I guess it's still in the car, wherever that is."

Logan was going ask her more about what the two goons at the ranch had wanted to know, but the cell door opened and the same cop who had escorted them there motioned them to stand up and walk out of the cell.

"Wait a minute," Logan said, making eye contact with the officer. "You've taken us in and held us for hours without telling us anything.

This is total bullshit! You have to allow us to make a call. We told you what happened to us, and you're not doing a damn thing about it. What the hell is going on?"

The officer stared at Logan. "Just do what I say." There was conviction in his voice. But there was something else, too. Disgust? Anguish? He didn't like what he was doing, or he didn't like them.

Logan noticed that there was something odd about this jail. There didn't seem to be any other prisoners, or guards, or people. It was empty. In fact, this was the quietest jail Logan had ever seen, not that he'd seen a lot of them. They walked through a series of halls that were identical. White textured drywall, green carpet. Built in a hurry. At a door that looked exactly like every other door they had passed, they stopped, and the cop who had been their escort opened the door and motioned them in.

The room was larger than the holding cells they had been in. Same neon lighting and color motif. Puke white with smudges. Green carpet. There was a long table in the middle of the room. At the far end there were two more officers seated. At least they appeared to be officers. They were in plain clothes. There were several file folders on the table in front of them, and they were studying them intently as Logan and Janine sat down at the table.

"So, where did you get the van?" One of the cops asked. Logan detected a note of hesitation in the man's voice. The words were rehearsed and spoken with some pseudo authority.

Logan told him the story about driving in the country and getting run off the road. He kept it brief, it was the only way he could tell it at this point. The officers listened but made no notes. They didn't appear interested in any of the details.

"You can't describe the men who held you?"

Logan and Janine both answered no. The cops seemed pleased.

"Excuse us for a second," said the cop in charge. The two officers left the room. When they returned their demeanor seemed to have changed. They looked more relaxed.

"Look, we've told you what we know. We've been polite. Now how about you telling us what's going on? You can't just hold us here against our will. What are the charges? When do we call our lawyer?"

The interrogators laughed.

"Lawyer?" said the beady-eyed cop. "Do you really want to call a lawyer? Some how I don't think so."

Logan thought about it, and decided the cop was right. "All right, then just let us go."

The cop in the suit picked through one of the files. "That will be up to you. Now, you've been through an ordeal, but you can't identify the perpetrators and you don't know why they ran you off the road. Right?"

"That's right," said Logan.

"And, you can't positively identify the place they took you to. Am I right?"

"We found our way out of there, and I think I could find it again. You want me to take you there? Logan was trying to be helpful.

"That won't be necessary. In fact, you might just as well forget you were ever there," said the cop, with conviction in his voice. "For your own good."

The beady-eyed cop smiled.

"Except for one thing," said the cop in charge. "We believe that you had something in your possession that a lot of people are interested in. Do you know what I'm talking about?"

The beady-eyed cop moved toward Janine.

"Wait a minute," said Logan. He didn't like the way the cop was looking at her. "There was an envelope. Is that what you want? You want the fucking envelope? It's probably still in the car we were in when we crashed."

"What was in the envelope?" The lead interrogator asked.

"I have no idea," said Logan looking right into the cop's dark eyes.

Janine turned her head and started to say something, then stopped. There was an awkward moment of silence. The cop who had been asking the questions stood up.

"Okay, here's the deal." The cop at the end of the table seemed to be in charge. "You've got yourselves involved in something that doesn't concern you. Now, you've got to get yourselves uninvolved."

"How do we do that?" asked Logan.

The cop chuckled. "Well, see that's the easy part. You go back to your job. She goes back to her mom, and neither one of you say anything to anybody. Not to your friends. Not to the cops. No one. You understand?"

Logan listened but couldn't believe what he was hearing. Leave it be? Walk away and everything would be okay? What the hell was going on? He felt like finding Detective Cassio and telling him everything he knew about what had gone on. But what then?

"Look, I told you guys what happened to us. We were on a drive in the country, minding our own business, and this van comes out of nowhere and tries to run us off the road. I lose control, we go off a cliff, and the next thing I remember is being held in a tool shed, beaten, with my hands and feet tied, and then listening to the same two guys beat her."

"Shut the fuck up!" Beady-eyes was on his feet. "We heard the story. We know what you said, but it never happened. Okay? If you say it did, then you're still involved. Understand? You don't *want* to be involved."

Logan thought about it. "Yeah, I understand. Whatever you say."

"All right, we've all got an understanding here right?" The lead cop's voice was level and void of any feeling. His eyes never seemed to blink.

"Yes sir." Logan put his hands on Janine's and asked her if she were okay. She nodded, sniffling, eyes half open. Tears ran down her face. It seemed like she was close to crying nearly all the time, Logan thought.

The detective picked up his portfolio and papers and went out the door. The beady-eyed one followed and shut the door behind them. The room was empty. Only an untouched glass of water was on the table.

Minutes passed slowly, and then the door opened again. It was one of the cops who had stopped them.

"Come on, let's go."

CHAPTER THIRTEEN

Swing Inn

The phone buzzed in the newsroom as Burt Reid was sipping his second cup of coffee. The latest edition of *The Newspress* was on his desk. It was a nice time of week. Thursday morning before the commotion started. A short interlude when an editor could take a breath, drink a cup of coffee, and enjoy what he did for a living. Soon the reporters would be checking in, the publisher would be sending dummies, the next edition would start taking shape. Soon a new set of events and information would find its way into the paper and last week's edition would migrate to the bird cage, or the recycled bin, or the trash, or into a pile with a life of its own.

The phone rang again, and a voice came over the intercom. "Burt, are you in there? Pick up three, please. It's urgent."

Reid hit the button and answered in his terse newsroom voice. "Reid."

"Burt, it's me, Logan. I need some help."

Reid instinctively grabbed a number two pencil from the desk. "Where are you? What the hell is going on? You sound like shit."

"I'm in Temecula, and I need a ride back. Can you come out and get me?"

Reid looked at the clock on the wall. "How does a half hour sound? Where are you?"

Logan gave the location and hung up. He sounded confused and maybe a little on the apprehensive side, thought Reid. He sort of had that "get me out of jail" tone to his voice. It was a tone he'd heard before.

Leaving some instructions with the crew in the newsroom, Reid gathered some essentials: his notebook, some sharpened pencils, and his wallet and keys. Then, as an afterthought, he asked if there was anything that needed to go up to the sister paper in Temecula. He grabbed the courier bag and looked inside. There were a few papers and a halftone. The picture of the over-the-side wreck in Warner Springs. He looked at it again. Was that Logan's visor on the dash? He wondered. He took one last sip of coffee and headed for the door.

It was a twenty minute drive from Fallbrook to Temecula, through acres of avocado and citrus groves on a road that wound around picturesque foothills of granite and quartz. Stone outcroppings dotted the hillsides, monuments of another time when the land was arid and life clung to the precious moisture of the river valleys. Local legend had it that the most predominant rocks on the hillsides were the great warriors and gods that were here before the white man, frozen in time in the form of stone to keep watch over the land.

Logan told Reid he would meet him at the Swing Inn Café, a local spot on the main drag in Old Town Temecula, where bootleggers and bandits mixed it up in the old days. Temecula had a colorful history dating back to the days of the missions. The Pony Express had ridden through Temecula. The Mormon Brigade had passed through with the likes of Kit Carson. During prohibition, Temecula was a favorite spot for Hollywood's elite who came for the speakeasies and hot mineral waters at nearby Murrieta.

Reid took the new Interstate north from where it met the eastern reaches of Fallbrook. In five minutes, he was through the Rainbow Gap and into an inland valley alive with horse ranches, vineyards, and a ever-growing number of residential subdivisions. He exited on Highway 79, which turned into Front Street. The Swing Inn was in the southern end of Old Town. He found a parking spot behind the office of _The Cal Rancho News_. Reid dropped off the courier bag at the office and bolted out the door before anyone could ask questions.

Logan was in a corner booth when Reid came in, and he wasn't alone. The restaurant was busy. Full of truck drivers, local ranchers, construction workers, and the ever present urban cowboys who had moved in from Orange County, all boots and buckles. No horse.

It was noisy, not a bad place to talk, but conspicuous as hell. A lot of rumors got started at the tables of the Swing Inn Cafe. Sunday morning diners wearing Saturday night clothes. The cops dined here a lot. Along with every order of country resident, including nosy reporters. It was not a good place to keep a secret, but it was a good place to find out what was going on in town.

Reid shoved in next to the girl. He ordered a cup of black coffee from a gum-chewing waitress in a pink dress. Breakfast dishes cluttered the table.

"I don't think we've met, I'm Burt Reid."

"This is Janine Anderson, she was the lady in the wreck at Kelly's," said Logan.

Janine managed a smile. Her eyes were red from crying, and her face looked tired and strained. Had she been hit in the face? Reid wondered.

Logan gave Reid a look that got his full attention. "Thanks for coming out here. We're stuck without a car. Hell of a deal."

Reid could tell that for some reason Logan did not want to talk specifics. He took the cue. "Well, I had to come out here anyway and see Louie. You want to get going? I don't really need anymore coffee."

Logan nodded and picked up the check on the table. He had a few dollars in his back pocket, a small miracle after all that had passed. Logan had a habit of stashing a couple of twentys away in a pocket, just in case. Reid had become used to Logan always making the first move for the check, but today there was something else. He sensed that Logan was anxious to get out of The Swing Inn.

They were out the door and around the corner in one smooth motion. Reid's Regal was in the parking lot behind the newspaper office.

"So what's up, Logan? You going to tell me what's going on? Are you in trouble, or what?" Reid was matter of fact. A reporter's tone. A friend careful to respect another friend's privacy.

"Trouble? Yeah, I guess you could call it that. We've been run off the road, held hostage, beat to shit by a couple of low-life thugs, and then arrested by some very strange Riverside County Sheriffs." He blurted the meat of the matter out, ignoring the cop's warning. "The cops question us, hold us, and then tell us to forget everything and go home. Not to discuss it with anyone, or suffer some dire consequences."

Reid's news antenna went up. This was the kind of stuff that made great stories. If it were real. Logan could tend to exaggerate at times. Still, he thought it better to talk in the car, with less chance of being heard. The streets of Old Town had ears.

They drove north on Front Street through Old Town and toward the newer area of Temecula, where the restaurants, banks, and real estate offices were located. Logan told Reid more about the ordeal and about the cops and their warning.

"That is really strange. But then some cops have strange methods, especially if they are working on something that involves more than one law enforcement agency. They could be competing with DEA or FBI," said Reid. "So you say they drove you to Old Town and let you go?"

"We could have walked from the station, it wasn't that far."

"Wait a minute, where did you say this station was?" asked Reid.

Logan told him and Reid quickly turned down a road and drove a few blocks. He pointed to a building down one of the main roads and asked if that was where they were taken.

"It could have been, I wasn't paying too much attention. They just put us in the back of an unmarked car and drove away. Let us out on the corner downtown. I used my calling card number to call you," said Logan.

"There's no sheriff station there anymore," said Reid. "They moved it all out to French Valley last year. This is getting stranger and stranger."

Reid looked at his old friend. "I don't mean to sound alarmed or anything, but why are you telling me this? Aren't you afraid?"

"I don't know," said Logan. "Maybe I'm so tired I'm delusional. But man, those bastards are up to their ears in some kind of bullshit, I can tell you that. They're not out to solve some case, they're out to bury it. Somehow, I just can't walk away."

Logan heard his own words sounding like they were coming from someone else. He was tired. So why not just heed the cop's advice? Put Janine on a plane or bus or whatever, and go back to work. Do the safe thing. Maybe it was Janine. Maybe he didn't want it to end with her. Maybe they had a future.

"I hear you," said Reid. "You've got to do what feels right. And if those cops are bad, then your life will be hell. I'm thinking we go to Cassio and tell him everything."

Logan stared out the window. "Maybe. But he's kind of a hard ass himself. He's just as liable to throw Janine in jail and then nail her with being a conspirator or something."

"He's not all that bad. In fact, he's a pretty good guy underneath that cop persona. But, you could be right. He might need some hard evidence before he'd deal. You have any ideas?"

"The envelope," said Janine from the backseat. "It's what everybody wants."

Logan told Reid about the pictures and formulas. "We were on our way in to talk to you about it when we got run off the road."

"So where is it?"

"We think it's still in the wrecked rent-a-car, wherever that is," said Logan. "Do you know where they would have taken it?"

"Depends on who towed it. Either it will be out at the reservation or at Pete's," said Reid. "I could make some calls."

"We need to get back to my place and get some rest."

"Logan! Look!" Janine gasped.

A red BMW with a smashed-in left front was driving down Front Street. No doubt about what car it was. They got a good look at the driver as the car passed. He was a big man with balding hair. The look in his eyes was intense. A contemptuous look. The look of a mad dog.

The phone rang in Sobrano's office. It was a white phone with a rotary dial. He had kept it as a memento of times gone by, and now it was actually worth something as a collector's item. Not too functional though, if you wanted access to digital dialing options. Sobrano didn't. He used it for voice communications only. Limited to a select group of people. He came in from the veranda where he was having coffee and going over some paperwork. The phone rang again. A loud, bell-like ring from the 1960s. He picked it up and said hello in English.

"I'm being blackmailed by Walter." Dillard's voice was haggard. Sobrano could tell that he had been using drugs. His sentences came fast and fragmented. Half thoughts blurted out. "He told me to let his sister go, I was going to but somehow our messages got crossed and those idiots just left them at the ranch in Anza. Some of my guys picked them up. Questioned them. Nothing, no book. No formulas."

He rambled on about not being able to contact anyone at Marleano's and that they needed to get everything out of there because Marleano was dead and the cops would surely be coming to check on it. Inside Sobrano's blood began to flow, but as always, he kept his composure well.

"Take it easy, compadre. No one knows who really owns that place and no one is going to be coming out there soon," said Sobrano in reassuring tones. "We will get the stash out of there, and then we will see about our friend Walter. Most importantly, my friend, I want to find the documents that he took from my office."

Dillard winced. What could the documents contain that wasn't already being bantered about by Walter? The formula was important to the success of Pink Polly, but the new chemist would surely come up with a viable solution.

"I want you to get your cop amigos to track down that wrecked car and go through it. I want those formulas and everything that is there. Tell them to look for a large envelope. Do you understand?"

"They're doing it as we speak," said Dillard.

Sobrano advised Dillard to get the plan in motion and then take some time off. Get away from his office and get some rest. Dillard hung up his private-line phone. He didn't like being told what to do. Sobrano was not his boss, and he did not like the tone of Sobrano's voice. He may supply the muscle, but Dillard had the power in the States. Dillard was about to reach for another cigarette when the phone rang. Sobrano calling back? He picked up the new cordless receiver and pushed the button.

"Something just came over the radio I think you should know about." The voice was one of his operatives in Riverside. One of the guys who had just let Logan and Janine go. "There's been a 1026 at Warner Ranch. Two 1144s. From the location, I am sure it is at the Marleano place. Pretty bloody from the sounds of it."

"Cut out that cop shit and tell me what happened." Dillard was nearing the end of his emotional rope.

"Sounds like your boys out there bought it. One was shot, the other's neck was sliced. Neighbors saw a red BMW speeding away. When they went to check up, they found the bodies. So far, there's no mention of any drugs."

Dillard listened. "Do we have any of our guys out there?"

"Negative. That's San Diego S.O. Unless you have someone I don't know about."

Dillard thought about it and decided now was not the right time. "Stay on it and let me know as soon as you find the car those two idiots ran off the road. I want the envelope."

He hung up the phone and gathered some papers from his desk and put them, along with his cigarettes, into his briefcase. It was going to be another long day, and he wouldn't be spending it at the office.

Reid dropped Logan and Janine off at the Blue Doors to freshen up. He would check on where the wreck had been taken. He went right to work, starting with the Fallbrook Sheriff's Substation. He knew the secretary well enough to win some favors. She confirmed that the call about a car over the side in Warner had come from Sheriff's dispatch to Fallbrook. That meant Pete had probably picked up the call. He thanked her and called Pete, who was still recovering from being hit on the head last week.

"Yeah, we got the son-of-a-bitch. My man had to race another Indian driver out to the crash scene, and there was almost a confrontation. But we got it. What about it?"

Reid convinced Pete to let them in the car to retrieve some personal items. Pete wasn't too happy about it, but agreed. He called Logan and said he was on his way.

It was past noon when they turned on Alturus and were heading down the eucalyptus-lined road. A dark sedan sped around the corner and nearly ran them off the road. Logan recognized the car immediately.

"Hey, those were the two cops that took us in! What in the hell?"

Reid regained control of his Buick after a reactionary swerve to avoid the sedan.

"Do you think they saw us?" asked Janine.

"No, they weren't paying any attention to us," said Reid. "Should we follow them?"

"No, let's get down to Pete's and take a look at that car," said Janine.

They pulled into the yard and the Doberman, chained to the office entrance, barked a greeting. Pete was nowhere to be seen. They got out, careful not to come too near the snarling dog. Logan followed Janine into the yard to look for the car. Reid stayed behind and yelled for Pete. The dog continued to bark.

"Reid!" It was Logan's voice from out in the yard. "You better come over here."

Logan was standing between two bashed-in cars. He had found Pete, knocked out cold, near the rent-a-car they had been looking for.

"He's breathing. Better call 9-1-1." Reid took off for the office. He went around to the back door and dialed the number. He reported the injury and location and then, without identifying himself, he hung up.

"We better get out of here before the cops arrive. They're still looking for Janine," said Logan.

"How about the stuff you were looking for?" asked Reid.

Logan had found the car just before he found Pete. They didn't have much time, but they had come this far. He looked at Janine. "Let's check the car."

The Toyota was parked between a blue-and-white Monte Carlo and an old VW. Both had seen better days. They reached the car and Janine went to the passenger side and looked under the seat. Logan was staring at the wrecked car. He couldn't believe that they had survived. The top was crushed in and the windshield totally broken. He reached in through the broken windshield and retrieved his visor.

"I thought that was yours," said Reid, observing from where Pete lay.

Janine had finished her search. "There's nothing here." She looked dejected. Logan walked over and put his arm around her. It was a comforting hug that lasted a few precious seconds. Then, it was back to the task at hand.

"Let's get out of here before the cops come," said Logan.

They got in the Buick and drove back down toward Bonsall.

Reid turned left on a road that led to the Interstate, then took the freeway north. He glanced at the fuel gauge. Full tank.

"What should we do now?" asked Reid. "I think Janine should go ahead and talk to the cops without the envelope. It won't be that big of a deal."

"No! I need to get the things my brother gave me. If the envelope is not here, then those bastards must have taken it. I need to have it. It's the only way this is going to end. Please help me."

Her voice was breaking up. She had that little girl look again, and it didn't help.

"Just drop us back at my place and I'll get the truck. We've got to find those guys."

Reid thought about it for a minute, and then said no. He was in it now, and he had left Pete back there unattended. Something he was sure that he would regret. "I've got the gas. Where are we going?"

Logan smiled. "Back to the seen of the crime."

They drove out Highway 79 through the muted colors of coastal sage and high-desert chaparral. The sun had risen in a clear blue sky. A nice day. Sunny but cool, with a gentle breeze. Summers here were hot, and winters as cold as it gets without snow. The bent trees and twisted Manzanita along the road attested to the strength of the afternoon breezes.

"Got to be careful where you drive in these parts. There are a lot more guns around up here than ever before," said Reid. "Louie at *The News* has done a ton of stories. Every week someone gets shot, either by accident or because they had trespassed. Hemet Valley Emergency is one of the busiest ERs in the county, and that's saying a lot."

"I'm pretty sure the place we were held was used for growing pot," said Logan. "There were a lot of shovels and hoes. Too many for just a ranch. And there was other stuff."

A large four-wheel-drive truck passed them on the two-lane highway. Logan caught a glance of the passenger as it went by. It could have been one of the cops he had seen at the station in Temecula.

"That guy in the truck, he looked like one of the guys that questioned us," said Logan.

"I'll try to stay with him. Maybe they will lead us to the place where you were held," said Reid.

They drove through Anza. Reid stayed a good distance behind the truck but kept it in sight. A car with a trailer full of firewood pulled out in front of them. It was an older model Chevy, not meant to pull a heavy trailer. Reid caught a glimpse of the truck up ahead, and then it was gone over a rise. Another truck had pulled on to the road. The two-lane road through the more populated area made it difficult to pass, and the guy with the wood was not going to pull over and lose all his inertia. Reid waited patiently and, after a few slow minutes, finally found a straight stretch of road. He passed the car and trailer. The guy honked his horn and waived, just to be irritating.

The truck was long gone. They were alone again on the road leaving the outskirts of town behind. Logan studied the hills. Trouble was they all looked like the hills around the ranch where they had been kept. He turned to Janine.

"Did the dirt road from the ranch come directly on to this highway, or did we take another road before we got on this one?"

"There was some sort of intersection, remember? We went left and then came to the highway."

There were roads that led off from the main road. Some were paved and had street signs. Some were dirt, with no signs. Logan checked each one carefully but didn't think any of them looked familiar. Janine called it before Logan.

"Is that it? The one below that line of hills."

It was an older road, probably paved in the sixties. Could have been built to serve a mine or gravel pit. Logan studied the groups of mailboxes that indicated the more-traveled dirt roads. Trying to remember the details of the road was hard. He had been preoccupied with getting away and with the aches and pains of being tied up for two days and nights. In fact, he didn't feel that well now. It was a wonder they had made it this far. He thought about Janine. She was a soldier. She hadn't complained, and she was probably hurting worse than he was, both physically and emotionally.

"That may have been it back there. It looked familiar, but I'm not sure," said Logan, indicating a road they passed. Reid spun a U-turn and turned down the road.

It might lead to a ranch or mine, or it might be a dead end. No way to tell, thought Reid. They followed it around a corner into a shaded area with pine trees.

"I'm pretty sure this is it," said Logan. "And I think we are getting pretty close to the house."

He suggested that they pull off the road, hide the car, and try walking the rest of the way. Reid complied and they found a spot to pull into the trees. At Logan's suggestion, Reid backed the car in so that it faced back the way they had come.

A short hike over the hill and they were looking down at the place where they had been held.

"That's it. I'm sure of it."

"And that's the truck we saw," exclaimed Reid. "How are you guys doing?" he asked. "Are we up for a little trek through the bushes?"

"We've come this far," said Logan. "But let's be careful."

No one talked. Logan led them through a mazelike course of large Manzanita and sumac bushes. The chaparral here grew in clusters and was not hard to navigate. Every few minutes, Logan stopped to listen. As they got closer, they could hear sounds. Voices, a screen door slamming, wood being loaded on a wheelbarrow. Normal sounds for a country spread. Then another sound stopped them all in their tracks. The distinctive crackle and static of a police radio.

For a split second, Logan felt relieved. Like finally there was a cop when you needed one. But the thought faded quickly as his eyes zeroed in on the source. The static was coming from the truck. His suspicions were being confirmed.

"Why?" whispered Janine, pointing in the direction of the sound.

Logan shrugged and didn't answer. Reid just observed, intently. After a minute, they maneuvered into a position to see better, careful to keep out of clear sight.

The breeze that rustled through the tops of the sumac was coming more from the general direction of the house than toward it. Good thing, thought Logan, it would blow any noise they made away from the compound.

They huddled beneath the cover of a large sumac bush. Their position had an unobstructed view of the buildings and yard. Logan studied the layout and saw the shed where he had spent two long nights and days. The place was a ramshackle conglomerate of metal and wood sheds, a garage, and a barn that was past its prime, all built around an old Sears-style cottage that had several add-ons. It might have been a working complex at one time. Dry farming, cattle, or a base for would-be miners or rock hounds.

Reid's concentration was broken by the sound of the screen door. A man left the house and walked toward the truck. He was average height with thick dark hair and a mustache. He was wearing sunglasses, and he had a slight paunch around the middle. The crackle of the radio stopped him for a split second as he listened closely. Some dispatcher jabber, answered curtly by a mobile unit.

Logan couldn't make anything from it. Reid could, but he motioned that he didn't pick up on what it meant. The man walked out toward a large pile of wood stacked near the truck. There was a half-full load in a wheelbarrow, and the man proceeded to retrieve the load and wheel it toward the house. The radio crackled again, and again he stopped to listen.

"That radio must be important to them," said Logan to Reid. "That guy is paying a lot of attention to it."

Reid looked worried. He was staring at the back of the guy with the wheelbarrow. "Is that one of guys from Temecula?" he asked.

"Could be," Logan said. "I can't really tell for sure, but yeah, I think that's one of them." He looked at Janine.

"He's one of them," said Janine. "I remember him."

Logan looked at Reid. "You know him?"

"Yeah. He's a cop in Temecula."

CHAPTER FOURTEEN

The Best Of Plans

The fight broke out a little after the lunch rush. Headband Dave had made a slightly suggestive comment to one of the horsewomen, and she nailed him with a right to the jaw. When he reacted with a backhand across her face, Gary Scott leveled him. Scott was an assistant trainer and knew Marsha well. Not that he needed to protect her. She did a good job of that herself. He just didn't like men who hit women, especially when the woman was a co-worker.

The horse crowd at The Paddock was a gruff bunch. They liked their chilies hot and their booze early. And they loved a good tumble. So when Scott hit Headband Dave, Little Jerry naturally blindsided a construction worker for no good reason, and the melee was on. Jim, the weekend bartender, called the cops. This kind of stuff never happened on the weekend. He wondered how Logan would handle this. And where the hell was Logan, anyway?

Molinski heard the police scanner go off in the newsroom as she was breezing through paste-up. She instinctively went to hear what was happening. Fight at The Paddock. Nice, she thought. A good excuse for a ride and a possible beer after the interviews. Too bad she would have to get right back to write the story so that Reid would have something to edit when he got back. Where the hell was Reid, anyway?

The fight ended as abruptly as it had started. A few bruised cheeks and scuffed knuckles, that was about it. Headband had gotten the worst of it. Marsha had concentrated her efforts solely on him. He, in turn, was cautious about defending himself after Scott's haymaker to his jaw.

Mori had broke the fight up with just a few words. "Stop this damn fight now, or you're all eighty-sixed for good! Now!"

The fear of being eighty-sixed from their favorite establishment stopped the horse people in their tracks. The opposition, mostly construction workers, never wanted to fight in the first place. So Mori's directive was adhered to without much opposition. Only Marsha seemed determined to keep pummeling Headband Dave.

The deputies left without so much as a formal report. Molinski arrived as they were walking out. She was disappointed but seized the opportunity to muscle up to the bar for a cold beer. The Paddock had the coldest beer in town. Logan and Lenny made sure of it.

Molinski accepted the beer and then asked the question of the day. "Where's Logan?"

"That's a good question," answered the weekend bartender. Jim was a mellow guy with a pleasing voice, and ever present smile. "No one has seen him since Saturday night. Never called in, nothing."

"Anybody checked the Blue Doors?" Molinski knew people who had gotten lost for weeks at the Blue Doors.

"He wouldn't be there," said Jim. "He's probably on one of his sojourns to Northern California or maybe Mexico, but he usually calls or sends cards. It's weird."

Molinski thought about Reid leaving hurriedly that morning after the call. Reid and Logan went way back. If one were in trouble, the other would be there for him. She sensed some sort of urgency in the situation. Something was up. But what? She took a long drink of beer. Another would be nice, but she needed to get back and see if Reid had checked in. She might have to put the paper to bed if he didn't get back in time.

"Hey, where the hell is Logan when you need him?"

It was Chicago Bob. He had his arm around Gary Scott and looked just like a drunk who had been in a scuffle. In fact, he had. Bob wanted to know who won the fight pool. There was no fight pool. But there probably should have been, although fights at The Paddock were rare.

There was much more action with Kelly's Corner. Bob's inquiry as to the whereabouts of Logan did not go unnoticed by the mob at the bar.

"Shit . . . He's in Mexico," noted Little Jerry with conviction.

It was 3:30 p.m. Getting close to Little Jerry's bedtime.

Gary Scott, the tallest and most level-headed of the horse crew, looked down at Little Jerry. He took Chicago Bob's arm and replaced it around the jockey. "It's not like Logan to just disappear. I think something might have happened. He might be in trouble."

Scott's voice seemed to carry over the bar. The others looked at him and listened. Suddenly the crew at the bar had something new to focus on.

"If he's in trouble, then we'll go and help him out!" Chicago Bob was earnest with this proposition. The others chimed in their agreement and a toast was made.

Molinski downed her beer and made for the door. She had work to do.

Logan had an anguished look on his face. Reid was squinting in the direction of the truck. The dark sedan that had almost run them off the road was in the drive next to the truck. It was obvious now that the four men gathered around the vehicles were some sort of law enforcement officers. They were gathered around the truck and listening to the squawk of the radio. Logan couldn't make out what was coming over.

"I don't think we have much chance of getting that envelope," said Logan with a weary glance at Janine. "Not without some serious reinforcements."

"That's it," whispered Reid. "Let's get a little closer, see if we can pick up some names or anything else in their talk. I'll tell Cassio what I've seen and heard and he'll send an army out here."

"We'll need to hear what they're saying and what they're so damn interested in on the radio," Logan said to Reid. "Janine, you stay here. If something happens, you'll have to go for help."

Reid was excited. Hell, this could be the biggest story ever. The two crept forward, staying low behind the large red shank bushes. There was plenty of cover. A horny toad ran across their path from under a bush. His camouflage was perfect. If the creature hadn't moved, they would have never seen him. Logan could smell the sage in the dry fall air. It was starting to get cool now. It would be downright cold before long. They kept their eyes on the group and their ears to the ground. It reminded Reid of when he was a kid, sneaking around playing Indian.

They got within about fifty feet of the group and stopped. The sound of men talking wafted up through the bush in muffled tones. It looked like two of them were about to leave in the truck.

"I think those are the guys we saw coming from the junkyard," said Logan. "They must all be waiting for something to happen, or someone to arrive."

Reid nodded and then pointed at the group around the truck. "I'm sure those guys are cops, too," said Reid. "They're not from Fallbrook, but I've seen them. Maybe out in Rancho or Temecula. Let's get closer."

The brush was cut away from the complex. Getting closer without being seen would be a trick. Reid waited until he thought it was safe, then made a move for an old clump of scrub oak about ten feet away.

He never saw the gopher hole. His foot sank in past the ankle, and at a full run, it took him down hard, face first, into the sand.

The resounding thud and accompanying groan did not go unnoticed. The men by the truck looked up and saw Reid sprawled out on the ground, reeling with pain. Two of them had guns in their hands as they ran toward the reporter.

Logan crouched low behind the red shank, but it wasn't enough. In an instant they had Reid handcuffed, and then Logan was looking down the barrel of a 357. His heart sank.

"All right, asshole, step out and put your hands up."

The voice was not pleasant. In fact, nothing about these guys or the situation was pleasant. All Logan could think about was that they had made a huge mistake. Now they were going to pay for it.

❦

Dillard was sitting at his desk at home smoking a cigarette when the phone rang. "Yeah? What the hell is it now?"

"We've got good news and bad news."

"Yeah."

"We've got the envelope."

"Yeah."

"It was in the car. Not much trouble."

"So what's the bad news?" Dillard hated these games. He didn't have the patience.

"We came back out to your place like you said, and low and behold, we catch two rather curious intruders trying to sneak up on us. They know us. We are going to have to do something."

The voice was matter-of-fact. A cop's tone. A voice that had been there before, knew what to do, and how to do it. Dillard liked that. He could depend on his guys. Not like those idiots of Sobrano's.

Dillard listened to the story. The intruders were a bartender from Bonsall and the editor of the local newspaper. Well known figures in their little area. There was no telling how long they had been out in the bushes, or how much they had heard. How they had found the place was a mystery in itself, but then the bartender had been with the girl. She might have known about the place. Dillard's first thought was to shoot them and ditch the bodies. There was no way to connect them to any of the operation. And his men could direct the investigation, or at least influence it a little. They would eventually find the girl, and she too would disappear. Simple.

"Take care of them. What about those dead guys, anything on them?"

"Still no talk about anyone else or about the car."

"Good." Dillard was thinking. "Listen, on second thought, put those two down in the cellar. And put that envelope in the safe. I'll be out there tomorrow."

He hung up the phone. He should call Sobrano and tell him that his precious envelope was in good hands. But maybe he should check it out a bit first.

The vote at the bar was unanimous. Big Gary Scott would drive. One more shot of peppermint schnapps and they would be off to find Logan. How it had come to this, Chicago Bob had no idea. They had started talking about Logan's absence, disappearance, or whatever it was, and then it came to them. Logan was in trouble. It didn't take long before it was concluded that they, the guys that knew him best, were the only ones who could help.

After much discussion, they had decided that their search should take them east. At least to Fallbrook. The Packing House bar was probably a good place to start. They were about to leave when Little Jerry had to mention it.

"What about work tomorrow?"

Gary looked suddenly deflated. Two hours of discussion about charging off to save Logan and no one, until now, had bothered to think about reality. They had to be up at 3 a.m. to take care of the horses. There were millions of dollars worth of horse flesh that was their responsibility. They were the grooms, exercisers, and assistant trainers that kept things going at the various ranches in the valley. In fact, it was already getting past their regular bedtime.

"We could go right after work tomorrow," suggested Chicago Bob. "We would be fresh, and hell, maybe Logan just might show up in the meantime."

There was a murmur among the troops. It seemed to be the best idea. The fact that none of them was sober enough to drive never came up. Only Marsha wanted to continue. But then Marsha always wanted to continue.

Janine watched as the renegade cops brutally directed her two friends into the main building. Reid could hardly walk because of his ankle, and they were not about to cut him any slack. He fell hard a couple of times. Logan mouthed up in protest only to get back-handed with the barrel of a gun. They disappeared, unwillingly, into the house. The door closed behind them and that was it for awhile. No sounds. No sight of anyone coming or going.

She moved slowly away from the complex. A cold evening breeze rustled up through the canyon below. There was a smell of sage and sumac in the dry air. It was a pleasant smell, clean and fresh. The smell of fall. A precursor to winter and colder days. Bush to bush, scrub oak to scrub oak. She was careful, but still moved quickly through the afternoon light. The thought of the two thugs in the truck crossing her path kept her alert and gave her strength. She reached Reid's car in half the time it had taken them to hike to the complex.

The car wasn't locked, but Reid had the keys in his pocket. She did a quick search and found a container underneath the bumper, behind the front license plate. A Hide-A-Key, with one key in it.

Less than hour later, she pulled in The Paddock parking lot. There were a few cars in the lot. Mostly for Mori's store. The bar was almost empty. Chicago Bob and Gary Scott had carried Little Jerry out about a half hour before. Lenny was behind the bar.

"Well? You look like you could use a drink," he said.

His words hung in the air waiting for an answer. His eyes went from warmth and humor to concern as he noticed the condition Janine was in. As beautiful as she was, she looked a mess. Her hair was stringy and her clothes dirty. Only her face seemed in place. She took a seat at the end of the bar without answering. She had really never talked to Lenny, although she felt she knew him through Logan's stories. He was a good person and, more importantly, a good friend of both Logan and Reid.

"We've never met. I'm Janine and I've been with Logan for the last couple of days," she wanted to explain in more detail, but decided to get right to the point. "Lenny, Logan and Reid are in trouble . . . . Big-time trouble."

Lenny took that as an understatement. Two sheriff's deputies had stopped by just the day before, asking about her. He told her about it and was surprised by her reaction, or lack thereof. She acted as if it were secondary. And it was.

"Look, it's a long story but suffice to say that I had something that a lot of people seemed to want. Logan was trying to help me stay out of trouble and the whole thing just blew up in our face."

Lenny looked into her eyes and could see the grief. "Where is Logan?"

"They've got him, and Reid too." Her eyes filled with tears. Lenny brought her some water.

"Who is they? And, what do they want?" Lenny tried to make some sense, but she was almost babbling. He poured a Stoley rocks and set it front of her. It seem to calm her down.

She tried to recall the last couple of days. The van that ran them off the road, the torture and interrogation by two punks, then getting away in the van. When she got to the part about the cops in Temecula, Lenny stopped her and asked for detailed descriptions. She told him as best she could.

"Lenny, we need to get the cops out there, or somebody, and get them before they kill them."

Lenny didn't like anything he was hearing. He poured black coffee and tried to make some sense out her story. His guts told him they needed the law on their side, but whom could they trust. This was one hell of a mess. He asked her again about where she had just driven from.

"If you're right and it's in Anza, then I'm not sure if San Diego S.O. has any authority," he took a deep breath. "Anyway, the way Cassio and his partner were talking, I don't think they're going to listen to you. At least not until it's too late."

It was a slow night in the bar. Only one other customer, a drunk fixated on the television at the other end of the room.

"This is a real mess," he sighed. "We're stuck for right now. If we notify the cops, you're going to jail. If we try to go out there, we'd be busted before we got to the house. There's no way we could sneak up on them in the dark."

He went to the cash register and produced a key.

"This is Logan's. Go up and get some sleep. Meet me back here first thing in the morning and come to the back door. Tony will let you in."

Janine took the key and thanked him.

"Wait a minute, are you hungry?"

She hadn't thought about it, but she was starved. But could she eat with all this going on? Maybe. It would be worth a shot. And then some sleep. That would be worth a shot, too. Hopefully with some food and rest, things would get better.

Lenny took little time in putting together a plate of carnitas and some tortillas in a to-go bag. She thanked him and went out the side door. His eyes followed her. He hoped he was doing the right thing. What else could he do?

The guy at the other end of the bar left a $20 bill and went out the back through the patio. He was a little odd, thought Lenny. Hadn't said much. Sat in the dark with his head mostly down. Seemed to be off in a world by himself. Lenny, had considered not serving him, but what the hell, it was a slow night. And the guy leaves him a twenty.

He went to the kitchen to talk to Tony and let him know he would be in early the next day. Tony smiled and handed Lenny a bag to carry to the trash. They talked as they walked across the unlit lot. An engine started in the dark. A single headlight illuminated the night, catching Lenny and Tony in its glare. The car's engine revved up, then its tires squealed as it spun out of the lot and on to the road. Lenny watched the taillights go off toward the Club. Probably a BMW, he thought.

"That one, he loco," said Tony.

Lenny nodded.

CHAPTER FIFTEEN

Team Players

It was a night laced with pain. The chain of events leading up to their predicament was taking its toll. Reid's ankle was killing him. It was an injury like none he had ever experienced. A constant, deep throbbing that never seemed to let up. Logan was withdrawn. Exhausted both mentally and physically, he tried to dodge the questions and slaps to the face. There was no place and no time to rest.

A cop's voice pounded through Reid's consciousness like a jackhammer. Question after question. How much did he know? What was he doing out here? Did he tell anyone where he was going? The combination was unbearable. Reid nodded out twice, only to be slapped back awake. Logan did most of the talking, but none of it seemed to make enough sense for their interrogators.

"So you don't know shit until you come out here and fuckin' step in it, huh?" The voice was measured and experienced. "You know how stupid you guys are? You should have just put the chick on a bus. You wouldn't be here. Now, you and your reporter friend are gonna pay the price. Too bad. You brought it on yourselves."

"Let's get on with it. You heard 'em. Nobody knows they're out here, except the girl, and she's going to be high-tailing it to Mexico before the sun comes up." The cop sounded sure of himself.

Reid and Logan sat slumped in their chairs, hands tied behind their backs, feet tied to the legs of the straight chairs. It was probably about nine o'clock, Logan figured. It had been at least four hours since they had been caught. Four hellish hours. Sleep would be good. Anything would be good except this.

The front door slammed, and the cop in charge came in with a dark look in his eyes. He took a buck knife from the drawer and cut the ropes that held Reid's legs. Reid was asleep, or passed out. Or too tired to move.

"Stand them up and follow me. Brownie, get some more rope."

Brownie was a big man, well over six feet, 200-plus pounds, with short black hair and a mustache. He hadn't said a word that Logan could recall, but then Logan had been busy listening to the cop who seemed in charge. Now it was Brownie's turn. He stood Reid up and kneed him hard in the butt. Reid moaned in pain and his eyes opened wide. He was not doing well, thought Logan. The ankle was going to be a problem.

They went down some steps and through a thick wooden door with a little screen grate at the top. It was a little breathing hole, or at least that's what Logan thought. There was a bare lightbulb burning from a socket in the ceiling. Four concrete walls and nothing else. A water mark ringed the concrete walls about two feet off the floor. Must have flooded here once or twice, thought Logan.

"Tie them up good, Brownie. I want them to be comfortable for the night." It was the cop with the beady eyes who had been so rude the day before.

This guy was enjoying this, Logan thought. These guys were real pricks. Logan's mind was past weary. Even the concrete floor would be okay, if they would just leave him alone.

The one called Brownie pushed them into two wooden chairs he had set back to back. Their feet were tied to the chairs. Bandannas were used to gag their mouths. Reid moaned like he was about to pass out. And then the door shut.

The sun comes up from behind the Laguna Range and shines down through a narrow canyon before it warms the dirt roads of Bonsall. Dark night shadows cling to the walls of the cliffs and rest beneath the lush overgrowth that lines the winding road. By the time the first rays lighten the shadows of the track at Bonsall downs, fifty Thoroughbreds have been exercised, fifteen or so sprints have been run, and at least one exercise rider has sworn off drinking. On a given day.

Today, something else was going on. Right from the start it had been different. Little Jerry was more alert than usual and only took one try to get up on his first mount of the day. Chicago Bob wasn't singing along with the oldies on the radio. In fact, his radio wasn't even on. Gary Scott was out of jokes. There was less talk out on the track. No match races. The collective consciousness of the horse people was focused. Today they were going to do something different. They had somehow made a commitment, and they were going to see it through.

By around 9:30 A.M. most of the crew had finished their work. Scott pulled his truck around in front of a row of bunkhouses and started removing various ranch implements and miscellaneous debris that had collected over the weeks since his last run to Escondido for supplies. Slowly but surely they started to gather. Those that were usually bound for The Paddock and its menu of chorizo, Spanish omelets, and authentic breakfast burritos were ready for something else. By ten o'clock they were set to go. Scott, Little Jerry, Marsha, and Chicago Bob piled in the front of the old Ford F-250 and headed out past the guarded entrance to the track. They waved at Frank as they went by. Frank gave them all the finger, like he did every day.

They pulled out on to East Lilac and headed down the valley. Past the entrance to The Club. Past the soccer field and the golf course. As a matter of habit, Gary pulled in the back entrance to The Paddock parking lot. Mori's store would have everything they needed for their mission to the backcountry.

Usually, they would pull in next to Logan's car and then start banging on the front door to the restaurant until Logan or Tony let them in. From there it would be omelets and bloody Marys, or beers, and the day would be officially started. Today Scott's truck rumbled down the steep entranceway and was heading around the corner to the front of the complex. Suddenly, Scott slammed on the breaks.

"What's Reid's car doing here at this time of day?" Scott's question hung in the air. "Lenny's here, too."

The immaculate '64 Thunderbird was parked next to Reid's Buick. Scott pulled in at a 45-degree angle and turned off the engine. This called for an investigation. They got out of the truck. Little Jerry, who had been sitting on Marsha's lap, was out first. He was just about always first. At everything.

They went to the back door and knocked. Tony, the cook, opened the door with a big smile as usual, showing his silver-capped tooth that reflected the morning sun. They asked about Logan, and Tony's smile diminished a little.

"No senior. Still nobody has seen him. He never call."

"Is Reid here? Or did he just leave his car overnight?"

A familiar deep voice sounded from behind Tony.

"Who the hell wants to know?"

It was Lenny. He came out to the where he could see the group assembled at the back door. He looked worried.

"Something's up, guys. Logan and Burt Reid are in big shit," said Lenny. "I'm going to see what I can do about it soon as Jim and Mori get here. We won't be open for breakfast anytime soon."

"We didn't come for breakfast," said Scott. "We saw the cars and wondered what was going on. Thought maybe Logan was back."

Little Jerry blurted out that they were organizing a search party of their own to find Logan and were driving to the country to check out some leads.

"Whoa, wait a minute now," said Lenny. "You guys could get yourselves in a lot of trouble driving around and asking questions. Those country people out there would just as soon shoot you as look at you. They don't like nosey strangers, even if they are a motley looking bunch like you."

Then he stopped. Like he'd just come up with an idea. He told them to wait a minute and disappeared back into the kitchen. Tony had gone back to chopping the day's vegetables. The morning sun glared off the screen door, making it impossible to see past the first few feet inside. But they could hear Tony humming and chopping, and the smells from the kitchen were good.

Lenny came back to the door.

"Gary, can you come in here for a second. The rest of you go over to Mori's and get whatever you were going to get. We'll just be a couple of minutes."

Lenny opened the door and motioned Gary in. Little Jerry mumbled a few words, then sauntered around the corner. Chicago Bob had already gone. Marsha followed without a word.

Scott walked through the kitchen into the dining room. Lenny went through another door that led to the bar. The restaurant was empty except for a waitress who was setting up. Dorothy. She was small, trim, and tan. Medium-length brown hair with streaks of blonde running through it. She was setting out napkins on the tables and placing a fork, knife, and spoon on each one. She looked up and smiled as Scott walked by.

When he came to the archway that connected the main dining room to the bar, he stopped. Janine was sitting at the first bar stool. He didn't know her, but he knew of her. He had seen her sitting at the same place once before. The day she crashed the BMW in the intersection. She had cup of coffee in front of her instead of a Stoly on the rocks, but she had the same faraway look. Beautiful but aloof. Troubled. Eyes that couldn't seem to smile. Scott felt a note of urgency in the air.

"We've got trouble, Gary. Maybe you guys can help."

Lenny was matter-of-fact. Without asking, he brought over two more cups and the pot of coffee. He poured them, and then refilled Janine's. There was cream on the counter. Scott took a sip and waited. For once, he was all ears.

"Some crazy renegade cops have Logan and Burt Reid held up at some ranch outside of Anza. Janine thinks they might kill them." Lenny's voice was naturally low, but Scott had never heard him speak with this kind of edge. "There's a whole lot to the story, and I don't even want to know it all. Except to say that some bad people have our friends and they need our help."

Scott listened intently as Lenny relayed what Janine had told him. He was familiar enough with the backcountry to have a pretty good idea what kind of place it was. They were probably less than an hour away.

"Tell me again what you remember about the ranch layout and the road where Reid's car was parked," Scott said, focusing on Janine. He unfolded a bar napkin and took a pen out of one of the glasses at the cocktail station. "Start with the buildings and surroundings."

He sketched a map of the complex, then turned it over and drew a larger scale map of the area. Janine helped fill in some details about various landmarks she remembered. With that, Scott had a rough idea where Logan and Reid were being held. He finished his coffee and then laid down the pen.

"There were four guys or five?" he asked.

"Four, I think. Maybe five. But four for sure."

"They had guns?"

"Yeah, they had guns. Hand guns. When Reid fell, they all pulled guns. I didn't notice them before. But the second they heard a noise, they all had guns in their hands."

Scott sat thinking for a while. Lenny refilled the cups and lit a cigarette. The bluish smoke drifted up through rays of sun streaming in from the patio doors, which Dorothy had opened. The restaurant was getting ready to open, and the smells of tortillas and beans were drifting out of the kitchen.

Lenny's baritone broke the silence. "I think we should give Cassio an anonymous call. Let him know the situation. If he can come and help fine, if not, we did our duty as citizens. In the meantime we go on out there and see what we can do on our own."

"This is a situation all right." Scott's tone was serious and the words came slowly. "And it calls for drastic action. What kind of fire power you got?"

Lenny pulled a 38 caliber from behind the bar, then slid a small 9 millimeter out of a holster in his boot. Scott smiled.

"I've got to make a quick stop back at the stable. Can you get Jim, the backup guy, in here to work for you?"

"He's already on his way," said Lenny.

Dillard phoned the office as soon as he woke up and told them he wouldn't be coming in today. Then he called the airport to get a plane ready.

He shaved and showered at the townhouse, put on a suit fresh from the cleaners: thin lapels, thin tie, religious pin. He combed his thin, blond hair straight back, and smiled at himself in the mirror. It was a big smile meant to compliment the honest look on his face that he had practiced so much. "Believe me!" he said to the image in the mirror. It was something he did almost every day.

Dillard was ready. The problem at the ranch was going to be addressed today. He needed to talk to John Low, the cop in charge, as soon as possible and arrange an accident for the nosey reporter and his friend. Then it came to him. Why not mix a little Pink Polly into it? They could fly the two snoops down to Mexico and use them for guinea pigs.

He called Low's number left a message for him to call him back. Low, as matter of routine, would not answer his phone. In fact, he had the ringer turned off. He had it set up to take messages. He used it for outgoing calls only.

Low called back at precisely at 9:30 a.m. Dillard listened as the detective briefly outlined what had happened. They talked in metaphors. The storyline was about fishing and the weather and a couple of snakes that had been captured.

"You're going to have to get rid of them. You can't risk them being around to hurt someone," said Dillard. "Maybe you should give them to the zoo or something, or to the university for study."

Low knew where the slick politician was going, at least he thought he did.

"They're fine for now. We've got them in a cage. I've got to make some calls and take care of a few things. I'll get back to you later. In the meantime, let's hope the weather holds, the last thing the lake needs is more water from another storm."

Dillard hung up. He needed Low, but not forever. He was too independent and ambitious. Someday he was going to have a little accident, in the line of duty so to speak. Dillard lit up a cigarette and sat back in the chair. It was just a matter of time, and he would have the machine in motion. Just a few bumps in the road, and then it would be over.

When Scott's truck rolled into The Paddock parking lot, there was no sign of Little Jerry and the others. Scott pulled in next to Lenny's T-Bird and parked. He knew where to find them, and he was a little worried. This was not a good time to put a buzz on. Not when there were people who needed help. He walked around the corner to the bar entrance. The door scraped on the cement as he opened it. Sunlight poured into the darkened room within.

It took a second for his eyes to adjust, but it wasn't hard to make out the familiar shapes at the bar. Janine was still sitting at the end. Jerry, Chicago Bob, and Marsha were perched a couple of stools away. Jim, the backup guy, had arrived and was wiping down the bar. To Scott's surprise, his three comrades did not have longneck beers in front of them. Instead, they appeared to be drinking coffee. In fact, there was a box of donuts being passed around. A rare sight, thought Scott.

"You guys ready?" Lenny's voice boomed from the kitchen. He appeared through the door with two large to-go bags. "You want to take some coffee?"

Scott nodded, and Lenny set out a couple of large Styrofoam cups. A few customers had come into the restaurant, but there was no one else in the bar. Lenny handed Scott one of the bags and pushed the large container of coffee across the bar.

"Here's the deal," he said in a low voice. "Janine will ride with me in Tony's pickup. You guys follow us out to Anza. Hopefully we won't have any trouble finding the place. Once we're there, we'll play it by ear."

Tony's truck was a Ford 250 like Scott's, except older. It had seen more than a few trips to Baja. Tony's family lived in a small town about an hour below Ensenada. Lenny had visited there, taking a load of clothes and canned goods down at Christmas time. The truck was old, but it had good tires and it ran like a top. Tony took care of things.

The freeway led north through a small pass with rock-strewn hills on each side. Lenny used the time to envision a plan of attack. It was hard to do without having the layout of the place. He asked Janine to describe it again. They would have no idea where Logan and Reid were being kept. That made it even more difficult. He thought back to his days in the Corps. Viet Nam was a bad dream he'd just as soon forget. He wondered about Scott; he had the look of a soldier about him. Something in his demeanor told Lenny that Scott was a good man to have on your side. He looked in the rearview mirror to make sure Scott and his crew were still following behind them. They were.

They had driven the twenty-odd miles to Anza Road when Scott flashed his headlights and honked. Lenny pulled over accordingly and let Scott walk up to the window.

"I've been thinking," said Scott. "We're going to need some kind of diversion or a show of force, or both. I know some people up here who we could borrow a couple of horses from. It might give us an advantage if this place is as far off the road as Janine said, and if we can somehow disable their vehicles."

Lenny nodded. It was a good idea. Horses would allow them to cover the ground quickly and give them the mobility they would need to scout the perimeter of the complex. They agreed that Scott would lead them to his friends, and they could figure the rest out from there.

Scott led the way up the Anza grade. It was a wide highway leading up to the plateau where the town of Anza stood at the foot of Mt. San Jacinto. The Double Bar R was a couple of miles east of town on a nameless dirt road. It was a beautiful spread: twenty-plus acres, large ranch-style house with numerous outbuildings and a large barn. There were extensive corrals and training facilities and a large oval track. It had all the makings of a small but first-class training facility. And there were lots of horses. Quarter horses.

Everyone but Scott was taken with the spectacle of the Double Bar R. He pulled up the circular drive leading to the main house and stopped. Getting out, he motioned for everyone to stay in the trucks. A large German shepherd, who had barked at them and chased them up the drive, was now at Scott's side, wagging its tail. Lenny recognized that it wasn't that the dog was a friendly sort, it was that it knew Scott.

"Man, this is some kind of place," he said to Janine. "I never would have guessed that Gary had friends like this."

Scott disappeared into the house. Five minutes passed before he came back out, followed by a tall, slender woman with graying blond hair pulled back into a tightly wound ponytail. She was wearing jeans, riding boots, and a western-style blouse with snaps instead of buttons. She smiled at the newcomers and held up her hand in greeting.

Little Jerry was first to get out, opening the door and rolling off of Marsha's lap. Janine and Lenny got out and stretched their legs. The air was clean and fresh.

"This is Mary Mactavish, owner of the Double Bar R," announced Scott. "She's been kind enough to offer us a couple of her horses and some trailers."

There were no formal introductions other than that. They were, after all, in somewhat of an urgent situation. However, given Scott's nature, there probably wouldn't have been much in the way of conventional cordiality anyway.

They were led around to the barn. Lenny and Chicago Bob hooked a couple of double horse trailers up to the Fords. Mary and Scott picked out four good looking quarter horses from the large pasture in back of the main house. In less than twenty minutes they had tack and gear loaded and were ready to roll.

Mary waved good-bye from the barn. She was not long on words, a good match for Scott, thought Lenny. Either that or she was his sister.

Lenny was in the lead again, with Janine scouting the road for clues as to where they were going. They drove through town hoping to be inconspicuous. But, two unfamiliar trucks pulling horse trailers were not the kind of thing that went without notice in the backcountry. There would be comments and speculation from the locals eating lunch at the cafe. Hopefully, the gang that had Logan and Reid would not have ears in town, thought Lenny.

Outside of town, Janine sat up and studied the mountain ranges.

"I think the road is coming up. It was getting dark when I left, but it has to be right up the road."

Sobrano looked up from his Latte as one of his men dressed in combat fatigues from the Mexican Army came in the room.

"The plane is ready. Our friend will meet us at the Palomar Airport and drive us out. He has everything we will need."

The mild-mannered Mexican Don sipped his coffee drink. He needed to go north and settle this matter once and for all. If only Walter had listened, none of this would have happened.

The white phone rang. Odd, thought Sobrano, Dillard shouldn't be calling this early in the morning. He answered in English.

"Hello."

"Your partner has your envelope, and he is ripping you off."

"Walter! Where are you, my friend? I was just thinking about you."

"Dillard is on his way to his ranch. They are holding some people hostage there, and in case you didn't know it, your boys, Ratface and Lobo, are dead. Oh . . . and the code is in the envelope."

Sobrano heard the line click and then nothing. Why was Walter giving him this information? Was it a trap? He felt his normally cool temperament begin to simmer.

"Get my bags," he shouted. "Pronto!"

Cassio, sat in his office chair, looking up at the board. It was filling up with information, yet there was no clear-cut pattern. Maybe some of these things weren't related after all. Maybe they were. He had two more homicides to add to a growing list. A strange drug kept showing up around the deaths. Downtown, out at Bonsall, and now at Warner Springs, where the bodies of two known thugs had been found along with some bindles of the pink stuff.

These two latest victims were known criminals believed to be working for Carlos Sobrano. The red BMW that had been in the crash and later stolen from Pete's yard had been sighted driving around Temecula. He had put out a report to apprehend whoever was driving it. But, like just about everything else up on the board, it had turned into a dead end. Now Pete had been hit on the head again and was back in the hospital. What did it all mean?

The phone rang. He let it ring twice before answering.

"Cassio."

"Your reporter friend is being held hostage at a ranch off Old Mine Road in Anza. It belongs to Senator David Dillard, but you can't prove it. Carlos Sobrano will be there around 3 p.m. I suggest you bring lots of backup."

The line went dead before Cassio could say a word. It was the second such tip he had received this morning. The first was more cordial, but had less information. He felt sincerity in the voice, but what could he do without more specific information. Now he had it. He wrote down the information on a yellow pad and then, by force of habit, wrote the address down on the board.

He pushed a button on the telephone console.

"Get me Captain Burman at Riverside S.O. It's urgent. And we need an assault team ready to go in twenty minutes. Code three!"

CHAPTER SIXTEEN

A Day Of Reckoning

R eid was not doing well. His ankle was swollen the size of a large grapefruit. He had never before experienced such pain. The cold dank cement room didn't help. He thought he had heard something like a small animal scratching at something in the corner, but it was too dark to see. He passed in and out of sleep, drifting from bad dream to nightmare.

Logan hadn't slept at all. He had spent the night trying to figure a way out. So far all he had for his efforts was rope burn. There was light shining through the small screen at the top of the door. And there were sounds of someone upstairs in the kitchen. He listened intently, trying to picture exactly what was going on. The voices were muffled; he could only guess what was being said.

He'd heard a truck leave shortly after they had been put down in the cellar. Who left? He didn't know, but he surmised that two of the thugs had left. Brownie and the other weasel-faced redneck were probably left to do the dirty work. They must both be awake now, Logan thought, he could hear the semblance of a conversation and the sound of the screen door slamming.

Officer Rogers was a tall thin man with hawkish features and eyes that were a bit too close together. Walking out into the midday sun, he looked around the chaparral-covered hillsides. A crow sounded a loud call from a tree. The bird mocked him as he walked across the courtyard to where the truck was parked. He felt like taking a shot at it but thought better. Brownie might not like that. He went to the truck and took his sunglasses from behind the visor. Johnny Low and Fat Pat should be back soon, he thought, then there might be a little more action. He walked back to the house, thinking that they should probably check on their prisoners. No harm in seeing if they were still alive.

He was halfway across the yard when something out of the corner of his eye caught his attention. Someone was walking up the dirt road toward the gate. The figure was a good four-hundred yards away, walking with head down, not appearing to be in any hurry. At first, Rogers thought it was a young man because of the walk, but then he detected the unmistakable outline of breasts. What the hell was a woman by herself doing out here, he thought. They were a good three miles from the main road and five miles from the nearest house. People just didn't walk out here alone. Especially a woman.

It didn't appear as if she had seen him. So he took a couple of quick steps out of her line of sight. She was still a ways away from the gate. The sight of a stranger approaching was a shock. Rogers thought for a second, then made a beeline for the back door.

"Brownie! There's someone coming up the driveway," he blurted out as he burst through the back door. "Some chick, just walking along."

"Take it easy, there's nothing to worry about. She's probably lost or something. Did she see you?"

"I don't think so. She was pretty far away and looked like she wasn't paying much attention to where she was going."

Brownie thought about closing the doors and pretending like no one was home. But then she might start snooping around and try to get in to use the phone or something. The best thing to do was to go outside and meet her, play the part of two ranch hands working on the house. Worse case scenario, they might have to give her a ride back to town.

The door slammed behind him as Brownie walked out of the kitchen. It was a loud noise that shot out a good distance. Loud enough to be heard from well down the driveway. Rogers followed him out into the large dirt courtyard, where the day before they had apprehended the two intruders.

From down in the cellar, Logan detected a change in the movements from above. A heated discussion of some kind and the door slamming.

Something was going on. He tried to focus on Reid to see how he was doing. His eyes were closed again. Hopefully he was sleeping, although that would be an accomplishment considering all the noise and the ordeal they had experienced.

Brownie and Rogers walked out into the courtyard to where the driveway was visible. Sure enough, a girl was approaching the gate. She was solidly built, wearing Levi's, T-shirt, and riding boots. A bit stocky but still shapely, thought Rogers. He couldn't help but notice her shape underneath a snug T-shirt, and it cornered his attention for a second.

"Go back and keep an eye on the house," said Brownie. "I'll see what she wants."

He walked down the dirt drive toward the gate. What the hell was a girl doing out here by herself anyway? She looked up and saw him but didn't appear to be startled. She was wearing sunglasses. The type that wrap around the eyes. No way to tell where she was looking. She didn't smile as he approached.

"Can I help you?" he asked as he approached the gate.

She looked up again. "Do you have a phone I could use?"

"Nope, no phone. Sorry. What the hell you doin' out here by yourself?"

"I was driving around. I have some friends that live out here somewhere. I was looking for their place. My car broke down. I've been walking around for hours trying to get back to the highway."

Brownie thought about it for a minute. This was a problem. It wouldn't be smart to let her come up to the house, and he couldn't leave. If the others came back and he wasn't here, there would be trouble.

Lenny wasted no time in sneaking over the hill. He kept his eyes on the ranch house and the thug talking to Marsha as he crept from bush to bush. He could get within about forty yards of the house without being seen.

Marsha put her leg up on the first rung of the gate while she talked to Brownie. She was attractive, he thought, and the raspy tone of her deep voice gave credence to his thought that this was a girl who had been around. A smoker, a drinker, who knows from there.

"I could probably give you a ride to town," he said, trying to keep his eyes on her face.

He spun the combination on the lock and opened the gate. He swung it all the way open so that he could drive out without stopping twice. They walked up the driveway to the dirt courtyard where a truck was parked.

"Wait here while I go get the keys," said Brownie.

He walked to the back door of the house. Marsha was close enough now to get a good look. The other guy must be inside somewhere. She casually glanced up at the hills, a small tight smile appearing on her lips.

"I'm going to give her a ride into town. It's the only way I can see to get her out of here quick," said Brownie. Rogers looked up from the table. He agreed with concern. "What in the hell is she doing out here anyway?"

Brownie related the story about looking for friends and her car breaking down. It was plausible. Still, nothing like this had ever happened before. Not many people drove around these country roads. But she seemed harmless enough.

"Soon as we go, I want you to go check on our two friends. Bring them some water. Somebody may want to talk to them some more. No sense in having them delirious."

Rogers agreed. He was just finishing up a sandwich. There was a bag of potato chips on the table along with a can of Pepsi. There were crumbs from the sandwich and chips on the table and on the front of his shirt.

"And clean this fucking place up. We're going to have some company today, and they could be here anytime."

Rogers knew how weird Dillard was. He could get irate at the slightest sign of a mess. Or he could be oblivious to everything around him. You never could tell.

The screen door banged behind Brownie as he walked out toward the truck. Lenny was close enough now to see every move. Peering through a bushy scrub oak, he watched the man walking. He had the gate of a cop, Lenny thought. No doubt the man had a gun, either on his leg or inside his jeans. The plan was for Marsha to get one of the guards to give her a ride into Anza. Lenny could then sneak into the house, or possibly lure the other guards out, if there were more than one. Scott and the others could then ride down from the hills and take the house.

They would then free the hostages, incapacitate the guards, ride back to the vehicles, and get the hell away from there.

It was pretty straightforward. And so far so good. Marsha and the guy were getting in the truck. From down the road came the sound of another vehicle. A car topped out over a hill in the distance. It was a newer sedan, not the type you see driving out in the country. The guy with Marsha seemed as surprised as Lenny at the intrusion. He got out of the truck to get a better look.

Brownie waited for the car to appear again. It had disappeared in one of the many dips in the road. Whoever it was, they were coming to the ranch, and they were coming pretty fast. The car emerged from a stand of chaparral and approached the gate. Brownie watched as the car slowed. It was a black Lincoln Towncar with three men inside. It slid to a stop in the dirt driveway causing a small cloud of dust to rise from around the car. The door opened before the dust had fully settled and out stepped Dillard. Low and Pat Brown were with him. None of them looked happy. All business today.

From up in the hills, Gary Scott crouched behind some bushes. Little Jerry and Bob were with the horses on the back side of a rise. Scott had been watching the car negotiate the dirt road for some time.

Whoever they were, they were trouble. Time to improvise. He patted the holster he now wore on his hip. A .45 caliber revolver his grandfather had given him was as clean and ready to shoot as the day it came from the factory. He also had a Winchester 30/30. Bob and Jerry didn't have any guns, but they had ropes and knew how to use them. Chicago Bob fancied himself a cowboy and was always roping something around the complex where they all stayed.

Scott recognized the driver from newspaper photos and TV. Senator David Dillard. The other two looked to be hard men, either military or cops. The odds were getting worse, he thought. This could get ugly. But there was no backing off now, they had Marsha. He took a red bandanna from his pocket and tied it around his head. Time to go to war. Looking down at Lenny, he gave him a thumbs up. Lenny smiled. It was a tight-lipped smile. A smile of determination.

Brownie left Marsha sitting in the truck as he walked out to meet the three new visitors. Rogers came from his perch at the kitchen table as soon as he heard the car come driving up. No one was particularly happy about seeing Dillard. Only Dillard appeared to be in good spirits. At least until he saw Marsha sitting in the truck.

"Hey, what the hell is she doing here?" The words spewed out of him. "What if she knows who I am? Jesus!"

"She does now, Einstein," said Low, just loud enough to be heard.

Dillard was hot. Exploding hot. A temperament fueled by drugs and ignited by indiscretion. Marsha couldn't help but look up, but she didn't say anything. Rogers was now out of the house and heading for the truck. The three converged between the car and the truck. Dillard took a twelve-gauge shot gun from the car.

Little Jerry and Chicago Bob watched from the top of the hill. At Scott's signal, they mounted and rode around a small hill. Scott dropped back to meet them and give them some directions. Lenny held his position less than twenty yards from the driveway.

"What the hell are you doing?" asked Brownie, looking at Dillard holding the shotgun. Things were going sideways fast, as far as he was concerned.

Dillard hurried over to the passenger side of the truck and jerked the door open. He grabbed Marsha by the arm and pulled her violently from the truck. She didn't resist. He pushed her up against the front fender and trained the gun no more than two feet from her chest.

"How did you get out here? Who the hell are you with?"

She didn't answer. Dillard gestured with the gun, eyes bulging.

"Take it easy. She said she was looking for a friend's house, got lost, and had car trouble," explained Brownie. "Why don't you just calm down and maybe we can all just work this out."

"I think that's a good idea," said Low, who seemed less in charge now.

Dillard poked Marsha with the gun. All eyes were watching and waiting. Dillard's finger was moving slightly up and down over the trigger. He poked her again with the gun. This time fear turned to anger. Marsha had a bit of a temper. Dillard looked over at Brownie.

"Well now, I guess we got us one more little guinea pig," he said to Brownie. "They gave me the newest test batch and we need to see if they've worked out the bugs. We'll need some rope and some other things, maybe we can have a little fun after all."

"Shit," muttered Low. There was no getting out now. Dillard was a complete dick, he thought.

The gun was about a foot from Marsha's chest as Dillard looked at Brownie and the others.

"Fun?" said Marsha quietly. She spit as she looked down at the ground. Then, in one smooth motion, her right hand came up slapping the barrel of the shotgun. In a quick and well-executed chain of moves she knocked the gun barrel out of line, punched Dillard in the face with a clean left jab, then kicked him hard between the legs. The gun discharged with a loud crack resounding from the hillsides.

Brownie and Low reeled from fragments of the blast and fell to the ground. Rogers jumped back and grabbed his side. Dillard hunched over in pain and Marsha kneed him in the face. She tried to grab the gun out of his hands, but he held on.

The shotgun going off and catching the cops with scatter shot was just the stroke of luck Lenny and Gary Scott needed. They sprung into action from the bushes. Both started blasting away as they ran commando style into the fray. All three of the renegade cops caught some more lead as they tried to duck for cover.

Dillard panicked. "You stupid bitch, I'm going to . . ." His words were cut off by a vicious right hand to the jaw, courtesy of Marsha. From the ground, Rogers fumbled to get the pistol out of his leg holster. He had been hit in the arm and was having more than a little difficulty.

Dillard recovered from the punch and grabbed the shotgun. He tried using the butt to shove Marsha, but she stepped back, and he staggered again.

Rogers got his gun out and pointed it up at Marsha. A shot rang out, and he grabbed his leg as he rolled with the impact.

The sound of horses' hooves caught Dillard by surprise. Three riders charged from the valley, running their horses as fast as they would go over the terrain. Chicago Bob, wearing a black cowboy hat, had a rope and was twirling it over his head. In a flash, the rope was over Dillard's head and pulled tight around his chest. He was pulled to the ground in a violent jerk. The next thing he knew he was looking down the barrel of large handgun held by a small man with a reddish beard. Little Jerry was in command. Janine jumped down from the large chestnut and looked around quickly.

The shooting stopped as quickly as it had begun. Scott and Lenny trained their guns on Dillard and Rogers. The others appeared to be out cold, or worse. Dillard thought about grabbing Marsha and using her for a shield but then thought again. He raised his hands.

Marsha walked over and took Rogers' gun. He had been shot in the leg. Brownie had taken a corner of the buckshot load in his shoulder. Low and his sidekick appeared to be finished.

Lenny barked out orders: "Chicago, you're in charge of tying these guys up. Janine, let's go see if we can find Logan and Burt."

They moved quickly toward the kitchen door they had heard slamming with such frequency in the past hour. It was a distinctive slap of wood on wood; the frame and screen serving as a sound box. A sharp tone that echoed off of the outbuilding across the dirt drive. This time, when Janine closed the door, she let it go easily, making almost no noise at all.

It took all of thirty seconds for Lenny and Janine to walk through the house. The sparsely furnished rooms were empty of people. They checked the closets and the showers and then walked back through carefully, looking for a doorway, or something they might have missed.

"Probably in one of the other buildings," said Lenny, noticing the worried look on Janine's face. "Don't worry, we'll find them."

They walked back through the kitchen and out to where the others were holding the three thugs. Lenny was about to let the screen door go when he noticed the stairway leading to what appeared to be a cellar. He shut the door quietly and walked down the stairs. There were no sounds coming from within. An unlocked padlock prevented the door from being opened from the inside. He removed it and opened the thick cellar door, making a scraping sound on the cement floor.

The light of day liberated darkness from the room as the door opened. Lenny could make out two bodies on the cement floor. It took a second for his eyes to adjust to the light, and then, with great relief, he saw some movement from one of the forms. Logan's eyes were open and even though he had a bandanna tied around his mouth, Lenny could tell he was smiling. Lenny moved quickly to untie his two friends. Janine came in and rushed to Logan. They hugged and kissed with few words.

"I think Burt broke his ankle. He's been delirious. We've got to get him to a hospital," said Logan.

"Man, it's good to see you guys. When she showed up last night at The Paddock, I was thinking the worst."

Janine gave Logan another hug and a kiss, then backed away. "I'm so glad you're okay. I've been so worried. I don't know what I'd do now without you." Logan looked into her eyes. Little moments could be great. She kissed him again, and then said, "Logan, did know where they put the envelope they took from the car?"

Logan hadn't given the matter much thought and said that he hadn't seen anything but the dark side of the concrete cellar for what seemed like a long time. They walked back up the stairs and out into the driveway. The sun was high in the sky, and Logan could feel the warmth of its rays as he walked out into the courtyard. Few times in his life had the simple feel of the sun done so much for his spirit. But it was a fleeting moment.

Looking at the aftermath brought him back down to reality. This was not a good scene. There were wounded men on the ground. Bullet holes in the vehicles. Dillard was tied up and sitting on the ground with a couple of tough-looking thugs that Logan didn't recognize.

"Are they dead?" Logan was looking at the two cops who had taken them in to Temecula.

"No, but they will be if they don't get to a hospital," said Little Jerry, who had been supervising the prisoners.

The sound of a motor broke the moment of calm. It was a deep sound. A truck. They saw a cloud of dust, then a dark brown Humvee military transport came over the rise.

"What the hell is this?" asked Lenny of no one in particular. Scott instinctively cocked his 30/30.

"Take it easy, let's see who this is," said Lenny. "On second thought."

Lenny turned on his heels and ran for the house. Scott, Janine, and Logan were right behind him. Chicago Bob, Little Jerry, and Marsha jumped on the horses and headed out the way they had come.

The hummer rolled into the drive and slid to a stop in a cloud of dust. When the doors opened, three well-dressed Hispanic men jumped out. They were holding automatic machine guns, and they sprayed a couple of bullets at the house, just to let the occupants know that they had arrived.

A man in a white suit, wearing a white Fedora, stepped from the backseat.

"What great timing," said Dillard. "I will have to note this in my book of great moments. Now get me out of these fucking ropes!"

Sobrano's men waited for his signal before untying Dillard, much to his dismay.

"Where is the envelope?" asked the mild-mannered Mexican.

Dillard shrugged and looked at Brownie.

"It's in the safe."

A shot rang out from the house, and one of Sobrano's men whirled as he was hit in the shoulder. Another bullet ricocheted off the hood of the Humvee. The newcomers dove for cover, then started firing a barrage of bullets toward the house.

"Nice shooting," said Lenny with a smile. "With a little luck, they'll run out of bullets soon and we'll be driving that Hummer right out of here."

"I wouldn't count on it," said Scott. "But we'll give them a run."

A flurry of bullets answered the shot from the house. All but Scott ducked for cover as windows shattered and plaster sprayed from the interior walls. They ceased with a command in Spanish, then there was silence.

Logan looked at Scott. "What now?"

CHAPTER SEVENTEEN

Pink Polly Strikes Again

A fly buzzed through the living room and back into the kitchen where it had first entered through a small hole in the screen. The minutes had passed slowly, interrupted only by an occasional burst of gunfire. Sobrano and his men were effectively pinned down thanks to the sharp shooting skills of the two former Marines, Lenny and Gary Scott. Logan and Reid lay on the floor, out of the line of fire. Reid was in severe pain and needed attention. Janine had crawled down the hall into one of the back rooms.

"Hopefully, Bob and Jerry made it back to the trucks and will be able to bring in some backup," said Lenny. "In the meantime, we've got to make sure these guys don't sneak around the back and try something cute."

Scott fired another shot and someone swore. Sobrano and Dillard were well hidden behind the vehicles and were carefully staying out of the action. One of Sobrano's soldiers suddenly stood up and, covering himself with a flurry of gunfire, ran toward a large oak tree in the yard. Scott tried to get a shot off but was repulsed by broken glass exploding from the window.

"Okay, so what the hell is he going to do now?"

"Maybe he just wanted to get away from his stinking buddies," said Lenny.

The thud of solid metal striking stone triggered a look from Scott.

"What was that? Oh shit! Hit the ground!"

An explosion shook the walls and blew out the one remaining window on the far end of the living room. The solider had thrown some kind of hand grenade at the house. Luckily, it had fallen short of its intended target and hit the small brick wall surrounding the patio. The patio enclosure deflected part of the blast, otherwise it might have blown a hole through the wall of the house.

"What was that?" asked a panicked Janine, crawling back down the hall.

"It was a fucking hand grenade," said Lenny. Reid and Logan were both wide-eyed and looking at Scott and Lenny. Smoke from the explosion drifted through the broken windows and brought a pungent sulfur smell to the room.

More pops of gunfire came from the direction of the vehicle, and then another thud on the patio. This time it was closer to the house. Scott and Lenny dove to the other side of the room just before the blast blew out a huge hole in the wall that protected them. Janine reversed her course and scurried down the hall into the bedroom.

In a flash, two of Sobrano's men were through the hole and in the room. Their guns covered the room, but they didn't shoot. They motioned Lenny and Scott to their feet and gathered up the weaponry. The third soldier, nursing a bullet-grazed shoulder, retrieved Janine from the bedroom.

They herded their new prisoners back out into the yard, where Sobrano, still looking clean and dapper in his white suit and fedora hat, waited with a smile. Dillard was smiling, too, but was looking much the worse for wear with a swollen lip and puffy left eye. His greasy blond hair was standing up like he had seen a ghost. Smoke from the grenade drifted up from the house. Parts of the house were still smoldering, but there was no fire.

Rogers, who had been searching the house on Dillard's orders despite having a wounded leg, emerged through the hole in the wall with a large manila envelope. Dillard shot him a stern look, but it was too late.

"Ah, thank you, my friend," said Sobrano, motioning Rogers to hand him the envelope. "Now, with just a few minor adjustments, I think it's time to say good-bye to this aberration of a plan once and for all."

The revolver came out of his coat holster as smoothly as a salesman producing a Mount Blanc pen. Rogers' eyes widened and he started to say something. But the bullet, slamming into his chest, took the wind from his words.

Dillard winced with the repercussion of the shot. He looked at Sobrano in disbelief. And then the gun came up leveled at him.

"What? Why are you doing this?"

"You know why, you cheating son of a bitch. You were after this because you knew it had something more valuable than that stupid formula. Did Walter tell you? Did you think you could just fly to Geneva and use the code numbers to my Swiss bank account?"

Sobrano was no longer smiling. Nor was Dillard.

"Our business with this Pink Polly has been a farce from the beginning. One thing after another. Your career is ruined. Only this could save you now. This could buy you some freedom."

"No, I swear to you, I didn't know. I just wanted to get the evidence and destroy it." Dillard was desperate.

Logan and the others watched the ordeal unfolding before their eyes while their Mexican guards covered the scene with their automatic weapons. Sobrano lifted his silver-plated revolver and aimed at Dillard's unsmiling face. Logan watched as a bead of sweat rolled off Dillard's forehead. Logan thought he looked like he was about to fall down on his knees and get religious, for real.

Logan's attention was diverted by a high-pitched whine followed by the sound of blades chopping through the air. A helicopter with the Riverside Sherriff's logo came in low from the same small valley that Little Jerry and Chicago Bob had led their charge. It swooped in and hovered over the drive, kicking up dust with each *thwop* of its blades.

"Drop your weapons and hold your hands over your head," blared a voice over a loud speaker. Wind from the chopper blades whipped at Sobrano's suit and blew dust in his eyes. Dillard dropped to the ground, then sprang at Sobrano. The gun flew from his hand.

Logan saw clouds of dust from the road leading to the ranch, and three sheriff's cruisers appeared racing toward the complex. The Mexican gunmen opened fire at the helicopter, then at the sheriff's cars as they approached. Logan and Janine dove for cover under a truck as bullets started spraying everywhere. Gary Scott had managed to get a gun back in his hands and took out one of the gunmen before taking a spray of automatic gunfire in the leg. Dillard and Sobrano were in a death clinch with hands at each other's throats, rolling on the ground. The gun was lying where it landed when Dillard had tackled Sobrano.

The first of the three cruisers sped through the yard and slid to a stop in front of the Humvee with the others close behind. Two black and whites from Riverside and a green and white from San Diego slid in a semicircle, facing the other three vehicles and the house. In a split second, six car doors sprung open in unison and guns were in action launching a barrage of hot lead toward the men who had been shooting. The Mexican gunmen tried to return fire as they ran for cover. Scott and Lenny retreated to the patio and now with them on one side and the six newly arrived deputies out in the yard, the remaining gunmen and their wounded compatriots were effectively pinned down.

Dillard and Sobrano were still grappling on the ground, but when the gunfire ceased they stopped. Using a loud speaker, Cassio gave orders for the group in the middle. Scott and Lenny stood up and laid down their rifles, watching the action with interest. Smoke was still rising from the hole where the hand grenades had been thrown. Dust from the arrival of the sheriff's cars drifted up through the air as the helicopter circled overhead.

What a scene thought Logan. What next? The sound of horses averted his attention.

Chicago Bob, Little Jerry, and Marsha rode in and stopped behind the deputies. The men who could walk dropped their weapons and raised their hands above their heads. There were still two laying motionless, victims of Dillard's errant shotgun blast and other well-aimed fire. Logan looked at Janine and smiled. "I think it's finally over, what a scene."

"All right now, everybody take it easy," directed Cassio through his megaphone. Logan nodded. "Everything happens nice and slow."

Cassio grouped Dillard and Sobrano together with those of their men who could still stand. One of the other deputies was on the radio, reporting their position and calling for medical aid. Reid, for the first time since they had taken him out of the cellar, was standing. He, too, was smiling at Cassio.

"That was close, Manny. Too close for me." Reid was almost overcome with emotion and pain. His voice trailed off as he surveyed the damage.

There were vehicles and weapons lying all over the dirt yard that had been like a war zone. The helicopter, which had been hovering over the action, veered off and flew slowly out toward the main road. A strange silence fell over the yard for a few seconds. For a brief moment there were no sounds of birds, no breeze, no voices, and there was no gunfire. Cassio broke the spell.

"So, quite an interesting bunch we have here." He was looking at Reid. "Looks like you might have one hell of an exclusive." Even he was smiling now. Cassio waved his hand over the disarray of men and vehicles. "Let's get some cuffs on these guys."

Again it was quiet. Gunfire and explosions had scared all the wildlife away within miles. The toll of the shooting had its effect on the humans, too. After so much action, there was nothing anyone could say. Emotionally, they were all drained. It was the calm after the storm. Logan watched as the deputies started handcuffing Sobrano's men.

Logan closed his eyes and listened to the silence. He was glad to be alive. An odd sound broke the spell. A low throaty hum of a car traveling at high speed. Suddenly the roar of an engine turned all heads. A half-demolished red BMW was speeding up the driveway in a swirling cloud of dust. Its left front bumper had been smashed back, giving the car a distinctive sneer. The trunk was open and slamming up and down with each undulation in the road. It came up the incline fast and made a swooping turn to intersect with the group of vehicles in the yard.

One of the deputies swung his rifle around and pointed at the incoming car, which did not appear to be slowing down. Cassio started to go for his loud speaker but thought better and dove out of the way. Panic struck at once, as everyone in the circle realized that this was some sort of kamikaze run and that the driver had no intention of stopping, or even slowing down. In unison, they all dove for cover. Dillard and Sobrano fell to the ground where they were standing rolling for cover as best they could.

Rocco was coming in hard. His bulging eyes scanned for a target. Dillard, where was he? His car. He saw the car. Aim for the car. Rocco was delusional. All he had thought about for the last three days was how he was going to kill Senator David Dillard and all his associates. Now it was time. He was going in with a bomb. Where was Dillard? He took his foot off the throttle long enough to pick up the plastic sack on the seat. He switched it to his left hand and held it out the window. He would launch the bomb and eject to safety. Where was that ejection button. He was flying low and fast. Time for some Napalm.

Logan and Janine had instinctively run for cover behind the small brick wall of the patio with Scott and Lenny. Reid was still on his way, hobbling the best he could. Logan jumped back up and went to help his friend. He checked the path of the incoming BMW to see where it might end up. He caught a glance of a wild-eyed man behind the wheel. He was the same guy they had seen driving the car in Temecula. His arm extended out of the window holding a plastic sack of what looked like sugar, or flour, pink flour. Logan grabbed Burt Reid and dove for cover just as the runaway car seemed to veer toward Dillard's Black Lincoln.

Rocco couldn't pick his man out of the crowd that lay sprawled about, but he knew the car. And that would have to do. He angled in. His descent would be steep, just like he had been told. Come in steep and hard, then pull up on the stick and let the bombs fly. These Viet Cong were going to pay now. He lined up the Lincoln and put his foot to the floor. He envisioned Dillard's face in the back window of the Lincoln. He was screaming. Rocco felt good about this. With his hand still out of the window, he slammed on the breaks and launched his bomb through the air. Time to eject. He reached down and pushed in the cigarette lighter.

The BMW slammed into the trunk of the Lincoln, its momentum causing it to stand up vertically and then somersault over the top of the black Towncar. There was an explosion and the impact launched the contents of the trunk into the air like a catapult. A covey of plastic sacks launched from the trunk and flew through the air. The red bomb of a car burst into flames and careened into the back of one of the pickup trucks.

"Jesus! Cover yourself!" Logan yelled at Janine. Then he heard one of Sobrano's men scream as he was crushed under the combined weight of the BMW and truck. Flames ensued and there was another smaller explosion. A dark smoke rose from the wreckage spiraling skyward toward the inbound helicopter. The chopper made a low pass and kicked up dust in the process.

In the immediate confusion, Dillard rose and ran to Sobrano's pistol, which lay in the dirt about three feet behind where him. Sobrano remained down covering his head. Dillard grabbed the gun and returned to Sobrano kicking him in the ribs. Sobrano turned over in pain. He saw Dillard, gun in hand, with the look of revenge in his eye.

"Don't shoot me, we can get out of here."

Dillard fired three quick shots. Sobrano's eyes bulged with the impact of the bullets. Quickly, Dillard reached down and grabbed the envelope. A gunshot rang out. One of the deputies had risen from behind his car. Dillard returned the shot, and the deputy ducked.

Looking around desperately, Dillard picked up one of automatic weapons that Sobrano's men had been using. He covered himself and ran across the yard. He jumped the fence and fired into the patio wall, sending pieces of brick in the faces of Lenny, Scott, Reid, and Logan. He grabbed Janine and pulled her to her feet.

"You're coming with me," he yelled.

Using her for a shield, Dillard made his way back across the yard toward the Humvee. A couple of the deputies took shots, but none were too close out of concern for the girl.

As gunshots sent plumes of dust and brick in the air, Logan dared a peek over the brick wall. Where was Janine? He saw one of deputies with a gun in his hand, but he was staggering like he had been hit. Cassio and the other deputies were still on the ground. He heard a weird ringing in his ears. The explosion must have knocked them out, Logan thought. Lenny and Scott were also slow to move into action. Something was wrong. There was a strange smell in the air as thick smoke from the burning BMW enveloped the courtyard.

Logan heard the motor of the big four-wheel-drive vehicle roar to a start, and the next thing he saw were the four wheels kicking up dust as the Humvee spun a turn. He instinctively jumped over the wall and picking up a gun, ran toward the vehicle firing off a burst of bullets. Dillard completed the turn and charged out of the yard.

Without hesitation, Logan jumped in the one remaining pickup truck and started the engine. He was reacting on pure adrenaline now.

He cranked the wheel to the right and put his foot into the gas pedal. In a split-second he was rumbling out the driveway in pursuit of a large cloud of dust. Cassio rose slowly from behind the sheriff's cruiser. He had been knocked flat by the percussion from the explosion. The fire was starting to burn out of control and would definitely spread to the buildings if it didn't get some attention soon.

Cassio opened the door to his car and grabbed the radio to call for backup and to order in some firefighting teams. Something stopped him. He didn't feel right. Had he been hit? No blood. His mind raced while his body seemed to be moving in slow motion. He needed to keep it together and get some help quick. With much effort, he radioed in their situation.

The other deputies were back in action now, as were Lenny and Scott, although all were moving and reacting as if in shock. The flames from the BMW and truck were burning with intense heat. Two of the deputies moved in an effort to get those left alive away from the fire. Sobrano's gunman, as well as Brownie and Low, were dead. Another deputy pulled Sobrano across the dirt to safety. He was in bad shape but still breathing.

Only one of the cruisers, the one closest to the collision, was out of commission. Cassio shook off his delirium and barked out some orders to secure the position. Then, putting one of the officer's in charge, he jumped in his car to give chase. Seizing the opportunity, Lenny and Scott jumped in with him.

"We know you probably won't like this, but we're going with you," said Lenny in his easy Texas drawl. "We came out here to save our friend, and we'd like to stick with it 'till the end."

Cassio looked at them and, although he would be breaking all kinds of rules, he put his foot to the floor and aimed the cruiser down the road without so much as a word.

CHAPTER EIGHTEEN

Visions

A pale November sky accented by wispy fall clouds hung over
the valley. Smoke spiraled slowly skyward, marking the spot
where men had died. A roadrunner stopped and cocked its head at the
chopping sounds of the helicopter, watching as the huge metal bird rose
and circled around the column of smoke.

Another sound turned the roadrunner's head. The high-pitched
whine of an engine and the swoosh of moving air. Instinctively, the bird
darted toward the shoulder of the dirt road. In an instant the Humvee
appeared, rising over the hill like a great monster in pursuit of fleeing
prey. It roared around a bend in the road, blasting dirt and rocks into the
sage where the bird had taken refuge. In a minute, it was gone, its great
clamor diminishing with another rise in the road.

More noise. Another beast topped the hill. The roadrunner hastily
retreated back across the road in the direction from which it had first
come. Its spindly legs carrying it quickly. Flightless wings flapping, the
bird made it safely across the road before the growling pickup truck
flew past. This time the bird did not stop but continued to run through
the clumps of sage and manzanita, disappearing into the high desert for
good.

Logan gripped the wheel with both hands. The cloud of dust in
front of him was distorting his vision and forcing him to drive with
more caution than he wanted. His blood was pumping, and for some
reason he was feeling strangely odd. He watched the brown clouds of

dust in front of him as they billowed up from the road. It was as if a thick brown fog was enveloping the truck. He eased his foot off of the throttle and let the truck slow while he fought to focus on the road.

The road appeared again, and he sped up a little. Taking deep breaths, he tried to clear his head. He had been through a rough ordeal and certainly was suffering from the adverse effects of little sleep and severe stress. Yet even that could not explain the way he was feeling. It was as if he were hallucinating. He felt as if he were watching himself driving the truck instead of driving it. What was going on?

The Humvee slid to a near stop before careening wildly on to the two-lane highway. A grind of gears, and the gunmetal gray vehicle stormed off in the direction of Anza. Inside, Janine was gripping a handle on the door with white-knuckled hands. Her face was tense and pale, almost as if there was no blood in it at all. Her body was stiff and her feet were pressing the floorboard like she was taking the big drop on a roller coaster. Dillard had a wild look in his eyes, not just scared or mad. More like that of a rabid dog, veins bulging red on white bulbs. Blood dripped from his shoulder, but he didn't seem to notice. Dillard's demented intensity horrified Janine, and she whimpered uncontrollably.

Logan topped out over the last hill in time to see the Humvee take off in the direction of town. He could see better now but was still feeling that strange sensation of being in two places at the same time. He remembered once back in the late sixties someone had put LSD in some punch at a party. It was the same feeling he had now. He could hear his heart beating and everything in front of him was surreal. Intensely sharp yet pulsating images that seemed to be moving continuously to the left as he stared.

Deep in thought, he slowed down. He watched the swirls of brown dust along the road, left by the passing of the speeding Humvee. The sound of the siren behind him jolted him out of his fog, and he looked in the rearview mirror to see a green-and-white sheriff's cruiser with red lights flashing. The cruiser was bearing down hard with no sign of slowing down. Logan instinctively veered to the side of the road, narrowly avoiding being hit from behind. The cruiser passed, spraying the pickup with dust and gravel as it went by. Logan caught a glimpse of three men in the car. It looked like Lenny and Scott with Cassio at the wheel. Logan, stunned by what had just happened, sat awestruck as the cruiser raced off toward the highway.

Lenny looked across the seat at Cassio, who hadn't said a word since they had left the scene at the ranch. Nor had he responded to several calls that came over the radio. Scott, too, was strangely quiet.

"How you doing, Manny?" Lenny asked.

Cassio didn't answer. His eyes remained glued to the pursuit. He had nearly run Logan off the road, barely acknowledging that he was there at all. Another call came over the radio, and Cassio ignored it. They came to the highway and, without so much as a look in either direction, Cassio swung the cruiser on to the road. A semi-trailer that had been heading west was forced into a skid of screeching brakes, skidding off of the road and on to the wide dirt shoulder. A gravel truck coming in the opposite direction nearly collided with the semi as it skidded across the road. Luckily, the driver managed to steer off into the sand avoiding a crash. Cassio's errant turn had nearly caused a gruesome accident, yet he was unfazed. Like it never happened.

Lenny and Scott had been tossed left and then right in their seats. Lenny came close to hitting his head on the ceiling as the cruiser bounced. Horns blared from both the gravel truck and the big rig. Lenny looked back at the scene and then at Cassio.

"Jesus, Manny, what in the hell are you doing?" He checked out Scott, who looked like he had seen a ghost. Stiff in his seat, sickly white skin, eyes staring straight ahead. It was as if he were about to blow up.

"What the hell is going on with you guys? Damn it, Manny, you're going to get us killed driving like that!"

Cassio kept his eyes glued to the road and said nothing. His foot was to the floor, and the cruiser was flying down the road. They passed two cars going up an incline and barely made it back into the right lane as a big rig came over the top of the hill. Even with the red lights and siren on, Cassio was driving so fast that other drivers barely had time to react.

⁓⟡⟐⟡⁓

A long-haired man in his late twenties was walking across the street in midtown Anza when he heard the sound of a speeding vehicle. He looked up in time to pick up his pace, first to a jog, and then to a run, before a dust-covered Humvee burst over a rise in the road. There was no slowing at the site of a pedestrian. Another car about to pull out of a restaurant parking lot stopped until the truck passed. Then, just as the Humvee had left the main stretch of town, another speeding car entered from the north. A sheriff's cruiser, red lights and siren on, coming at full speed in pursuit of the Humvee. The long hair scratched his head and went back the direction he had come.

⁓⟡⟐⟡⁓

Logan was mystified by Cassio's action. Nearly running into him on the road and then narrowly escaping what could have been a head-on collision with a truck and a big rig. He had let the pickup slow to a stop and was parked in the middle of the road when Chicago Bob and Little Jerry rode up on their horses.

"Hey, Logan. Are you okay? Logan! Wake up, buddy."

Little Jerry slid off the big red quarter horse and walked up to the window. "Hey, Logan! Shit, what's wrong with him? He's like asleep or something."

Bob got down from his horse and walked to the front of the truck. He pounded on the hood. Logan's head came up and his eyes opened. It took him a second to focus, and then he saw his two friends standing there.

"I don't know what happened. I was following the hummer and then I think Cassio tried to run me off the road." Logan pointed to the highway. "And then they almost had a huge wreck out there."

The big rig and the gravel truck were still where they had come to rest on their respective shoulders. The two drivers appeared to be rehashing what just happened. Marsha came riding up and remained on her horse.

"Marsh, take these horses back to the truck, Jerry and I are going with Logan."

Jerry gave his friend an inquisitive look, then nodded in agreement. Marsha gathered up the reins of the two horses as Jerry jumped in the passenger's side. Chicago Bob took his rope off the saddle horn and threw it in the back of the truck.

"You still got your gun?" Little Jerry asked.

"I got my gun and I got my rope, and I'd like to use them to hang somebody's ass."

Bob shoved a mumbling Logan into the middle of the seat and got behind the wheel. The truck was a late model 4x4 Ford with a V-8 and plenty of horsepower. The cop, or ex-cop, that owned it had equipped it for off-road driving. It had both a scanner and a CB radio. Bob reached down and turned the scanner on.

"Looks like they went toward town, maybe we'll hear them over the radio." He gunned the big V-8 and, rolling down the window, he took off his hat and waved it at Marsha. "Don't wait up for me, darlin'!"

Marsha smiled back and gave him the finger. She would just as soon have been in the back of the truck with a chance to get another shot at that asshole Dillard. Now she was left to pick up the pieces and get the horses back to their owner.

With Chicago Bob at the wheel, they left the dirt road and motored off toward Anza. Little Jerry took a flask from the inside of his jean jacket.

"Medicinal," he said as he took a sip. He handed it over to Bob, who took a drink and looked back at Jerry.

"I don't think he wants any," he said, tapping Logan on the chest.

Logan remained somewhat incoherent and was still mumbling about Cassio's driving.

The Humvee shot down the hill from Anza at better than eighty miles an hour. Its heavy tread tires made an eerie screaming sound that wavered in pitch with each undulation in the road. Janine remained cramped in the corner of the truck. She looked at Dillard, who was still beyond any rational form of behavior. He was gripping the wheel and smiling as if he were on some wild ride at an amusement park.

"Where are you taking me?" she blurted out over the incessant howl of the engine and tires.

Dillard did not react for a few seconds and then, still looking straight ahead, said, "You'll be just fine."

He steered the big vehicle on to Highway 79 and went east toward the desert. Janine glanced down at the guns on the seat. Before she had a chance to blink, Dillard had the pistol in his hand and was aiming it directly at her face.

"Don't even think about it. If you want to live, stay quiet and don't move."

The tone of his voice was convincing. She turned her head and looked out the window. She was scared. More scared than she had ever been.

CHAPTER NINETEEN

Road Kill

The scanner scratched out its report in the newsroom about 2 P.M. A team of sheriff's deputies were involved in a shoot-out in the east county. Molinski could hear gunshots being fired in the background as Cassio's voice called for backup. A few minutes later, he was calling for an ambulance, then just as it sounded as if things were in control, the sheriff's helicopter reported another vehicle approaching at a high rate of speed. The next transmission reported an explosion and more gunfire from the scene.

Pam Molinski hadn't heard of a firefight like this since she was in the army. This was an extraordinary event, and she desperately wanted to be a part of it. She listened intently, taking notes. Where was Reid? He would love this. O'Malley came in wearing his gray fisherman-style vest that held multiple roles of film. He had been out on assignment shooting a "grin and grip" for the Village Section editor. He looked perturbed.

"Have you been hearing what I've been hearing?" O'Malley's tone was excited. "That's a little out of our territory, but it does involve some of our deputies."

Molinski nodded and started going through the story as she had been hearing it. O'Malley collaborated and filled in on some of the things he had surmised from the transmissions. Between the two of them, they had a fair description what may have happened. The one puzzling factor was the fact that there had been no more contact with the pursuing sheriff's unit since Cassio had first reported that he was in pursuit. There had been numerous attempts by both dispatchers and other units to contact him, yet there was no reply.

"He's in pursuit, we know that by the reports from the town of Anza," said Molinski. "You'd think they would have followed in the chopper."

"It stayed at the scene to back up the deputies on the ground. They should have dispatched another unit by now."

Another report came over the scanner. It was from a helicopter that had flown out of San Diego. The Humvee and sheriff's cruiser were in sight and appeared to be headed east on Highway 79. Still no response from the pursuing unit.

"What happens if it gets dark?" asked Molinski. "That chopper is going to have some trouble keeping them in sight."

"They've got some tools," said O'Malley. "Night vision goggles, and a 10,000 candle searchlight. They should be okay."

Louie from _The Cal Rancho News_ walked into the newsroom and jumped into the fray. He'd been on an errand to pick up some supplies for the sister paper, but news has a way changing schedules for a newsman. An experienced editor who had once worked for the Associated Press, he listened as Molinski and O'Malley related the events of the last three hours. Every couple of minutes, the scanner would break in with new information. Ambulances and backup units had arrived at the ranch. There were four dead, none of which were identified. Coroners from both Riverside and San Diego counties had been dispatched. Another ambulance was on the way as there were at least six people in need of medical attention.

The phone rang in the newsroom and Molinski answered. Her face immediately broke into a smile. "Reid!"

Reid's voice was hoarse, but he was still the consummate reporter. "I knew you guys would be there. Have you been listening? I want you to follow the story, get O'Malley and follow the action using his scanner."

Molinski agreed excitedly, and then listened as Reid gave instructions of how to get to the scene. He was on his way back to town with one of the deputies but had convinced him to stop at the first pay phone.

"Call Louie and tell him to get Charlie rolling out here for pictures and a story."

Typical Reid, thought Malinoski, all news and no story.

"One step ahead of you, boss. They're both here and in action. Now what about you? What the hell are you doing there?"

"It's a long story, but you can catch up with me later. I have a feeling I'm going to be in Palomar Hospital for a couple of days. Just get out there and cover this before the other guys. We've got a big time jump with lots of inside stuff, so let's go!"

Molinski handed the phone to Louie, who spoke to Reid for a couple more minutes. Molinski and O'Malley gathered up their tools and bolted out of the room. Louie hung up with Reid and called his ace reporter at home. Charlie would need no encouragement, he was a newsman and this was the best story to come along in years. Who knows where it would lead.

It was twilight when the Humvee rolled through Julian, ignoring the stop signs and traffic signals. Janine was petrified. She had lost count of the number of times they had almost crashed in the last two hours. They had outrun the pursuing sheriff's car, at least it was no longer in sight. She hoped it was still back there somewhere. By now there had to be others involved in the chase.

The Humvee's motor sputtered and coughed. Thank God, we're out of gas, thought Janine. Dillard glanced down at the dash and flipped a switch. The engine stopped and then started again. The fuel gauge went back to the full position. Janine let out a sigh. Dillard laughed.

"It's David Dillard, Senator David Dillard, or let's say former state senator after this," said the voice on the radio. The helicopter pilot acknowledged. The dispatcher went on. "We think he's heading for a place he was linked to in Descanso. We're sending some units there to wait. We'll also set up a road block at the bottom of the grade. He should be there in about twenty minutes."

"Roger that, I'll keep him in sight. I have Unit E 220 about a mile behind the suspect. Has anyone been able to raise him? Over."

Despite repeated tries, Cassio, in Unit E 220, was not responding. Still he remained in pursuit and was negotiating the high-speed chase with considerable expertise.

Lenny studied Cassio. He had not spoken since they had left the scene of the shooting. The whole time he seemed to be fighting to maintain his concentration on driving. Scott had been mumbling but was now silent. In fact, he appeared to be asleep. Head down, nodding and swaying with each bump and turn.

"There must have been something in that damn smoke," said Cassio suddenly, his voice low and without emotion. "Fumes or a gas. I've got one hell of a headache."

"Nice to have you back," said Lenny. "Now if Gary here would just pull out of it, we'd be back in business. You might want to radio in and let them know where we are. They've been trying to raise you since we left the ranch."

Cassio had the cruiser heading up the long winding road that led into Julian, an old mining town atop the Laguna Mountains. The last mile into town was relatively straight driving and Cassio was making up some time. The helicopter had reported that the Humvee was through town and headed down the backside of the mountain.

"Might be headed for Descanso," said Cassio. "Dillard has some connections out there; at least his name came up in a bust there. Of course, at the time, we didn't believe it."

He radioed in and shared his intuition with the dispatcher and was told that units were already in route to the Descanso location. He muttered an agreement, then slowed the car down to take a right turn on a side road. Lenny didn't say anything, the sergeant knew what he was doing, now that he was back from his trip.

Chicago Bob was happy. He was tooling down the road in a fairly new truck and on an adventure. The shooting and blood back at the ranch hadn't seemed to affect him. He was steady by nature. They were at the foot of the mountain and about to start their accent. Little Jerry was less jovial. He had been sipping his flask of schnapps and was slipping into one of his muttering moods.

It was almost dark now, and Logan watched the lights from the truck illuminate the road. He felt like he was at a drive-in movie. It was a black-and-white picture. The trees and bushes that lined the road cast grotesque shapes that seemed to loom up from the edges of the screen. Down the middle was the ever-moving double yellow line. Like a snake, it led them in their pursuit. What was his destiny? He was with friends, he knew that. But where were they going? He sat back again, closed his eyes, and took a deep breath. There was something out there that was scary, but he just couldn't quite remember what it was.

Far up ahead, and on the other side of the mountain, a dark Humvee raced down the road. Its engine and tires issuing a constant scream into the night. The moon was rising in the east. A near-full harvest moon. Normally a beautiful sight. But on this night, the pale yellow disk brought no good tidings. Janine relaxed her grip on the seat. Not that she was no longer scared, she just couldn't physically maintain her composure any longer. Like she had been in an accident that just kept happening. There had been near head-on collisions, high-speed drifts through turns, near misses with cliffs. She had closed her eyes over and over again, thinking this was it, she was going to die. Now, driving down a fairly straight road into the desert, she resigned herself to the fact that if they were going to crash, it wouldn't matter if she were holding on tight or just sitting there. So she relaxed.

Dillard remained glued to the wheel, but the crazy look in his eyes had gone. He appeared more concerned now, contemplating. Where was he taking her? Did he even have a plan?

The road made a long, sloping curve before it straightened off into the southern desert. Dillard was taking the turn fast, but not so fast that the vehicle was out of control. And that was good, because as they came around the corner there were a string of red flares lining the sides of the road and two Highway Patrol cars forming a road block.

A blinding searchlight flashed on the Humvee. Four patrolmen had guns aimed from behind their car. A fifth had a loud speaker and a pistol.

Dillard instinctively hit the breaks, and the tires locked up in a skid. The Humvee drifted sideways and was heading for a broadside collision with the two cars blocking the road. Dillard fought the wheel, then took his foot off the brake and hit the throttle. The massive vehicle lurched and then sprang back around, drifting to the opposite side in a correction. Now they were heading directly at the two cars and they were going in fast.

As one, the patrolmen realized that the oncoming truck-like vehicle was not going to stop. In unison they dove for cover. The Hummer hit the road block dead center catching the front-quarter sections of both Highway Patrol cars. The cars jolted up on to two wheels and then spun on impact as sparks flew from the metal contact of the massive steel bumper on the front of the military vehicle. The Hummer barely slowed as it roared through the obstruction, knocking the cars to the shoulder of the road like bowling pins.

Inside, Janine had screamed and grabbed the door handle expecting to be thrown through the windshield. She felt the impact and was jostled forward in her seat, but the truck just kept going. Only a slight concussion-like shock wave of noise and air interrupted the din of the huge rubber tires on the asphalt as the Hummer sped off into the moonlit desert.

When the report of the collision came over the radio, Cassio and company, just minutes away from the scene, were first to arrive. The helicopter had gone back to its base to refuel, but there were few roads in the desert and virtually no place to hide. They would have no trouble finding Dillard, and when they did, there would be some scores to settle, thought Cassio.

The five patrolmen were shaken up, but there were no serious injuries. One of the units was drivable; the other would need some major body work before it was back on the road.

"That son-of-a-bitch came through here and knocked us out like a couple of fucking marbles," said the patrolman who had been holding the megaphone. "I don't know what the hell he's thinking, but I don't think it fazed the bastard."

Cassio nodded and acknowledged the power of the large military vehicle. They would have to take that in to consideration. He got on his radio and asked for an ETA on the helicopter, then went over a road map with the Highway Patrol officer. Scott and Lenny helped the other officers pick up some of their belongings, including their guns that had been dropped or thrown in the heat of the moment. Afterwards, they leaned up against the sheriff's cruiser and lit up cigarettes.

"You feeling better?" Lenny asked Scott.

"I don't know what happened, but I really lost it for awhile. It was scary." Scott complained about a headache, but other than that he was okay. Functional at least, and more than willing to continue.

Lenny looked out into the desert. The moon was inching higher in the sky now, lighting up the landscape that more resembled the moon than anything on earth.

"I think he's going to Mexico," said Lenny, looking down the long black line of highway that disappeared into the horizon. "With that damn rig, he can just about make his own road."

CHAPTER TWENTY

Cold Moon

Alarge yellow moon had just topped a ridge behind downtown Julian when a dark blue Ford truck missed the driveway and bumped over the curb. Chicago Bob, weary from a long hard drive up the mountain, had taken the quick route into the gas station. A little short of the turn. No damage done, but the jarring impact with curb had knocked Logan and Little Jerry's heads, bringing them abruptly back into reality. They had been experiencing various forms of sleep and near sleep for about the last hour. Jerry let out a "shiiiiit," and Chicago Bob smiled for first time in quite a while.

Rolling to a stop in front of the pumps, he jumped out of the truck and instructed Jerry to put in $20 worth of gas. Logan reached for his wallet, but his pocket was empty. Lost in the fracas, no doubt.

Chicago Bob watched Jerry dutifully gas up the truck and then went in to buy some coffee and a jug of water from the store. It was a good stop. Less than five minutes and they were back on the road, feeling much refreshed.

"I heard that Dillard ran a CHP roadblock on the backside of town," said Bob. "They think he's headed for Descanso. Do you know it?"

"I don't know much right now except that my head is ringing like a mission bell," said Logan. He took a sip from the coffee. At least he felt a little more in control of his thoughts. He wasn't seeing things move like before. Little Jerry was also lucid again and in fair spirits. Chicago

Bob privately wondered if the little jockey had picked up a new pint of schnapps at the store.

Julian was a quaint little old town founded in the late 1880s when gold was discovered on a hill that now overlooked the main street. Most of the buildings had been completely restored, and the town was a haven for tourists. Especially during autumn weekends, when the apple harvest was in and all the stores were stocked with apple delights. If it could be made with an apple, it was made in Julian.

It would be a nice place to live, thought Logan. A nice place to own a ranch or small farm and raise a family. If you had the right partner. His thoughts went to Janine. He had gotten to know her quickly in the short time they had been together. There was a passionate attraction between them from the start. She had opened up to him about her past. Could he accept that? Probably. People make mistakes, but people can change. Would she be willing to have children? They hadn't discussed it. He was almost forty and she was in her early thirties. A good time?

Now she was with Dillard. A mad man capable of anything from what Logan had seen. Did he take her merely as a shield, or did he have other plans? He remembered the look of panic when Dillard scooped her from right beside him. That was about the time he had smelled something funny in the air. Maybe that was when he got dosed with whatever it was. He felt helpless as Dillard dragged her off, and now he felt helpless again. What were the chances of getting her back?

Static from an incoming message came over the radio. It was a dispatcher talking to one of the units on scene where Dillard had run the roadblock. Cassio and one of the CHP units were in route to Descanso, where they were meeting up with a team already in place at the ranch owned by Stephen Casey. Or formerly owned by Stephen Casey; he had been murdered at The Downs.

"Whatever happened about that?" asked Bob. "That was a bazaar deal. Guy gets in a fight with his girlfriend and winds up dead in an avocado grove."

"Shit, it was a professional hit. One bullet to the back of the head," said Little Jerry. "Got it from Tuffy, he knows everything that goes on at The Downs. That Casey guy had been drinking at The Club with Big Mike and Spike. Probably into the shit, too."

Little Jerry was amazing, thought Logan. Just when you thought that he was incoherent of all that went on around him, he would produce information or observations that were the result of some cognitive thinking.

"I don't know Descanso, so we'll just have to follow our noses," said Bob. "Maybe we'll get lucky."

⚜

The desert night was clear and cold. At 10:30 p.m. it was light enough to drive with no headlights. A large pale moon hung from the sky like a luminescent globe in a dark room. A shape moved across the valley floor, grinding its way up a dry riverbed toward some steep cliffs that jutted off the eastern ridge of the Lagunas. Far off to the east, the lights of Descanso twinkled.

A few miles away, Cassio pulled the cruiser off the main road and on to a wide soft dirt road that led to the ranch once owned by Stephen Casey. It was a good bet that was where Dillard would be. In fact, he should have already been there. Sheriff's units on scene had been hiding out, waiting for more than an hour. Yet no one had shown. Cassio had been cruising the main roads and side roads in and around the town.

They pulled into the empty driveway. The place was deserted. Except for the dozen or so SWAT officers hidden about the premises. Cassio blinked his lights twice and backed out. He called into dispatch to see if the chopper had any better luck.

"I think we better get some rest and pick this up in the morning," said Cassio, looking over at Lenny. He was tired and so was Scott. The agreement was unanimous. Everyone was tired. It had been a grueling day. One that no one would ever forget. Death is not an easy thing to witness, for anyone. Cassio took the road that would lead them back out to the Interstate. They would be back in San Diego in about an hour.

"You guys are going to have to find your own way back to North County, or wherever you're going to go. I can't have you along as ride-alongs anymore. Sorry."

They passed a late-model blue Ford pickup that was parked on the side of the highway. It had pulled well off the road into one of the turnouts. As tired as they were, no one noticed that it was one of the trucks from the ranch. The one Logan had commandeered to chase after Janine.

Inside, Logan, Chicago Bob, and Little Jerry were asleep. They had stopped driving around 11 P.M. Too tired to continue. There had been no new updates over the scanner.

"Don't worry, Logan. We'll find them. Just need a little rest and some sunshine so we can see where the hell we are. We're not giving up." Bob's words gave Logan a little boost. Maybe things would work out. One way or another, tomorrow would be one hell of a day. He closed his eyes and was asleep within minutes.

CHAPTER TWENTY ONE

Day Of The Dead

The sun came out of the eastern desert like a large red ball. A few clouds hung around the horizon, hovering over distant purple mountains. A single star glimmered in the dark sky to the west.

Logan felt a nudge in his ribs. It didn't hurt, but everything else he could feel did. His throat was dry and sore and his head ached. Another nudge and he opened his eyes. Little Jerry, a veteran of many worse nights, was smiling.

"Shit, let's get some coffee and go catch that bastard."

Logan had to smile. Here was this guy he really didn't know all that well. A guy who he would have never dreamed would have had the fortitude and courage to pull off what they had accomplished so far. And now, after a day of outright terror and an incredibly uncomfortable night, Little Jerry was ready and willing to get back to it. Shit!

Chicago Bob muttered and opened his eyes. He yawned and looked woefully up from under his black cowboy hat.

"You boys ready to ride?"

Logan laughed. As bad as he felt physically, the absurdity of waking up with Chicago Bob and Little Jerry in the front seat of a pickup was enough to lift his spirits. Nothing needed to be said.

Bob started the truck, and they headed into town to look for a place to eat. A Jack-in-the-Box for coffee and breakfast did the trick. They ate inside, happy to get out of the truck for awhile.

They were finishing a second round of breakfast burritos when Logan saw it coming down the highway. The big brown hummer was in a hurry to get somewhere. Logan could not see through the tinted windows, but he could feel Janine there. And she needed him.

"There they are! The son-of-a-bitch," said Logan through a mouthful of egg.

In split-second they were back in the truck. They had been quick and the dark shape of the Hummer was still visible about a half mile down the long straight road. Logan was vaguely familiar with the area. The road led east but would soon turn to the south where it would eventually intersect with Interstate 8. They followed from a distance, careful not to get too close. Dillard may recognize the truck.

⁓⊱≈⊰⁓

It was 7 A.M. when Manny Cassio walked into his office, coffee in hand. He sat down in his chair and got on the phone. He wanted all the information possible from anyone involved with the case. Within minutes he had reports coming in from the ranch where the shootout had occurred. He paced back and forth between his big board and his phone, adding bits and pieces of information as it came in.

Red-headed Pat Brado came in about eight, looking a bit tired, or stressed, thought Cassio. Brado was not his partner, but they worked on a lot of cases together. They had been working this case, too, but Brado had not been able to give it his full attention because of other commitments.

Brado looked up at the board. It was filling up with information, and he was always interested in Cassio's methodology. Brado admired the way the sergeant could take charge of a case. The board gave him insight into the interactions involved in any given set of circumstances.

"What does the board say?"

Cassio looked at Brado and considered the question. "It says that some very big players were involved in a speculative venture. When it didn't work out, things went to hell."

"What's the upshot now?"

Cassio looked at his fellow detective. "We get Dillard and we have wrapped up the bunch. And there might even be some assets in the pot that we can divvy up for the department. Buy a new chopper or something."

"I'll take that hummer," said Brado.

Cassio smiled and went back to the phone. Brado studied the names on the board and the colored lines connecting them. Somebody was going to go to jail.

The fax machine was spewing out reports from the various officers involved. There were reports from the crime scene, reports from last night's unsuccessful stakeout, and there was correspondence from Mexican authorities concerning Sobrano and his men. The feds were going to be all over this one, thought Cassio.

Brado had been glancing over the reports as soon as they came in. Sorting and stapling them, and then stacking them neatly on Cassio's desk. In between calls, Cassio would glance at each one and then put it in a designated pile to be examined in more detail at a later time.

Cassio looked up and noticed Brado going over one of the faxes more carefully than he had with the others. He was reading this one with interest. Then, as he felt Cassio looking at him, he stopped. Without looking at the sergeant, Brado went back to the machine and retrieved another incoming fax. He shuffled the first fax into a pile with some other papers.

"Let me see that one," said Cassio.

Brado handed him a stack of papers. There were two separate fax transmissions and some other papers that must have come from one of the other desks.

Cassio checked through them. The first was from the sheriff SWAT team commander. Pages from the second fax were dispersed among the other papers, but Cassio arranged them according to the automatic date/time stamp from the fax machine. Once arranged, Cassio noticed that there was no automatic return number from the sending fax machine. There was no cover page, but his name was scrawled at the top along with the word urgent underlined three times.

The first page was handwritten. The second looked like a map. Cassio shrugged. He read it quickly, then looked at the map. He read it again, then the map again. Looking at the big board he gripped the edge of the desk as if making a decision. Brado studied him with interest.

"What's going on? Something important?"

"This fax, it's a tip about Dillard. It says that he is heading for a ranch near the border. There is an airstrip there and a plane. If he gets there, he's off to South America."

Cassio picked up the phone and ordered up a team of deputies. No time for a meeting in the briefing room, he would have to give instructions on the fly.

"I'm going with you," said Brado, grabbing his coat.

Within minutes, there were three sheriff's cruisers heading east from San Diego Sheriff's Headquarters. Cassio estimated that it would take about two hours to get to the destination. They used red lights and sirens to make time.

<hr />

Logan watched the road ahead as the dark shape of the Humvee snaked its way around the foothills. Chicago Bob stayed back far enough so that the truck would not be seen. There were few cars on the road, and Dillard was making time. Bob looked at the speedometer. Eighty. If a cop was around, they would both be getting tickets. Of course, Dillard had demonstrated a propensity for not stopping for cops.

So far they hadn't heard much over the scanner. Just routine dispatch. The SWAT team had pulled out earlier and was heading back to San Diego. Logan's blood was pumping. They were on their own now with no course of action but to act and react. Right now they were following Dillard and waiting for an opportunity. Any opportunity.

"The Interstate is up ahead. It will be interesting to see which way he heads," said Bob. "If he goes east, he's probably headed for mainland Mexico. West and he could be going back to San Diego or Baja."

The Humvee took the freeway on-ramp to the east and merged into traffic. The Ford pickup with Chicago Bob at the wheel followed. They gained a little ground because Dillard had seemed to slow a bit to keep pace with the traffic. There were more cars on the road now, and they couldn't risk getting closer. Bob carefully avoided direct line of sight with Dillard's rearview mirrors.

About twenty minutes passed before the Humvee changed lanes and headed for an exit. It was in the middle of nowhere. One of those exits that has a number instead of a name. Or it just hadn't been named yet. A lonely exit that you would only find in the desert. Dillard veered across two lanes and took the exit.

Bob crossed a lane and pulled off on to the shoulder. It was a good move. If they followed now, Dillard would see them for sure. From the shoulder they could watch him from a slight elevation and stay out of sight. Hopefully, he hadn't noticed them.

Still gripping the wheel with both hands, Dillard glanced down at his gauges. Plenty of fuel, but the engine was running very hot. It was just a matter of timing now. If he could make it to the desert lab, he had a chance. He looked over at Janine. She was beautiful. Maybe he would take her with him. Maybe not. She would serve her purpose if the time came.

He had planned to go overland in the night, using the off-road capabilities of the military vehicle to navigate the desert. A small, boulder-strewn stream bed had changed that. They had driven into it without warning and even the Humvee was no match for the sand and rocks. It had taken him nearly two hours to get out and it was almost by sheer luck. Now he was back on the right road and with a little more luck he would be on his way to Central America within hours.

So far he had not seen any cops. Not even the usual Highway Patrol speed traps. He had been lucky again. He kept the engine at a steady pace, hoping it would not overheat. No doubt that the radiator had been damaged. No telling what else might have broken when they crashed into the dry riverbed.

Chicago Bob checked his gauges. The truck was running smooth. He had about three quarters of a tank of fuel. He followed carefully now, trying to stay out of sight.

It was a cat and mouse game, but for some reason Logan felt more like the mouse at this point. Dillard was a dangerous man. The most dangerous kind. Desperate. A true sociopath caring only for himself and with utter disregard for human life. Who would have thought that a man who portrayed himself as a righteous, religious, ultra-conservative politician could be such a monster? Whatever was ahead, it was going to be difficult, to say the least.

They came over a small pass cut through a black lava mountain. As they topped out on the hill, slowing so as not be seen, they noticed a plume of dust from the flats below. A large dark vehicle was cutting across the desert floor. There was a road, more of a track than a road, but a route that was traveled. It led off to the east. Logan followed it with his eyes to a cluster of hills. It looked like there were some trees there and possibly some buildings.

"Looks like he's heading out there." Logan pointed at the dark peaks rising out of the sandy flats. "Maybe a ranch or something."

"We should sit tight for awhile," said Little Jerry. "Let him get out there a ways before we start. Then we go slow until we get close enough to go in with a bang." He patted the pistol that he had taken from under the seat.

Logan hadn't thought of it until now, but they only had one weapon. What in the hell were they supposed to do? Jerry reached inside his coat and produced a small automatic. "Can one of you guys handle this?"

Logan was surprised, but he took the gun without asking about it. It was obvious that it was part of Little Jerry's everyday attire. Yet he would have never guessed.

They waited five minutes before coming off the pass and down to the turnoff on the dirt road. There was little chance that they would be seen. At least not for a while.

Did Dillard know he was being followed? Not likely. They had been careful to stay back and out of sight. Still, Dillard was a strange one, with odd senses. Logan worried about Janine. Was she okay? She had been through a lot now. When this was all over, he should take her on a vacation. Maui, Mexico, Colorado . . . someplace where they could just relax for a couple of weeks. He could borrow the money and buy cheap plane tickets. Hell, he knew a great travel agent in Fallbrook that could help put a package together. That was it, a vacation.

The truck bounced over the dirt road, heading for the small cluster of hills. There were three small peaks, jutting off the desert floor like fins on a sea creature. They rose abruptly for no apparent reason. Trees of the conifer family grew around the base and halfway up its sides. They were spindly pines, clinging to the sides of the mountain. All else was barren except for the occasional patch of desert sage. Wind gusted across the road in front of them. Off in the distance a tumbleweed broke loose its hold to life and rolled off with the wind. The only signs of the Humvee were the tracks of its huge tires on the dirt road and a hint of dust hanging over the road.

As they approached the group of hills, it was apparent the road led through to the other side. There were no buildings in the immediate area. This could be good or bad for the searchers. It might offer the opportunity to surprise Dillard if they hadn't been seen. But if they had, then he could be lurking in the hills, watching their approach. They could be sitting ducks.

Chicago Bob slowed the truck instinctively as they approached the slight incline leading in to strange cathedral-like desert terrain. The place had the look of an old mining concern. The angles of the slope, the odd color of the rock outcroppings and dirt all had the appearance of some ancient alluvial event. Logan had read about such places. The road was harder now, more rock than dirt. It led between the first two hills, rising slightly on the slope to avoid what appeared to be a narrow creek bed that washed out of the small valley. A likely place for a flash flood.

They wound around the red-colored slope and through some bone-like gray pines. Shade from the trees seemed to have an eerie green tint. A spindly thorned tumbleweed rolled across their path.

"Shiiiiiiitt . . . this is a weird place," said Little Jerry. "Gives me the creeps for some reason."

Chicago Bob agreed but kept the truck loping up the middle of the road. No telling what was around the next bend. They could all be dead in a matter of seconds. Or they could be heroes. No time to think about it.

"You know, you guys don't have to be doing this," said Logan in a detached voice. "This is my own doing, and it could be, well, there could be some consequences. We could all get shot."

Little Jerry looked at Chicago Bob. "Shit this is the most fun I've had all month."

Chicago Bob laughed. "Fuckin' A."

The road climbed steadily through the hills toward a blind corner. Would it top out over another valley? The trees were fewer toward the top, and there was more wind. They came around the bend and Chicago Bob slammed on the brakes. In the valley below was a ranch-like spread with four or five buildings nestled together in a complex of sorts. There were several large barnlike structures, but no corrals or evidence of livestock.

Dillard's Humvee was parked in front of what looked like the main house. No other vehicles were visible, but there were plenty of places that could hide a truck or two. Logan looked the scene over. Out away from the complex was a large stretch of desert floor clear of rocks and tumbleweed. An airstrip. It made sense now because one the buildings along the strip was large enough to house an airplane.

Had they been seen yet? No telling. The road down to the complex was steep and could not be traveled fast. Once at the bottom, it was a straight shot at the ranch. What kind of firepower did Dillard have? Logan tried to remember.

Backing up around the corner from which they had come was not an option. The only thing to do was to creep down to the bottom, hoping not to make too much noise, and then charge in.

"As soon as we stop, we split up," said Bob. "You and Jerry can cover me. I'll make for the side and try to get around back. Don't shoot until he shows himself."

Chicago Bob eased the truck down the winding road. Logan kept his eyes on the main house, waiting for a shot to ring out. Any second a bullet might rip through the cab and send them tumbling down the slope.

Dillard's eyes swept the room. There were just a few things he could use, then he would be gone. He needed to find the keys that opened the barn. Janine stood inside the door, staring at the floor like a zombie. She sobbed softly and tears rolled down her cheek. He had slapped her across the face twice since arriving. The force of the blows and the intensity of his actions left little doubt what might happen if she tried anything. And, as he had pointed out, she was alone, and this was a desolate spot. Dillard paid little attention to her as he ransacked the desk in the living room.

They heard the sound at the same time. An engine. The sound of a truck or large vehicle approaching at a high rate of speed. He ran to the window as the dark blue Ford Ranger slid to a stop beside the Humvee. Three men jumped out quickly and spread out. Dillard reached for his pistol and fired a shot through the closed window. Glass shattered and the rap of the gun filled the room. An answering bullet broke an upper pane of the window and lodged in the wall behind the desk. Janine dropped to her knees and crawled to the safety of an overstuffed chair.

Little Jerry fired two more shots from behind the Humvee, then ran for the side of the main building. It was a good move, but Dillard was ready and came up firing. Halfway to the building, a bullet caught Jerry in the leg. He fell face first into the dirt and slid to a stop. His gun tumbled to the ground and came to rest a few feet in front of his body.

Logan sprung to action, running to the corner of the house. Chicago Bob moved to Jerry. He picked up the gun and grabbed Jerry's legs. Dillard's ugly face appeared in the window, and his black automatic weapon began spraying bullets in the yard. First they came at Logan, then Chicago Bob. Logan heard a thud land a few feet away and saw that Chicago Bob had lobbed Jerry's revolver to him. Logan picked it up and tried to get a shot off but was forced instead to dive for cover on the side of the house.

The gunfire stopped for a second, and Logan looked around the corner. Chicago Bob was down and laying beside Little Jerry. Logan swore. It was now or never. He never considered himself brave, but when trouble had come to him, he had not backed down. There was something inside him, an unknown emotion that catapulted him into action. It had first happened when he was a teenager, when an older boy had threatened his sister. He had attacked in an uncontrollable rage. The boy was three years older, a foot taller, and forty pounds heavier, yet Logan had managed to break his nose and give him a black eye before having his own nose broken. Nevertheless, the bully never bothered his sister again.

Logan came to his feet and ran around the corner. How many bullets were left in the gun? He watched the window where Dillard had been shooting from, but it was empty. He slowed to a walk and looked back at Chicago Bob, careful to keep his attention on the house. Bob was trying to point at something. What was it?

The air went strangely quiet. No sound except that of the cold November wind blowing around buildings and through the yard. Had Dillard been hit? Where was Janine? No time to ask questions. What had Chicago Bob been pointing at? Logan went to the door on a low run. He leaped and kicked the door open in a well-timed blow. Gun in hand, he swept the room for a sign of the gunman. He stopped when he saw Janine huddled in the corner, hands over her head and whimpering. Dillard must have gone out the back.

"Janine!"

She looked up surprised. "Oh, Logan."

He moved to her and they held each other. She felt so good in his arms. She was crying almost hysterically. In the moment, he forgot about Dillard. He just wanted to hold Janine as tight as he could. At this point, he didn't care about Dillard. For all Logan cared, he could run off to Mexico, or Guatemala, or wherever the hell he wanted to go. Dillard was an ass, and he would surely meet his own end.

"Isn't that nice, a reunion." The voice was nasally and the tone was as sarcastic as it was cold. An evil voice. The transformation was complete. David Dillard, former state senator, defender of the religious right, a once-powerful conservative political power had changed his colors.

Logan and Janine froze as one.

"Just go. Get the hell out of here. You've got what you need. Just leave us alone," yelled Logan, unable to quell emotion.

"And risk the chance of having you testify against me? Not that they're going to find me." Dillard was grinning sardonically. "I don't take chances like that, friend."

He motioned them to stand against the wall, while he snapped a fresh clip of bullets in his gun.

"By the time they find this place, I'll be a long ways away. And there won't be anything here to connect me with you." He chuckled. "This is going to be perfect."

"What are you going to do?" Janine's voice was tortured. "You can't kill us . . . please."

"I can't?" Dillard pulled the trigger on the automatic weapon. Flames leaped from the barrel and a demonic syncopation filled the room. Bullets shattered the wood behind Logan and Janine, but none hit them.

Dillard grinned while he shot. His eyes were glazed with power. The smallish rifle had become a part of his body and was spitting venomous bullets at will. Janine was screaming and covering her eyes. Logan held her with his right arm. He was rigid, but his eyes were open and he was staring at the madman with the gun. He could feel the eruption within him about to happen. He could leap for Dillard's throat and smash his head to the floor. The bullets would not hurt, and he would kill David Dillard with his bare hands.

The madness stopped as quickly as it began. The smell of sulfur from the gun stung Logan's nostrils. Dillard remained in the slightly crouched position he had assumed just before going into his fit of rage. Logan knew that it could begin again in an instant. They could be dead. Or he could lunge at Dillard and make a play. He studied Dillard's eyes for a clue of what was to come. If he pulled the trigger again, Logan would lunge. He shifted his weight to the balls of his feet.

Smoked drifted up toward the ceiling, highlighting a stream of afternoon sunshine that shown through the blown-out window of the room. Silence again. A void of sorts, and then Dillard let his breath out and laughed. He stood up and the dementia left his face. In a calm voice, he told them to follow his directions and things would be better for them.

"So what are you going to do?" asked Logan. "And how is it going to be better?"

"I'll tell you what I'm going to do. I'm going to give you a chance to live," said Dillard in even tones. "I'm going to put you in that tank out there, and I am going to tie you up so that you're nice and secure. Then you are going for a little drive in the desert. An off-road adventure, you might say."

CHAPTER TWENTY TWO

Change of Plans

L ong gray lines of moisture drifted up from the south, forming tiny strings of clouds that usually signal a change in the weather. The afternoon was moving on as Manny Cassio led his caravan off Interstate 8 and on to the unnamed road heading south toward the Mexican border. There was nothing out this way save for a few old mines and maybe an abandoned ranch. A smuggler's route. A place with little law, and less forgiveness.

Was he on a wild goose chase? Somehow he had a gut feeling about the fax. It was obviously from the same source that had been providing information about Dillard and Sobrano all along. So far that information had been proving right. Especially considering what had happened out at the ranch in Anza.

This was a complex case, he thought. Murder, mayhem, drugs, political corruption. Where would it end? There were so many things that seemed to be related, yet didn't quite add up. Three of the men killed at the ranch had turned out to be cops or ex-cops. Dillard, undoubtedly, had more law enforcement people working for him, either knowingly or not. He was a powerful man. That was about to change.

"It's funny," he said to Brado who seemed to be entranced at the passing desert, or just off in his own thoughts. "When that guy Casey told us about Dillard, it seemed so unlikely. Yet here we are chasing him down. What do you think of that?"

"I think he was a powerful guy who got caught up in his own hype," said Brado. "I never would have believed it. I never would have believed he even used drugs, much less was involved with dealers like Carlos Sobrano. Right now I just want to see that the bastard gets what he deserves."

"So what do you bet that Dillard had one those cops shoot Casey?"

"Not much," said Brado, again looking out the window. "How far you think this place is?"

"I'd say about a half hour."

Brado let out a sigh. Cassio wondered about him. Sometimes, he was just a little off. He let his thoughts drift back to his board downtown. The one with the lines. They were connecting in his mind now. The recent rash of overdoses and bazaar suicides occurring in San Diego. Evidence in those cases was sketchy. They were all drug related, but what kind of drug? His own intuition led him to believe it was all connected to a drug ring determined to bring a new drug to market. A drug that would take over where cocaine and methamphetamine left off. A drug that would be controlled and distributed by one powerful multi-national organization. But the drug didn't happen. It had backfired and caused the fledgling organization to deteriorate from within. A core meltdown. In the end, it seemed that the powers were fighting each other for control. But for control of what? Not the drug. Dillard had grabbed an envelope from Sobrano before he made his escape. What was in the envelope? Something that might be worth more than the drug?

Logan listened to the insane man's plan. He would tie them down in the Humvee, set it in gear, and then point them out toward the endless desert.

"You got a fifty-fifty shot," said Dillard with a sly smile. "With a little luck, you'll just run out of gas and somebody will find you in a couple of days." He laughed. "Or weeks." More laughing. "Or months."

Logan thought about it. Maybe Dillard would get them in the car and shoot them in the head. But that might be too humane for this psycho. He wanted them to suffer. The desert was full of hidden ravines.

Dry washes cut through the desert floor like mini Grand Canyons. A vehicle could be swallowed up in one and never be found. A million ways to die.

There were few choices. Dillard made it clear if they didn't cooperate he would shoot Little Jerry and Chicago Bob first and then Janine. Logan agreed, then lapsed into what he hoped would appear as a subdued state of cooperation. Inside he was raging with anger and adrenaline. It would come quickly then. From left field, as an old friend used to say. A meatball.

"Out the door people," Dillard motioned with his gun. Logan grasped Janine by the shoulders and squeezed gently. He hoped to convey somehow that he had a plan and that he was going to do something to try to get them out this. His touch was gentle but firm. A reassuring touch of trust and love and conviction. She headed for the door with Logan behind. Dillard's finger twitched on the trigger as he pointed the gun at the base of Logan's neck.

"Not so fast, Dillard." A voice from the back of the room halted the procession.

The little caravan stopped abruptly. Janine whirled around and Logan caught a glimpse of hope in her eyes.

"Walter!"

Logan turned and looked at Dillard, his gun still pointing at his head. He watched as Dillard's finger twitched on the trigger. His eyes were bulging, a bead of sweat rolled down his cheek. He opened his mouth, but before he could get a word out, a blast from Walter's pistol shattered his right arm. His body whirled around clockwise with the bullet's impact. The gun in his hand spit out bullets that just missed Logan's right ear. The gun hit the floor, followed by a limp body. Dillard's blood dripped from the wall where it had splattered, and from Logan's chin.

Logan kicked the gun away from Dillard, just in case the snake came back to life. Janine was already in her brother's arms.

"Oh, Walter, what the hell were you thinking? Why didn't you stop what was happening to me? I thought you might be dead. This has been such a fucking nightmare." Logan heard her words. Something was different about them. Hard words.

Dillard looked up from the floor. "You . . . You ruined everything. You were a bust from the start."

Walter leveled the gun in Dillard's direction. He was smiling.

Logan looked at Walter and suddenly realized he had seen him before. But where? Then he got it. "Inside ooot" He had an accent then. Walter was the Canadian snowbird on the driving range. It seemed like weeks ago. And the hat. The Tam o'Shanter hat. No hat now, no accent. Logan suddenly felt confused. Why hadn't Walter come forward then and helped out?

"We've got to move quickly now, sis. They'll be here soon to pick up the pieces," Walter looked at his sister. All business. "Where's the envelope?"

Janine moved quickly to Dillard and rolled him over on his back with her foot. He was alive but in no mood to fight back. Reaching inside his jacket, she pulled out the envelope and held it up. Walter turned the gun from Dillard to Logan. He motioned to Janine.

"There's some rope in the drawer of the desk. Take it and tie them up."

Them? Logan looked at Janine, and then at Walter and the gun. What was going on?

"Move and I'll shoot you." Walter's voice was smooth, with no trace of an accent. He had a thin knowing smile and a look in his dark eyes that sent a shiver down Logan's back.

Janine walked to Walter, careful to stay out of the line of fire. Her face was expressionless. She moved as if Logan was not there. Deliberate. Uncaring. Void of emotion. A very different person than just a few moments before. Gone were the tears. Gone were the actions of a scared, helpless innocent. She was moving now as if under a spell.

"Janine, what are you doing?"

"Don't talk to her. Don't say another word or all cap your ass."

Logan stared in disbelief. Janine moved in silence, but the look on her face was telling enough. It was apparent that Walter was in control and that he had a plan. And it looked like Janine was part of it. He motioned at Logan with the gun.

"Nice and easy now. Help us out here and you'll be okay."

Logan didn't know what to do. What was Janine doing? What was going on? A minute ago he was going to lay down his life for her. Now she was tying him up. For what? To be shot? She was like a different person.

What choice did he have now? Walter would surely follow through with shooting him, and from the looks of Dillard, he was a good shot. Janine rolled Dillard over and tied his hands behind his back, then sat him up against the wall next to Logan.

"Very good," said Walter. "Now if we just had some of our Pink Polly for you, it would be all set," said Walter. "Sorry about that, but then maybe it's better this way."

He looked around the room then motioned Janine to go out the rear door. She left the room without looking back. Walter walked over to Logan. "Thanks for taking care of my sister. You guys created all the distractions I needed."

Walter stood up and walked to the back door. Logan watched as he stopped and turned.

"Sorry guys, change of plans."

The gun came up, and Logan felt the whiz of a bullet next to his ear then felt the blood splatter from Dillard's forehead. The roar of the gun was deafening, and then he saw the black hole of the barrel pointing at him.

From outside, Chicago Bob heard the shots. There was one then minutes later there were two more. He was drifting in and out of consciousness. He had taken two bullets and had lost blood. And there was the matter of the last forty-eight hours or so. Still he tried to stay awake. He heard the sound of an engine. A big engine. It was an airplane. And then it was gone.

CHAPTER TWENTY THREE

The Blue Chameleon

The chameleon is an old-world lizard that has the unusual ability to change the color of its skin to suit its needs. Chiefly arboreal, it uses its independently movable eyeballs to identify possible prey and, of course, other predators. Once identified, the chameleon blends in to the environment and remains almost invisible until the moment it needs to move. The unsuspecting insect that happens by is usually whisked off by a large dark tongue before it can react.

Logan had been told a story at the bar once about the blue chameleon. Seems that on Maui there is a Hawaiian legend about a Blue Chameleon. It can not only change its color, but can change its shape and size to suit its purpose. Its prey includes all the animals of the forest, including man. Deep in the jungles of Hana, the Blue Chameleon waits for whomever and whatever crosses its path. Once it has revealed itself, as the legend goes, the only way one can avoid a horrifying death is to let go all fear and doubt. To stand defiantly and meet it face-to-face. Only with faith and courage from deep within can one survive.

Reid came out of the room, and the look on his face told the story. Dorothy from The Paddock and Lenny stood up as he approached. They had visited the hospital several times a week since Logan had been in the coma. It was going on three weeks.

"The wound is healing, but the bullet grazed the bottom of his brain, and the doctor can't say how much damage has been done. He says it might be a good idea to start making plans."

The intent was obvious. Logan's sister would have to make the decision. She had flown in for a few days but needed to get back to her work. She called Reid almost every day for updates.

"It's got to be really tough for you," Dorothy said to Reid. "You guys have been friends a long time. He used to tell me stories while we were setting up the restaurant. You guys going to Hawaii, and Mexico." Her voice drifted off.

Minutes later Dorothy and Lenny said goodbye and Reid walked back into Logan's hospital room. The doctor was gone. Logan was on his back. Tubes and wires invaded his once strong body. It was hard to fathom how a person could lose weight and go so white so fast. Reid sat for a minute with his friend, and then looked at his watch. Another deadline.

It was a recording that wouldn't stop. A phone that kept ringing and ringing with nobody there to answer it. The sound of an engine. A loud sound. Not that of a car or truck. What was it? There was pain. Looking across the room he could see a shape. Dillard? Was he smiling? Laughing? Janine smiling and then drifting away. Laughing?

He felt himself drifting off and into a strange void where he floated about. There were voices and what seemed to be prayers. Sounds he couldn't make out.

Off again, running from the Blue Chameleon. Running through a field of knee-high weeds. It was nighttime, but there was an eerie light so that he could see as if it were day. Moonlight. Running and floating, he crossed the field toward a single tree. It had a long branch protruding from its trunk, and there was a swing. A young girl was swinging. Her back was to him, but as he approached he could see that she had two braided pigtails. Her hair was light brown. He ran on. She swung away. And then he ran past her and on toward the end of the field. He heard her laughing as he passed. He looked back and the huge lizard was still there. It had large red eyeballs, and its tongue lashed out at him as he watched.

He jumped and the wind blew his long hair back as he floated over a field of flowing wheat. Flying now, through the air. There was a family having a picnic below him, and he waved at them. They waved back. On he flew until the sensation of flying turned to falling. He felt a surge of fear race through his body. He was falling and falling out of control. The ground was coming, he could see it, then it turned into a blue ocean.

He came over the top of the wave and landed hard on the backside. He felt a wash of air and hard spray of water. He couldn't see. When he opened his eyes there was another larger wave looming in front of him. He needed to paddle hard to make it over. Panic. It was a big wave and getting bigger. Fear. The wave was going to break on him. He struggled to paddle faster. The translucent giant kept rising and then right in the middle of the green wall he saw his fear. The Blue Chameleon. Its eyes were looking directly at him. They had him, and he had them. Suddenly the fear left. He was calm. He wanted this wave. He was going to ride this wave. He was riding the wave . . . a big long wave.

Dropping, falling, down, down, black. Black. Faraway sounds. Voices. Calling his name? Light. It was a foggy day. Seagulls called and smell the salt air reached from the beach. There were people there. Friends. Old friends and new friends. His dog Blue was there. Blue Dog. A black and tan cocker mix that he had for almost fifteen years. His dad was there, smiling and wearing his Navy uniform. Just like in the picture at home. Everything was going to be all right. He had made it through. The nightmare was over. One of his friends from down on the beach was calling him. He had a surfboard for him. Maybe it was time to go out again.

Strange feeling. Something was happening. It was a funeral. His funeral, just like he had talked to Reid about in one of those morbid conversations over many beers. He had always said he wanted to be cremated and his ashes thrown out to sea. It was happening. They were doing that right now. It would be all right, he thought. Someone from above called his name.

"Logan! Come on, Logan. Logan."

Sunlight was shining through the fog, and he heard the voice again. Who was it? He heard his name again, and he could see a face. It was too close to tell who it was, but he knew him.

～✹✺✹～

Burt Reid backed away from the bed and looked at the doctor.

"Can he hear me? Why isn't he responding?"

"He might be hearing you and he might not. I've read about cases where the patient wakes up and remembers every detail of what happened while he was in the coma. But you just can't tell. I do believe that if he is going to come out of the coma it will take his friends and family to make it happen."

Reid looked back at the person in the bed. Logan had been unconscious for almost four weeks. But today, for the first time, Reid had hope. Logan had mumbled something and had made a movement. Reid had called for the doctor immediately. Progress, any progress, was reason for hope.

The coma was taking its toll on Logan's body, and although they could keep him alive, there was no guarantee he would ever have a real life again.

Reid's visits were a ritual. He had been there to see him almost every day. Lenny and the crew from the stables had also been down. With no immediate family in the area, this band of friends were the closest thing to relatives Logan had. The doctors had said that he might regain consciousness at any time. Then again, he might not. He was alive and breathing on his own, which was good.

But today there was more hope. It may have been his imagination but he thought Logan had moved his lips. Then the doctor came and Logan was much the same. Reid glanced at his watch. Maybe tomorrow. Reid turned for the door.

"Reid . . ." The voice was weak and hoarse, but it lifted Reid's chin like a shot.

"Logan!"

Reid ran over and grabbed his hand. Logan managed a smile.

"I was at the beach. You were there, and Dad, and Blue . . ."

Reid's eyes filled with tears. He couldn't help it. They had been through a lot together, and Reid had been thinking lately what it would be like if Logan died. When it all came down to it, friends and family were all that mattered. For really the first time in his life, Reid had been thinking about how precarious a condition life was. He squeezed Logan's hand.

"Welcome back, buddy."

CHAPTER TWENTY FOUR

Thanks . . . Giving

The table at the Double Bar R was set for a banquet. White linen tablecloth, Franciscan China, and polished silverware befitting a royal entourage. There were flowers and two sets of wine glasses and fifteen high-backed chairs surrounding the table. Smells of turkey and potatoes enveloped the room each time the large swinging door to the kitchen opened. Classical holiday music poured from the stereo, and a fire roared in the huge stone fireplace.

Mary Mactavish was directing a crew of cooks and servers like it was a dinner rush at a steak house. It had been a time coming, but now the diverse set of people that had shared a bazaar bit of history were together in one place. Two months had passed since Logan had come out of the coma. Things were slowly getting back to a normal pattern, although some things had changed permanently.

"You know, for all his prowess and cunning that Walter was a lousy shot," said Cassio, talking to Logan. "Lucky for you, but I wouldn't have minded seeing that slithering bastard, Dillard, get his."

"I can't believe it either, I could have sworn he was dead. What the hell." Logan raised his glass. "The son of a bitch is still going to get his, Manny. Believe it."

"Yeah, it's got to be hard on a guy like that. He won't get much respect. That's if he ever makes it to prison. Sobrano has a long reach, and Dillard's been spilling his guts, from what I hear."

Logan had heard the story from Reid as soon as he got home. Dillard had been removed as state senator and charged with no less than five major crimes. He was also being indicted by a Federal Grand Jury and would undoubtedly be facing a long time in prison. Word had it that Sobrano's organization had put a hit out on him. Dillard would not be safe anywhere he was sent. Sobrano, a survivor of three gunshot wounds, faced the same charges as Dillard and was also being processed for extradition to Mexico for prosecution.

"Congratulations to the new commandant," said Lenny, stepping in from the porch to join Logan and Cassio. "I hear if this case keeps unraveling, they're going to make you the sheriff."

Cassio laughed. "No way the cowboy is going to step down. Anyway, haven't you heard? I'm coming back to Fallbrook so I can keep an eye on you guys."

There was a good group of deputies there, and it was time he settled down in one place, Cassio explained. Brado would not be coming with him, though. In fact, he was under investigation by Internal Affairs. Several bits of evidence had turned up that connected Brado to the deputies at the ranch in Anza and to Dillard.

"You know this case made me aware of something I never thought about," said Cassio. "All these people weren't who we thought they were. Dillard, the brother, the girl, Brado. On the good side, who would have thought this rag tag bunch would turn out to be crime-fighting heros!"

"Yeah," Logan said with a smile. "We're all just a bunch of chameleons. Part of life I guess."

As the day went on, Logan soaked in the stories and got caught up on how it all unfolded. He'd missed a lot.

Reid and his team had chronicled the events of the two weeks in November and were up for several awards. The story made the national newswire, and TV, radio, and newswire reporters were climbing all over *The Newspress* newsroom. His only complaint was the story and aftermath had him working seven days a week. But it was a once in a lifetime opportunity, and he relished it. The story, like the prosecution, was continuing, and Reid would be with it all the way through.

Lenny had taken a well-needed vacation to San Felipe, where he delivered a trailer-load of clothes, food, and presents for the people of the village there. Once back from Mexico, Lenny had settled in to his routine behind the bar. Of course, the stories about the incident were horrendous. Lenny had a tendency to editorialize a bit.

The crew from The Downs had returned to work, doing what they did best: train the world's fastest Thoroughbreds and tell long, inspired tales about the adventure. Little Jerry had recovered but would walk with a permanent limp as a result of the gunshot wound to the leg. Chicago Bob was fully recovered and as ornery as ever. Marsha had a new girlfriend and was thinking about taking up golf.

After a long weekend of partying, Big Mike and Spike decided to head for the low desert. They had announced to the crew at the corner that they were going to get some golf in before the snowbirds blew into town. Word on the street, however, was they were both headed for Betty Ford. Pink Polly had paid her last respects in spades.

The blow up in the backcountry made national headlines, and for a few days every local within miles was being interviewed. Newcomers to the area would never be treated the same. In San Diego, there was a small military funeral for Rocco. A distant cousin had claimed the body and made arrangements. Only one other person attended. A thin, rather haggard looking blonde wearing tight blue jeans.

Logan had much of it since he returned to work in mid-February, but it was good to hear it all again. He had missed Thanksgiving while in the coma and spent Christmas in the hospital. It took him a while, but he managed to settle back in at The Paddock. Mori had been supportive, and Jim, the backup bartender, had filled in on a regular basis. Logan had been a bit depressed at first. Janine weighed heavily on his mind.

She and Walter were said to have been seen in Costa Rica, according to Cassio. International authorities were apprised of the whole Swiss bank account scam and were watching closely. Even if she and Walter were successful in getting the money, they were going to have a tough time spending it. Logan had taken her betrayal hard. At first, he went through periods of depression, waking up in the middle of the night and not being able to get back to sleep. The fact that he had been such a fool was hard to get over. Eventually, the depression had turned to anger, and the anger to indifference. Then something happened to replace the whole thought process.

Logan had been setting up the bar in the morning. It was his third day back and he was still a little weak. He was filling the ice bins when Dorothy came to the bar and asked for a towel to wipe some tables. Logan handed her the towel and for some reason their eyes met in a way that he had not experienced before. He looked at her, and it was as if he was looking at her for the first time. Suddenly he noticed her smile and how well it complemented her eyes. She was lovely. So diminutive and sweet. They had always been friends, and she was an excellent waitress. Sharp wit, good personality, never one to let a busy day or demanding customer rattle her.

Their eyes had met for only an instant. But something transpired there. Those soft brown eyes that had the look of goodness in them. Eyes that would be there for him, always. Without thinking, Logan asked her to dinner. She agreed with no hesitation, and they had been dating regularly since.

Gary Scott rose from his chair near the fireplace and walked to one of the twin bars. He filled his glass with a fine Chardonnay from the Temecula Valley. It was a magnum-size bottle, and he called for Chicago Bob to pass it around the room.

"I'd like to make a toast, so please fill your glasses and join me," Scott spoke with authority.

Little Jerry took over the duty of filling the glasses from Chicago Bob, who had over-filled Marsha's glass, spilling wine on the fine hardwood floor.

"This is to the best group of friends a man could have, and I want to say that I admire each and every one of you," said Scott.

Little Jerry needed no more encouragement and raised his glass in a salute.

"To the dance of life!" he said. A chorus of cheers broke out, and glasses clanked.

"Wait a minute. I have more," said Scott. "I've come to a decision that I hope you will all support. Anyway, I've decided to join Mary here at the Two Bar as her ranch foreman, trainer, and . . . as her husband."

There was a concerted expression of surprise, followed by an another outburst of cheers and clanking. Little Jerry, who had been taking a sip of wine during the announcement, almost choked. Chicago Bob hoisted the oversized bottle to his lips.

"There's more," said Scott. "I want all of my crew, to join me here at the ranch. It will mean a change of lifestyle for you, no more drinkin' and gamblin' at 10 A.M., but I think it will be a good thing for everyone."

Lieutenant Cassio raised his voice among the commotion. "Well one thing's for sure . . . not having you guys around will make my beat one hell of a lot quieter. But it's sure going to cut into Mori's business and Logan's tips."

Laughter filled the big room, and then Mary Mactavish announced that dinner was served. There was turkey and prime rib and all the trimmings. There were more toasts and some spilled wine and a flurry of conversation. By the time the pumpkin pie arrived, Little Jerry was curled up on the couch in front of the fire and Chicago Bob had joined some of the ranch hands on the veranda for cigars.

Logan squeezed Dorothy's hand and gave her a kiss. "I'm going outside with the boys." She smiled and retired to the kitchen, where Mary and some of the other women were going over future plans.

Logan met Reid and Lenny outside. It was a beautiful March afternoon. Crisp air with a hint of sage and chaparral mixed with the smell of hay. There were thin clouds high in the sky, signs of a late northern storm. Southern California could use the rain, thought Logan.

Reid pulled out a packet with some fine Churchill-style cigars. "This was a great day. I don't know when I've had a better meal," he said, offering a box of matches to Logan. Mori came out and joined them but declined the cigar.

"You know, they're just about to put a signal at Kelly's Corner," he said. "And there's talk about a new gas station going in across the street where Perry's used to be."

Reid confirmed that he had heard the same thing.

"One more wreck at Kelly's Corner and they will have to move quick or they'll lose federal funding," said Reid. "Once a signal goes in, business will boom on the corner. You'll be a fat cat, Mori!"

They all laughed.

"Well, that's it." Mori turned to Logan and put his hand on his shoulder. "I'm not getting any younger, and Flo and I have heard your stories about Hawaii and Hanalei Bay. I want to enjoy life while I'm still young. What would you say if I made you and Lenny here an offer to become working partners with me in the restaurant? Of course, I wouldn't be working. You run the place, and eventually, you take it over for good."

Logan looked at Lenny. He didn't have to think about it. The restaurant business was his trade. It was all that he knew. Same with Lenny.

"What do you say, Lenny?"

"I say, let's get on back and get to work, partner."

Jim, the backup bartender, wiped the counter down with a towel. It was an exceptionally slow day. All the regulars were up at the party. He would have liked to be there, but he would hear all about it when they got back. And he needed the money.

The afternoon peace at The Paddock was broken by an all too familiar sound. A screech of tires, and the inevitable clash of metal meeting metal could mean only one thing. There was another TC on Kelly's Corner. Jim sprang to the window and peered through the louvers.

"Minor . . . truck T-bones a station wagon. I'd say only minor injuries," he said to no one in particular.

A couple of farm workers ran out from the front of the store to help. It wasn't a big wreck, but it was big enough. Jim turned around and looked at the clock.

"Who won the pool?"

THE END